Violet's War

Rosemary J. Kind

Printed in the United Kingdom

First Printing, 2021 Alfie Dog Limited

The author can be found at: ros@rjkind.com

Cover design: Katie Stewart, Magic Owl Designs
http://www.magicowldesign.com/

ISBN 978-1-909894-46-4

Published by
Alfie Dog Limited
Schilde Lodge, Tholthorpe,
North Yorkshire, YO61 1SN
Tel: 01347 838747

DEDICATION

To women footballers everywhere.

AUTHOR'S NOTE

This book, and the one which follows, would not exist without the story of the Dick, Kerr Ladies Football Team. However, the novels are not about that team, but are an entirely fictional story set against the backdrop of events in the period 1915 - 1921. I have deliberately begun the story ahead of the Dick, Kerr team taking to the field; they were not the first team during WW1 but were undoubtedly the most famous and most successful. Libra Lines was a well-known Coventry player as early as 1912 and continued to play throughout the war.

To put the numbers of supporters in context, on Boxing Day 1920, 53,000 spectators attended the Dick, Kerr Ladies Team match at Goodison Park whilst there were thousands more outside the stadium unable to get in.

The teams playing in this story are all fictional.

When I first came across the story of the real Dick, Kerr Ladies Team I felt compelled to look into it in some detail. As a child, I loved playing football. I was a 'tom boy'; I spent all my time on the field with the boys playing football. When I was about 10 years old, on behalf of a number of the girls at school I approached our teachers to ask if we girls could play football instead of netball and have an official girls' football team. This was about 1975 and the answer was a plain and simple 'no'. Girls were only allowed to play netball. It was a sad indictment of the times. I wish I'd known about the Dick, Kerr Ladies Team back then. Maybe I wouldn't have given up.

For information, the news headlines used are to give a flavour of what was being reported around the time of each chapter. They do not always correlate to the specific day the chapter begins. I have taken them from *The Daily Mirror* and *The Sunday Pictorial* because those were the newspapers Billy and his father read. The songs used are music hall and other popular songs from the time.

I generally avoid jargon and acronyms; however, I have used the following:

A Blighty one - an injury which is sufficiently bad for a soldier to return home.

AWOL - Absent without leave.

Woodbines - a favoured brand of cigarette.

NOTE:
The characters are all fictitious and any resemblance they may have to persons alive or dead is entirely coincidental. This book is not intended to suggest that the events portrayed happened in reality. It is purely a work of fiction, rooted in elements of real history.

CHAPTER 1

The boy I love is up in the gallery,
The boy I love is looking down at me,
There he is, can't you see, waving his handkerchief,
As merry as a robin that sings on a tree.
The Boy I Love Is Up In The Gallery - George Ware 1855

10th April 1915 - The Allied Warships set a Fort on Fire - The Daily Mirror

"Billy!"

Violet was kneeling by the step, and as the coin Billy tossed landed in the bucket the dirty water splashed up into her face.

"Heads or tails?" He stood over where she was scrubbing, his face the picture of innocence.

Violet sighed. She put the Cardinal red polish aside and sat back on her heels. "Now what have you two been up to?" She looked from her husband to his best mate Stan and back again. "I take it you won then." It was a statement rather than a question. She could tell the result of the Billingbrook United match by their tipsy grins. She shook her head in mock exasperation; at least it was nearly the end of the football season. "Why don't you play with your son, Billy Dobson, and give me some peace? I need to finish up here or I'll have your mam to answer to." Violet nodded to where their son was clumsily trying to move a

1

hoop as big as he was, with a stick which was considerably longer than his arm. At only four years old, Tommy showed more determination than skill.

"Heads or tails?" Billy repeated. He stood firm, his hands now pushed deep in his trouser pockets and his cap askew.

Violet frowned and dipped her sore, red hand into the bucket, taking out the shilling. He wouldn't give up until she humoured him. Without looking, she placed the silver coin on her palm, still covered by her other hand, then looked up, waiting for what was to follow.

"Heads I come back victorious, tails I die glorious in battle." Billy clutched his heart and fell to the floor at Stan's feet, laughing.

Stan prodded him with his boot.

Violet blinked and got up slowly from the step. Feeling sick, she looked down at the shilling, then returned her gaze to Billy, who Stan was now pulling to his feet. Wide-eyed, she tried to remember which way up the shilling had been lying at the bottom of the bucket, but when she thought it was a practical joke it hadn't seemed important. Now it felt like everything. Moving to stand close in front of Billy, she looked him in the eye. As her heart raced, in a measured tone she said, "Billy Dobson, what have you done?"

As Violet looked first to her husband and then back to Stan, grim realisation descended. "No, no, no. Tell me I'm wrong." They had only been talking the previous day about the number of men 'taking the King's shilling' and joining the army. She beat her fists against his chest. "Tell me you've not signed up." She could feel hot tears starting to run down her cheeks. "You stupid, bloody idiot. I don't want you to be anyone else's hero. I want you to be my

Billy, at home here with me and Tommy."

She turned to Stan, who shrugged and had the good grace to look a little sheepish.

"This is your doing, Stanley Bradley." Violet pulled herself up to her full height and faced Stan. She pursed her lips tight and felt a bolt of steely determination.

Stan's eyes widened. "Er, I'm off then, Billy mate. See you later."

Before Violet could utter any one of the words which were bubbling up inside her, Stan ran in Tommy's direction, pretending to chase the giggling child before hot-footing it away down Victoria Street, waving to Tommy before he turned the corner and was out of sight.

Slumping down on the partly-scrubbed step, Violet buried her face in her apron and felt Billy sit beside her.

When Billy spoke, all signs of cockiness had gone. "They were all doing it, the lads. There was talk at the match about it being the right thing to do for King and Country and all that. There are posters up everywhere. You know the ones, 'Daddy, what did you do in the Great War?' I just thought…"

"But you didn't think, did you? You never bloody well think. How am I going to cope and bring up Tommy with you away? He's four years old. He wants you here with him, not fighting in some foreign land. And are we just supposed to manage, living with them?" She indicated with her head along the hall to where her in-laws were no doubt sitting with their feet up. "You know she hates me. Her arthritis seems very selective in what it stops her doing."

"The thing is…" Billy said, but Tommy tripped over the hoop and started howling.

Violet brushed her arm across her eyes and stood up to

go to their son. She wiped the dirt off Tommy's knee and scooped him into the air. "Shall we ask Daddy to kiss it better?" She carried Tommy ceremoniously toward his father, who gave the knee a perfunctory kiss, before continuing with what he was saying.

"The thing is, I thought you'd be proud of me."

The diminutive but forceful figure of Billy's mother, Elsie Dobson, appeared from the dark of the hallway. "And what's our Billy done for us all to be proud of?" His mother ruffled his hair as though he were still a child.

He brushed his mother's hand away. "Mam, please. I've signed up, but for now I was talking to Vi."

"I can see that. You're stopping her working." Elsie turned to her daughter-in-law. "I thought you'd have this step finished by now. Run along, Tommy, leave your mam to do her work."

Vi gritted her teeth. What she'd give right now to just stand there and scream. How much worse would his mam treat her with Billy away from the house? She took a deep breath and picked up the brush from where she'd laid it aside. No doubt her skirt would have red on it from where she sat down, but it was too late to worry about that now.

"We'll talk later, love," Billy said, getting up off the path and out of the way. "I'll play with Tommy for a bit. We can kick a ball about. Sorry." He sounded chastened as he raised an eyebrow toward his retreating mother.

Vi shook her head. Billy had more than his bloody mother to be sorry about. She scrubbed the steps harder than she ever had before. Her hands would be raw by the end of this. She hadn't even asked him when he'd have to leave. Why did he want to go and be a hero? Lovable rogue she could deal with, but he wasn't hero material.

"Mam, Mam, look at me." Tommy was trying to copy

his dad, kicking the football. He swung his right leg back and then connected with the ball. It rolled a few feet in front of him.

"Well done," she called over to him, before returning her attention to the step. And who precisely would kick a football with Tommy when Billy went away? It wasn't as though Billy's dad ever came outside to play with his grandson, despite his obvious interest in football. She wondered how much of his keeping his distance was down to Billy's mam; she wasn't a woman to cross. Alf had found some way to stay married to her for the best part of thirty years, although Vi couldn't see how. For a moment she wondered whether Alf had played with Billy when he was a child. She couldn't picture Alf any younger than the late fifties he was now. His age seemed to suit him, mellow and mature.

She drifted back to thinking about Billy. Someone had inspired her husband's passion for football. He wouldn't miss a Billingbrook United home match for anything; he was always at their Whittingham Road ground, on the terraces with Stan. A tear dripped down onto the step and she sniffed rather than risk smearing the red polish on her face wiping it away.

She was still scrubbing when Billy came over.

"Come on, love, let's go in before you scrub the step away."

She moved a stray lock of hair from her sweaty forehead. "Mind you go in around the back and stay off this step until it dries."

Billy picked up the bucket and reached out a hand to pull her to her feet.

She looked at him and sighed, accepting the help. "What'll I do without you, Billy Dobson?"

"Mam and Dad will look after you."

She shook her head as they went down the narrow alley to the back gate.

"Here he is, our little hero." Billy's mam poured a cup of tea from the pot and passed it to Billy. "You'll be fine, love. Dad fought in the Boer War and he came home safe. You'll be just fine."

Violet wasn't sure if her mother-in-law believed what she was saying or not. It was possible Billy's mother was as scared as she was. Maybe they could support each other; it would make a change from the insinuations she wasn't good enough for Elsie Dobson's precious son. She cleaned up in the sink and poured her own tea. Tommy was playing in the yard. Perhaps now was a good time to break the news to them all that she was expecting again. The others had gone through to the front parlour, a rare privilege indeed. Maybe Elsie was in a good mood. Vi went to join them.

"When do you have to go?" Violet asked. She was fidgeting with her teaspoon, not wanting to hear the answer.

There was a long pause and she almost wondered if she'd spoken aloud.

Billy's voice was quiet as he answered. He seemed far more sober now than he had a short time earlier.

"Monday." He looked at his feet. "Stan and me, we have to be at the station with the others at eight o'clock. There's a special train which will take us to the barracks. I don't know much more than that. I didn't think to ask anything."

Violet swallowed hard. She'd known that was most likely to be the answer from what she'd heard from the girls at work; they'd had more than enough time to talk in the hat factory. Nine months of war meant orders were low. Not that talking was allowed during working hours. She nodded.

"We're very proud of you, aren't we, Dad?" Elsie Dobson left a pause for Alf's acknowledgment but hadn't finished speaking.

Billy's dad grunted without raising his eyes from the newspaper.

"You'll come home on leave, of course, but don't you go making babies every time you do. We don't need any more than Tommy running around the house at our age. Tell him, Alf."

She narrowed her eyes as she turned to Violet, who shivered under the glare.

Dad looked up from the sporting pages of the *Billingbrook Mercury*, marking his place with a finger from the hand holding his still smoking pipe. "It says here…"

Mam huffed. "Never mind what it says there. We don't want her ending up like that Queenie Tunnicliffe popping babies out every five minutes."

"Mam, that's Vi's mam you're talking about." Billy moved to stand between his mother and Vi.

"Aye, and it's better she hears it from me than somebody else."

Violet balled her fists. It was nothing she'd not heard from Billy's mam before, but it still hurt to hear her own mother spoken about with such derision. Vi was more than happy being part of a big family; it was what she and Billy wanted too. Her parents' house might be cramped, but they'd all been happy. They were close and kind and everything Elsie Dobson wasn't. Violet held back a tear. Now wasn't the time to tell them she and Billy were expecting their second child, that much was certain. She stood up from the settee and without a word took her tea into the kitchen.

Violet's hands were shaking and the cup rattled in the saucer as she looked out of the window to where Tommy was still kicking his ball around the yard. He was no trouble. It was not as though Billy's mam wasn't used to boys; she'd brought Billy up. Besides, she'd offered to mind Tommy while Vi returned to work. They hadn't asked her. Her own mam would have been happy to do it.

Violet watched Tommy and smiled. It would be no time before he got the hang of kicking the ball. As long as he kept it away from the windows when he did, or they'd all be in trouble. She grinned, wondering what Elsie would have to say about that.

Billy came up behind her and slipped his arms around her waist. "Sorry, love. She doesn't mean to be unkind."

Violet frowned. "Yes, she does. That's exactly what she means to be."

He laughed nervously. "Yeah, I suppose you're right."

"No one would be good enough for her Billy and I certainly know I'm not. She never stops making that clear."

Billy was quiet for a moment. "I am a bit special." He ducked as Violet gave him a gentle clip around the ear.

He became serious again. "The way it's looking, I'd have been called up eventually. Volunteering seemed like a good idea. It's not like there's much work on at the moment. I'd probably have been laid off soon, and it's not looking much better for Dad; at least this way there'll be some money coming in. When it's all over, we can find our own place. Have a proper start as a family. How about it?"

Violet turned to face him and looked into his lovely green eyes. She smiled weakly. "I say I'd still rather you weren't going. I don't need you trying to be some big hero. I just want you here as my Billy." She stroked her fingertips down his cheek. "We'd have managed somehow."

Billy moved her hand to his lips and kissed it. "Why don't you, me and Tommy take a picnic out somewhere tomorrow? We should call in to your mam and dad too, so I can see them before I go. What do you say, love?"

Violet sighed. "I still say I don't want you to go, but seeing as you are, yes, that would be lovely."

Billy hugged her to him. "We'll be all right, you'll see. I'll be home before you know it."

"Just make sure you are, Billy Dobson, and that you bring back the same number of arms and legs as you start with." She pulled away. She didn't want to cry. She had to be strong for Tommy as much as for herself. She went out into the yard and kicked the ball back to her son. He broke into a broad grin now he had a playmate and ran after the ball to kick it again. It had always been Billy who played out here with Tommy; she didn't like to think of what not having him around would mean to their son. She couldn't see his grandpa changing his habits now. Perhaps she could learn and then teach Tommy. She was sure her own dad would tell her what to do.

Billy came out and leaned against the wall, smoking a cigarette and watching them. Kicking the ball again, Violet was smiling despite everything.

"Is that washing dry?" Her mother-in-law's shrill tone broke the moment.

Violet's shoulders dropped. She passed the ball back to Billy, catching it on her skirt and had to try again. Whilst the boys continued to play, she took the clothes from the line and folded them into the basket. It would be good to get away from this house for a while the following day. Elsie Dobson wouldn't like her not being there to cook Sunday dinner, let alone that her precious Billy would not be at home as expected. Violet wondered if there was anything they could use for a picnic; even a bit of bread and jam would do if it gave them a break. It would make the outing more fun. She'd wait until Elsie had gone to sit down and then see what she could find. She didn't like being secretive, but she hated the constant conflict which happened otherwise.

A home of their own would make a world of difference.

CHAPTER 2

All 'round my hat I will wear the green willow
All 'round my hat for a twelve month and a day
If anybody asks me the reason why I wear it
It's all because my true love is far, far away.
Traditional

11th April 1915 - Battleship's Death Agony - Sunday Pictorial

Elsie stood in the doorway, her hands on her hips. "You'll be needing that dripping for the potatoes. That's all there is."

Violet gritted her teeth as her mother-in-law looked at what she was doing. Gripping the worktop, she took a deep breath. "Mam, we've already told you. Billy and me, we're taking Tommy for a picnic. We won't be here for dinner."

"Then you'd best leave that dripping well alone. Somebody is going to have to cook with it."

Violet could have sworn Elsie's eyes had been replaced by a pair of the gimlets out of Billy's toolbox, the way they bored into her. "Jam it is then," she muttered, reaching for the pot of damson from the shelf. She left her hand on the jar, waiting for Elsie to find a reason against that and only took the jar down when none followed.

As Violet put the spoon into the jam, Elsie tutted. "And why you think you can take our Billy off on his last day with us before he goes away, I don't know, young lady. His place is here and you well know it."

Violet opened her mouth to answer, but was prevented by Billy coming along the hallway.

"And what are my two favourite women talking about?"

Elsie glared one last time at Violet before turning her candy floss smile around to her son. "I was just making sure Violet had found everything you need for your little outing." She brushed an imaginary hair from Billy's shoulder in a proprietorial fashion.

Violet wished Billy would stop letting his mother treat him as though he were still a small child, and returned her attention to making sandwiches. Once Elsie was out of the way, Violet went to the small pantry under the stairs, to see whether there was something more interesting she could add to their treat. Anything she took was bound to incur Elsie's wrath, but that would be tomorrow's problem. For today, she planned to enjoy one last day as a family before they had to say goodbye to Billy.

A cloud lifted for Violet as they left the house and walked through the alley out into Victoria Street. She carried the small basket as Billy and Tommy kicked the football along the road. One of the neighbours was bound to complain about them kicking the ball on the Sabbath, but as far as Violet saw it there were more important things to worry about today.

There were few delivery vehicles in use being a Sunday and Violet almost felt a holiday air about the day; it was easy to forget there was a war on, when the sun shone. The war would become all too real the following day, but just for now, Violet wanted to pretend this idyllic life would go on forever.

It wasn't a long walk to the stepping stones which crossed the river on the edge of Billingbrook, although, it was more a stream than a river when it hadn't been raining heavily. On the other side there were trees which formed a canopy over some rocks, providing an ideal spot for a picnic. Billy scooped Tommy up and carried him over the stones.

"I want to do it," Tommy protested.

"You'll have to be a bit bigger first," Billy called as he took a stride to the next stone. "I even need to help your mam. You wait there." He put Tommy onto the bank near to where he'd already expertly kicked the football, then went back to take the basket from Violet so she could hitch her skirt and cross safely.

"Where does the water go?" Tommy asked as Violet sorted out the basket.

"I don't know really. I think it joins the River Ribble, at least that's what my dad told me."

Violet smiled, watching Billy with Tommy. He never seemed to tire of answering the boy's questions; she suspected Billy made the answers up when he didn't know, but wasn't completely sure. From tomorrow she'd have to do her best instead. There'd be no saying, 'Ask your dad,' if she didn't know the answer.

"Ribble, ribble, ribble," Tommy called over the gushing of the water.

Billy crouched down to his son's level. "When I come back, it'll be about time to take you on a fishing trip, Tommy lad. I'll show you how to use my rod and we can catch some dace or a chub."

"What's a chub?"

Violet sat on the stone, watching the two of them and

wishing this moment could go on forever.

Once the boys had spent plenty of time poking about along the riverbank, Billy flopped down at the base of the rock and rested his head against Violet's dangling legs. "I hope you brought lots to eat. I'm starving."

They made short work of the picnic and as it was not warm enough to sit idle for too long, they were soon back on their feet and ready for adventure. Violet wondered where the boys got their liveliness, but then having a baby on the way wasn't helping her levels of energy. As she strolled along the path through the wood, Billy and Tommy played hide and seek amongst the gnarled trunks of the trees. She didn't mind that every so often she left the boys behind and then they came running up to her laughing, sometimes side-by-side and sometimes with Billy carrying his son in a piggyback.

The route they'd taken brought them back into Billingbrook further around to the east, where the terraces had given way to row upon row of tiny back-to-back houses. Violet noticed that a few of the front steps were dull and dirty. It hadn't been like that a few years ago. Her mam had always tried to keep a tidy house, neat and clean the way it should be. The Tunnicliffes' front step was still bright with polish and however little her parents had, they set out to be respectable.

After the clean air around the riverbank, Violet registered the strong smell of waste and dirt; she'd never noticed when she'd lived there. She felt sad, realising a little of how Elsie Dobson saw her daughter-in-law's family. Violet wasn't ashamed of her parents, quite the opposite, but she wished she could help improve things for them.

"Hello, Mam," she called, as they went straight in at the

front door to her parents' home.

"Oh, Frank, if it isn't our Vi. Come in, love. Billy with you?" Queenie Tunnicliffe stood up, from where she'd been dozing in the threadbare chair, to greet her daughter.

Tommy ran around his mother's legs and bowled into his grandmother. "Nanna."

"You little rascal." She picked him up and embraced him, while his aunts, who were only aged five and seven themselves, jumped up and down in excitement.

"Where's Bobby?" Vi asked, reading the look of concern on Tommy's face.

Bobby was Vi's youngest brother and was the same age as Tommy.

"John's taken him out to give us all some peace." Frank greeted his eldest daughter. "The only problem with having so many kids is wanting a snooze on a Sunday afternoon."

The twinkle in her Dad's eye told Vi how small a problem he thought it and she felt homesick for the bustle of this tiny welcoming home.

"Sit down, Vi love." Queenie nodded to one of the younger ones, who moved off the chair to make space for Vi. Billy squeezed in next to her.

"Oh, Frank…" Queenie clapped. "While I make some tea, you show our Vi what Maisie Evans gave you."

Dad was beaming as he reached behind his chair and brought out a large box. He opened it with a reverence that Vi had rarely seen in her father. As he lifted out a beautifully cared-for accordion, Vi gasped. "Dad, whyever did she give you that?" She went over to look more closely.

"Careful there, love," Frank said quietly.

Even Tommy looked up from where he was playing and stared at what his granddad was holding.

"It's what you've always wanted, but..." Vi shook her head in wonder, as her father put the strap behind his neck.

Queenie came over, carrying the tea pot covered in a knitted tea cosy. "Maisie's husband Ted had left instructions with her that if anything should happen to him, God rest his soul, then she was to give it to our Frank. He knew how much Dad wanted one and... well, they had no children of their own, poor dears." Queenie's voice faltered as she put the pot down. "He died on the Front — Ted. Maisie heard last week." Queenie swallowed hard and went back to the kitchen area. "I'm glad our John's too young to go. Mind, I'd not stop him if he said that was what he wanted to do."

Violet sat down hard on the chair.

"Maisie said if I could play a tune or two at Ted's wake, then it was all mine." Frank began to play a few notes, then looked across at his daughter. "Are you all right, love? You've gone pale."

Billy went and put his hand on Vi's shoulder. "It'll be all right, Vi. I promise."

Violet was crying now. She began speaking through her hiccupping sobs. "That's what we came to tell you." She had to pause for breath. "Billy wanted to see everyone before he goes. He's signed up."

"Oh, lad, when do you go?" Frank lifted the accordion from around his neck and came forward to shake his son-in-law's hand. "And don't you worry, we'll keep an eye on Violet as best we can."

"Thanks." Billy hesitated and looked to Vi. "I'm off tomorrow."

"And I'm expecting another baby." Violet hadn't meant it to come out to everyone, but she just felt overwhelmed.

Mam gasped and sat down heavily. "Oh, Vi, the baby is great news — and like your dad says, we'll help all we can."

Billy knelt down in front of her. "Why didn't you tell me?"

"I've been trying to find the right time, I only found out last week. I didn't expect you to sign up."

"And I wouldn't have if I'd known. I'll be back soon, love — I promise." He put his arms around his wife. "It is great news."

Violet sniffed and wiped her eyes. With more force than she'd intended she said, "You don't know you'll be back soon, and I have to cope in the meantime."

"Whatever does Billy's mam say?" Queenie asked, pouring the tea.

Violet harrumphed.

"Now we'll have none of that, Vi. They're good people. You know they are."

Violet couldn't help but wonder at the ongoing respect of her own mother for someone who was wont to do her such disservice. "Billy's mam has made it quite clear that one child is more than enough. That's why I hadn't told Billy yet."

"They love Tommy," Billy said, as the boy came and sat by his dad. "They'll be delighted. We should tell them when we get back."

Violet shook her head and frowned at Billy. "Let's leave it. I don't want any upset with you going tomorrow."

Billy looked hurt, and Violet wondered if she was misjudging his mother's reaction. "Let's not talk about it now. I need that cuppa."

Queenie passed a cup to her daughter, who took it gratefully. Her dad picked the accordion up and started very quietly playing a tune.

Vi smiled. "You'll be entertaining the whole neighbourhood with that before long."

"He's already invited everyone for a singalong next Saturday. You should come over. You'll need a bit of cheering up with Billy away. Ena will be here, you know what she's like for having a good sing."

Ena was Vi's sister, and now they were both married they rarely saw each other. "I'd like that if I can get away. Shame it's Sunday today and disturbing the peace would be frowned on." She could see her dad was itching to open up the accordion and play it at full volume.

"There's no harm in keeping the Sabbath," Queenie said, folding her hands in her lap. "There's six other good days in the week." Then she smiled and a twinkle came into her eye. "I don't suppose anyone would mind too much if it was a hymn you were playing though, Frank."

Violet loved how proud of her dad her mother was.

Frank stopped what he was playing and looked up. "Righto. Well, I need to play this one for the funeral, so a bit of practice…" And he launched into 'Abide with me, fast falls the eventide'.

Violet loved the bustle of the family crammed into the one room; she'd grown up used to everyone falling over each other and hardly able to find their own space. She sighed. Seeing Tommy now playing with his uncle Bobby as though they were brothers reminded her why she still hoped for a big family herself. Her family didn't have much, but they had each other, and that made them richer than money ever could. Being the eldest she'd had to help bringing the others up, and she loved them all. At least with Ena now married and John working at the mill, her parents could find enough food to go around. She shuddered, remembering the times they'd gone without meals. Even then, she couldn't remember being unhappy.

By the time they left the family chatter and laughter for the walk back to Victoria Street, they were all in a party mood. Billy carried Tommy on his shoulders; the little lad would be ready for bed by the time they arrived home.

"I wish Tommy and me could live with my parents while you're away," Violet said as Billy dribbled the football as he walked.

"And where would they squeeze two more in? Three when the baby's born? How far gone are you?"

"About three months."

"It'll give Mam and Dad something to look forward to. You'll see." Billy retrieved the ball which had rolled to the side of the road.

Vi held her tongue. Maybe she was wrong, but that wasn't the response she was expecting.

"What shall we call it?" Billy asked.

"I don't know, I've not started thinking yet." That wasn't true, of course she'd been thinking about it. Would it be a girl or a boy? She'd love to call a girl after her own mother, but that wouldn't go down well with Elsie Dobson. "I thought we'd have ages to think about it. I wasn't expecting you to be away."

Billy stopped and lifted Tommy down from his shoulders. "You kick the ball for a bit, son." Then Billy turned to Vi and looked serious. "I know everyone says the war'll be over soon, but if it's not, you will tell him about his dad, won't you? Or her. I mean, every day, you will make sure the baby knows something about who I am for when I come back? Even if it's still too young to understand."

Vi looked into those eyes she loved so much. She

wasn't used to seeing Billy with a worried expression on his face. "Of course I will, silly. Both of our children will know they have the best daddy in the world, even if he is a silly Billy for worrying."

He kissed her passionately, then laughed. "That'll give Mrs Hedges something to talk about, us kissing outside her house in the street." He waved to the house they were outside.

"Billy! She might not have seen us."

Billy shook his head. "Oh, she saw us all right. I saw the nets twitch." He waved again and then focussed on Tommy and the football, singing as he walked.

'…in life, in death, oh Lord, abide with me.'

They were back at Ivy Terrace all too soon for Violet. "I'll put Tommy to bed, he can't keep his eyes open."

"Then we can tell Mam and Dad about the baby. It'll be fine, love, you'll see." Billy led the way down the alley to the back door.

The yard might be small, but Violet did realise it was better for Tommy to have some space to play that didn't involve being in the road. It was good not having to share the privy with seven other houses too; that was something she didn't miss. She sighed and just hoped that Billy was right about how his parents would feel.

When Violet came down from putting Tommy to bed, there was a steely silence as she joined Billy and his parents. She wondered if he'd already told them, but as he indicated the seat next to his she realised that they'd been waiting for her. Billy was looking serious and the look didn't suit him.

"Mam, Dad, I want you to look after Violet for me while I'm away…"

"Don't we always?" Elsie Dobson said, looking self-satisfied.

Violet thought that was a matter of opinion but said nothing.

"That's as maybe, Mam," Billy went on. "It's just…" He hesitated and Violet could feel his hand shaking in hers. He took a deep breath. "We don't know how long I'm going to be away for and she's… we're… expecting our second child."

Elsie Dobson didn't bother to hide her gasp.

CHAPTER 3

Keep the Home Fires Burning,
While your hearts are yearning.
Though your lads are far away
They dream of home.
There's a silver lining
Through the dark clouds shining,
Turn the dark cloud inside out
Till the boys come home.
Keep The Home Fires Burning - Lena Guilbert Brown Ford (1914)

12ᵗʰ April 1915 - French Soldiers Make Rings as Souvenirs - The Daily Mirror

"Well, you already know my thoughts." Elsie Dobson screwed her mouth into a tight knot.

Violet looked at Billy, who had turned to his father for a reaction.

Alf took his pipe from his pocket and began filling it with tobacco. He looked across at his wife and then continued to work on his pipe. Violet held her breath, waiting to see what Alf would say. She was used to him taking time before answering, but that didn't make it any easier.

Alf finally nodded. "We'll take care of the lass and the children. Don't you worry, Billy lad."

Billy broke into a broad smile. "Thanks, Dad. I told Vi you'd be pleased."

Violet almost snorted. Her mother-in-law was still looking like thunder. Pleased was one word that no one, other than Billy, would use to describe Elsie Dobson's mood.

"I'll be off early in the morning, so I'll say my goodbyes now." Billy shook his father's hand.

Alf nodded, but said nothing.

"If you expect me to miss you going off in the morning, you have another think coming. What mother wouldn't be there to see her boy going away?" Elsie remained where she was and glowered at Violet.

Violet sighed. She and Billy had already agreed they wanted the time for the goodbye to be theirs and theirs alone, but there was no way Billy would say that to his mother. Vi thought about how she would feel if it were Tommy. She could see why Elsie would want to be there, but she wished they could have the time to themselves. Billy was twenty-three now, with a family of his own.

As they lay in bed that night, Violet was glad to feel Billy's arms around her. Here, she could feel safe and secure. Snuggled under the blankets with Billy, it felt as though the war was happening to somebody else and she was immune to all of it. If only things could stay that way.

She knew she had to be strong, but oh how she wished he wasn't going. She lay awake long into the night, listening to him snoring and wondering what the future would hold.

While Billy prepared to leave the house the following morning, Violet held tight to Tommy's hand. They'd understand her being late for work today, she was sure they would, but she still felt a little concern. It wasn't as though the hat factory was overstretched with orders, and it was obvious they were going to have to let some of the girls go.

Vi was determined she wouldn't cry. Not just because she didn't want Tommy upset, but because it would inevitably elicit some comment from Elsie.

She could feel her lips quivering as she stroked Billy's face. "Just come home safe, love. And make it soon." She smiled and gritted her teeth.

The odd little group stood waving as Billy headed off along Victoria Street. He turned his head back to them every few yards until he met up with Stan at the corner. Then the two of them stopped, waved back to Vi and turned into Edward Street, out of sight.

That was the point Tommy burst into tears. Violet cursed herself; he must be picking up on how she was feeling. He couldn't understand what was happening.

"And you needn't think you're leaving him with me in that state, while you swan off for the day."

"Mam!" Vi protested. "I'm not swanning off, as you call it. I'm going to work."

Alf appeared from behind Elsie. "Tommy can come to work with me for a bit, we're not busy. I'll bring him back here in an hour or two."

Violet blinked and let out the breath she'd been holding. Maybe Dad intended to keep his word to Billy. She'd never known him to intervene on her behalf before. "Thanks, Dad."

He nodded and led Tommy off to the workshop where he worked as a cartwright. Vi wondered how much longer Dad would have a job at all; between the war and the new motorised vehicles, there wasn't much call for carts.

Every few minutes Violet wondered what Billy was doing now. She chided herself and tried to focus on getting ready to leave for the hat factory. If Billy had gone to work as normal, she wouldn't have been so distracted. At least for the moment he'd still be in England. She just wasn't sure where.

By the time Vi arrived at Strywell & Sons, she was over an hour late and no one could have mistaken the fact she'd been crying. She was called into the office of Mrs Prendergast, the overseer for the girls on the first floor. Vi hadn't even removed her coat and wondered if she was about to be given her papers.

The office, which was glazed on all sides, allowed Mrs Prendergast an eagle's view of the girls, an aspect she never ceased to make best use of. As managers went, Mrs Prendergast was not an unkind woman, but no one would have accused her of being soft.

"Well, Mrs Dobson, how do you account for the time?" The office was as stark and severe as Mrs Prendergast herself looked. What few papers there were on the table were perfectly aligned and the two bound ledgers on the end of the desk were precisely stacked.

Violet was determined not to cry in front of Mrs Prendergast, but she was struggling to hold on to her emotions. "Billy... my husband... signed up... gone..." she managed with a deep breath between each word. She coughed and composed herself a little. "It won't happen again."

Although she could have been mistaken, Vi thought Mrs Prendergast's face might have softened.

"You're quite right, it won't happen again — not and you keep your job here. I shall dock the time from your wages, including long enough for you to make yourself presentable before you join the girls. If you go out looking like that, they'll all be downing tools." Without further word, Mrs Prendergast sat behind her desk and picked up some paperwork.

Violet realised she'd been dismissed from her interview and wasn't sure whether to say thank you or just leave. As quietly as possible, she left the office and headed to the rest room to freshen up. She knew Mrs Prendergast would clock when she reached her bench, and Vi was well aware that if it caused any disruption to the other girls then they'd all have pay docked. She splashed some water on her face and dried it on the towel. Her hand was trembling as she tried to reapply what little make-up she wore. It might have been easier to give it up as a bad job, but she wanted to cover the sorrow that her face insisted on showing. She couldn't afford to lose this job. It was hard enough to find work when you were a married woman, even without all the layoffs which were occurring as a result of the war.

She had long since grown used to the smell of the adhesive as she glued as many of the hat brims as she could. She'd worked in a number of departments over the years, and although this was far from her favourite part of the process, there was no point in complaining if she wanted to keep working. The factory was a noisy place, but from machinery sound rather than chatter; there'd be nothing said until break. One visit to Mrs Prendergast in a day was more than enough for anyone.

When the claxon sounded for the end of the shift, Violet couldn't wait to go home to Tommy. She'd focussed hard on her work, trying not to think about Billy, but as she put on her coat, she wondered where he was and when she'd hear from him.

It would be their first night apart since they'd married. He'd been nineteen then and she was eighteen. Of course, she'd already been expecting Tommy, but they'd talked about marrying even before she'd found out. It was Elsie's disapproval when they were first courting that had made them wait before they married. They'd wanted a place of their own, so that it wouldn't matter what Elsie thought. Then Tommy had come along, and they'd had to beg for a place to stay. She sighed. She wouldn't be without Tommy for anything, but it hadn't made it easy. At least tonight with no Billy, Tommy would still be there to cuddle up to.

By the time Vi returned to Ivy Terrace, the day had taken its toll. All she wanted to do was to kick her shoes off and have a sit down. Tommy came running to the gate before she'd even opened it.

"Mam, Mam, can we play football? I've been good all day, I promise."

Vi looked down at her son and smiled. Still only four and already the obsession was taking hold. "You play out here a while, Tommy. There are a few things I need to do. Maybe we'll have five minutes before you go to bed." She hated seeing him looking disappointed.

"Grandma says I mayn't kick the ball against the wall or she'll put a hat pin through it."

"Oh, did she now?" Vi said through gritted teeth. "Then perhaps it's best you play with the hoop until I come out."

"Oh, Mam."

"Don't 'oh, Mam', me, young man." Vi's patience was starting to wane.

"But Dad would have…"

"And don't tell me what Dad would have done. Dad isn't here…" Vi could get no more of the sentence out, so left her son in the yard and hurried indoors.

"Is that you, Violet?"

"Who else do you bloody well think it is?" Vi muttered under her breath, but made no audible reply to her mother-in-law. She was going upstairs to her room for five minutes before she did or said anything else.

"You'll be needing to put the potatoes on." Elsie's voice sounded like Stan's nails had done on the slate at school years ago. Stan had always known how to wind her up, and it seemed her mother-in-law was no better; she'd had plenty of practice.

Violet pretended she hadn't heard and carried on upstairs. A short delay before eating wasn't going to kill them.

Once in her room, Violet took a few deep breaths. "Stay strong," she muttered as she removed her hat and coat and exchanged them for her apron. She ran her hand over the coarse fabric of Billy's jacket, which was hanging in the wardrobe. "Best not to take much with me," he'd said when he was sorting his things the previous night. "It's not as though I'm going on holiday." That had made them laugh. When did the likes of them ever go further than the outskirts of Billingbrook, never mind on holiday? He'd promenaded with her around the tiny bedroom, pretending to be all la-di-da.

She took the jacket off its hanger and for a moment hugged it to her. She put it to her face to breathe in the scent of him, but could only smell Woodbines. Then she sighed, put it back on the hanger and closed the wardrobe door, as though safeguarding the memories it held.

Once Vi had put the shepherd's pie in the oven to cook, she went out to spend five minutes with Tommy. "Just a few kicks, then it's up to bed for you, my lad."

His beaming grin as he kicked the ball lifted her spirits. It went off at an angle from his foot and clunked against the watering can.

"What was that?" Elsie shouted.

Violet held her finger to her lips, so that Tommy remained silent. "I was just watering the vegetables, nothing more." It was the first thing she thought of and unlikely for April, but as all was quiet from inside, she nodded to Tommy to carry on. She hoisted her skirt to kick the ball back to Tommy and realised she was smiling, genuinely smiling for the first time that day. Vi saw Tessie, the girl next door, watching her through the bedroom window and waved to her.

Tessie must be about fourteen or fifteen now. Violet couldn't remember. She'd been in service at one of the houses on the edge of Billingbrook from when she left school a couple of years ago until recently. The house had cut down on domestic staff once the war started and Tessie was let go in February. She was still looking for work as far as Vi knew. Unlike Elsie, Tessie's mam's arthritis was bad, but she never complained. It must have been hard for them.

"Mam!"

Tommy sounded exasperated and Vi realised she hadn't been paying attention. "One last kick, then you're off to bed." Vi kicked the ball using the side of her foot rather than her toe, and was surprised to find it heading where she'd intended, landing right at Tommy's feet. He kicked the ball one last time and looked pleadingly at his mam. Today Vi wasn't prepared to have a discussion about it; she needed a bit of time to herself. Besides, if there was no Billy to fall back on, she had to be firm. She picked up the ball and held out her hand for Tommy to join her going in.

Thankfully the lad didn't grumble, and once in bed he was asleep in no time. She wondered what his grandpa had had him doing earlier in the day and felt grateful.

Violet ate her meal with Elsie and Alf in near silence.

"That was lovely, love," Alf said as he passed her his plate so she could finish clearing up.

Once Vi had put everything away, she took herself off to her bedroom. Tommy was sleeping soundly. She watched him for a moment and then found some paper and a pen and sat at the small dressing table to write. They couldn't afford for her to waste what paper they had, so she thought carefully about what to say before she began. Vi had never written to Billy before; she had no idea where to start. To be fair, she didn't write anything very much, though thankfully she was capable, even if a little out of practice. She didn't want to make Billy worry about her and long for home, but neither did she want to make it sound as though she didn't care and they weren't missing him.

'Dearest Billy,

Tommy wants me to learn how to play football so I can teach him as you would. What do I know about the game? You would think having spent all my time around you and Stan I would at least know the basics. I'm going to speak to my dad to see what he tells me to do. Any tips you can give me would help.'

Vi put the pen down and let her eyes follow the stems of the roses on the wallpaper. She wondered where Billy was and what his bed for the night would be like. She presumed he'd have some training to do before they sent him over to France, but you heard stories... She shuddered. Taking one day at a time was the only way to face this, for Tommy's sake as well as her own.

Violet's eyelids were drooping, so she decided to finish the letter in the morning before she went to work. Tommy always woke her early. Although it would be difficult, she might be able to steal a few moments to write before the day took over.

When she got into bed beside Tommy, Violet felt as though nothing would keep her awake. By the time her head reached the pillow she had begun to imagine what lay ahead for Billy. She must have drifted off eventually, but when Tommy woke her next morning Violet felt groggy and still in need of sleep. She poured some cold water into the bowl and washed her face; that would soon bring her round. Then, sighing, she took the chamber pot down to empty it in the outside privy.

When Violet came home from work on Thursday she found an opened letter on the hall table in Billy's handwriting. She looked at the envelope underneath and realised it had been addressed to her. she was shaking as she went through to where Elsie was knitting a jumper for Alf.

"You opened my post." She was still incredulous that they would consider doing that.

"Well, that's a fine way to say good evening to us, I must say." Elsie lay the sleeve she was working on aside. "What were we supposed to do, wait for you to come home? He clearly meant it for all of us."

Violet could feel her anger rising. "If he'd meant it for all of us, he'd have addressed it to all of us. Kindly leave my post for me to open when I come in." She could feel her nostrils flaring and turned and left the room before she said something far worse. She took the letter upstairs to read.

'Dear Vi,

Not much to tell so far. I can't even tell you what's going on. Stan says that's because they check our letters, but the truth is, it's because I've no idea. We're training, that much I can say. We don't know where we'll be going or when. For now the barracks, in a place called Cannock, is home, although the cooking isn't as good as yours.

Look after Tommy and tell him his dad loves him. I wish we could have had one of those photographs taken of the three of us, so he could see what I look like. I hope he remembers me when I come home.

Billy.'

Violet felt a tear roll down her cheek. Why hadn't he told her he loved her? Why only Tommy? She knew he wasn't a big one for writing, but even so. She took a deep breath and was determined not to feel sorry for herself. She wiped the tear away and folded the letter. Maybe he'd say more when he wrote next time. She'd read it to Tommy later.

Putting the letter in its envelope, she placed it in her handbag where she hoped it might stay safe. Then she went to start the housework, before she heard Elsie's complaining voice.

As she worked, she focussed her thoughts on taking Tommy over to see her parents on Saturday. She was hoping to learn a little bit about football from her dad. She wanted him to show her how to play, but she realised she didn't even know what the positions were called or any of the rules, things it would have been easy for Billy to explain to their son if he asked. Vi wanted her dad to play some more cheerful tunes on the accordion as well, perhaps some of the music hall songs that she so enjoyed. They wouldn't stay into the evening when the neighbours were getting together, as Tommy being overtired on Sunday would not make for a happy day, but she was sure her dad could play the accordion just for them. She began to sing to herself as she worked.

CHAPTER 4

Goodbye Dolly I must leave you, though it breaks my heart to go,
Something tells me I am needed at the front to fight the foe,
See, the boys in blue are marching and I can no longer stay,
Hark, I hear the bugle calling, Goodbye Dolly Gray.
Goodbye Dolly Gray - Will D. Cobb 1897

12th April 1915 - The Docker Dons His Khaki Uniform - The Daily Mirror

"Well, Billy lad, I bet you wish you hadn't listened to me." Stan slapped his shoulder as they walked away from Victoria Street toward the station. "Mind you, the way they were stirring us all up to do our patriotic duty, I don't suppose I'm completely to blame."

"Not now, mate," Billy spoke quietly. He didn't have to pretend in front of Stan. He'd save the bravado for later. Stan knew how hard he was going to find leaving Vi and Tommy behind; he and Stan had been mates too long for secrets. It was different for Stan, he had no one much to say goodbye to. He was the youngest sibling and all his brothers and sisters had left home; as for his old mam, she and Stan weren't close, or at least not that Stan ever let on.

"D'ya think we'll be in the barracks local like?" Stan asked, not being able to be silent for long, a trait which always surfaced when he was anxious.

Billy lifted his head and looked ahead. "I'm guessing if we're catching the train, they must be taking us away from Billingbrook. They wouldn't use trains to take us from the town centre to the barracks, would they? I don't suppose the barracks here is big enough for all of us, if the queue on Saturday for signing up was anything to go by." For a moment Billy's spirits lifted at the thought that the station might just be a meeting point. If they stayed local, Billy wondered if they'd be allowed home; he hadn't wanted to raise Vi's hopes by telling her that could happen. He thought of the red brick barracks on the edge of the town. It was an imposing place, but there'd been hundreds of men joining up. He doubted that the Billingbrook Barracks could house them all.

Billy pitied anyone planning to catch local trains that morning. The station was completely overrun by young men and lads, most with a holdall of possessions. He recognised some of them from the terraces at Billingbrook United, but knew few of them by name.

"Look lively there, lads."

Billy raised an eyebrow to Stan. "This is it, then. We're supposed to do as we're told."

Stan laughed. "That's never happened yet. They'll have their work cut out with me."

Billy looked at the sergeant, smartly dressed in uniform, who was barking orders and he hoped Stan wouldn't push his luck too far. "This isn't school, Stan. It won't just be a wrap over the knuckles or a tanned backside." He painted on a face that hid the churning worry he was feeling. He'd taken many a teacher's caning on Stan's behalf.

"Name?"

"Billy Dobson." Billy stood a fraction taller.

"William Dobson, Sergeant," the soldier barked back, emphasising the 'Sergeant'.

By the way he was still looking at him, Billy could only assume he was supposed to repeat what he'd said. "William Dobson, Sergeant." He paused and shifted his weight to the other foot.

This time the soldier nodded and directed Billy to join a dishevelled group of local lads, many of whom were a few years younger than he was. Stan, even having witnessed Billy's exchange, omitted the 'sergeant' the first time he replied. Billy knew it must have been deliberate, but was relieved that his mate seemed to have got away with it. It was good that the sergeant didn't know Stan as well as Billy did right then.

"Did you just change your name?" Stan asked as he caught up with Billy. "You've never been William Dobson in your life. You weren't even christened that."

"If the sergeant wants to call me William, he can bloody well call me William and I'm not going to argue." Billy sighed. He couldn't face confrontation, not today.

Stan opened his mouth to argue but Billy shot him a look, and from Stan closing his mouth again it was clear he'd understood.

There was no sign of the train, but as the soldier in charge moved away from the station's entrance it was apparent that he had the contingent he was expecting. Despite the number of men milling around, Billy had no difficulty hearing the instructions as the sergeant addressed them.

"From now on, lads, you are part of the 14th East Lancashire Battalion, the Billingbrook Pals. You will live and breathe your battalion and follow my orders. You are now heading to Cannock. Any questions?"

Billy couldn't imagine any of them wanting to ask questions at this stage. For the moment, even Stan seemed lost for a cocky reply, although Billy feared that was unlikely to last long.

"Where the bloody hell are we going?" Stan asked Billy as he rolled a cigarette.

Billy gave him a look. "I think we skipped that class when we were in school. How the heck should I know where Cannock is? I can tell you two things — it's not here, and they don't have a football team that plays against Billingbrook. That's all I can tell you."

"Staffordshire somewhere," one of the other lads chipped in.

Billy looked the youth up and down. The way he was dressed, the lad was from a better part of town than he came from, let alone where Stan lived. "Right, thanks. What's wrong with Lancashire? You'd have thought we had places as good as anywhere in Staffordshire."

The youth laughed. "I think it's the Germans we're supposed to be fighting this time, not another English county. I'm David Moore." He stuck his hand out for Billy to shake.

Billy was a bit surprised, but took the proffered hand nonetheless.

"Well, Davy boy, this here is Mr William Dobson." Stan smirked and gave a mock salute.

"Give over, Stan. Billy Dobson," Billy said, shaking David's hand. "Don't mind Mr Stanley Bradley." He pulled a face at Stan.

Stan followed suit and shook the lad's hand, after having moved his cigarette out of the way.

"You two already know each other?" David asked,

looking from one to the other.

"Just a bit." Stan laughed. "Best mates since he caught me stealing an apple from Agnes Braithwaite when we were six."

Billy saw the look of horror on David's face. "He was hungry, he'd had no breakfast. I made him give it back, but I shared my lunch with him."

"He did better than that," Stan said and looked at his feet. "He gave me his whole sandwich."

They were spared any further comment on the subject by the steam engine coming into sight around the bend in the track. They stood back as the engine came alongside the platform and let out a very satisfying sigh of steam. It sounded as though the train was glad of the rest once the brakes were applied.

"Well, here's a first," Billy said as he opened the carriage door and climbed up.

"Have you never been on a train before?" David asked as he followed.

"We've never bleedin' been out of Billingbrook before, never mind on a train." Stan let out a low whistle as he looked around him. "So this is how the other half lives." He laughed and slung his bag onto the rack above the seats.

As the train rattled south from Lancashire, Billy tried to enjoy the scenery. Stan had bagged the window seat in their compartment, but the window was down and it gave a good enough view of the countryside as it passed. He wondered when he'd next see the hills above Billingbrook, or take Tommy down to the river. Why had he ever done this? Of course fighting for King and Country was vital, but he hadn't needed to go yet. What on earth had made him want to join up? All that bloody propaganda. He should have seen past that and he probably would have done, if he hadn't had a beer or two. Well, he was here now — he was not going to be found wanting, whatever the outcome. Someone had to keep Stan out of trouble, and it may as well be him.

"Smoke?" David offered the cigarettes to Billy and then Stan. Both took one and lit up.

"Ta," Billy said, waving some of the smoke away. He wondered what had made David sign up. The lad was either excited or nervous, the way he seemed so eager to please.

"Mother didn't want me to join up," David said as he took the packet back from Stan. "Father said he thought I'd be called up soon anyway and I'd be given better training if I went now. His is a protected business, but he knew I wanted to do my bit."

Billy wasn't quite sure what to say in reply. "How old are you?"

"Eighteen," David said.

Billy shook his head. He'd become a dad when he was not much older than Davy, and yet the lad still seemed so very young.

"I'm supposed to be learning the business with Father, but he says that can wait until I come home."

Billy suspected he'd know the lad's entire life story long before the train arrived at their destination; David seemed to have attached himself to Billy and Stan. Billy supposed it wouldn't hurt to take the lad under their wings. He was obviously bright and that might come in useful.

"Are you the eldest?" Billy asked.

"Eldest and youngest — I'm an only child. That's why Mother would have rather I stayed at home. I've promised to write." David smiled.

Billy tried to imagine what it must feel like to watch your only son going off to war. What if it were Tommy when he was older? It would be unbearable. With a jolt he realised why his own Dad hadn't come out to say goodbye to him. His Dad had seen war and wouldn't want that for his own son. Billy stared into the distance out of the window, thinking of home.

From the moment the train pulled into the station for their garrison, no one could have been in any doubt that their life belonged to the army. Stan had that look in his eye and Billy started to wonder just how wrong things would go and how soon. For his own part, he preferred the path of least resistance. As a kid, that had often meant following Stan's schemes, but now he would simply follow instructions.

As the sergeant bellowed commands to the disparate band of men, they coalesced into a ragged group and shambled from the station toward the distant buildings. Any thoughts Billy might have had that their introduction would be a gentle one were dispelled when they were directed to the massive parade ground.

"Attention!"

An experienced soldier standing in front of their lines smartly stamped his left foot down close to his right foot. Billy copied the action. Over the next second or two he heard a scraping of feet into something resembling an appropriate stance.

"I," barked the soldier facing them, his voice several decibels higher than Billy had ever heard a man shout, "am your drill sergeant. By the time I've finished with you, you pathetic apology for a platoon, you will be proud to call yourself soldiers."

"LEFT TURN."

Again the experienced soldier in front of them completed a smart left turn, and Billy and the rest of the platoon attempted to copy. The drill sergeant then began to stalk along their lines, intermittently barking at slouching lads until all the fifty or so of them were standing uncomfortably straight. Billy didn't dare move his head, but let his eyes stray across the parade ground to see multiple platoons going through the same initiations.

They marched. They halted. They turned. They marched. Before they next stood easy and were directed to the canteen, they had undertaken two hours of drill.

"My bleedin' feet," Stan said as they sat on benches to eat.

Billy looked at Stan's shoes. No wonder his feet hurt; the shoes looked as though it was only hope that was holding them together. The issue of their uniforms couldn't come soon enough by the looks of Stan.

"We'll sleep well tonight." Billy felt like he could have slept where he was now. He needed to at least write a letter to Vi before he did that.

They'd barely finished eating before the door opened and a voice boomed, "Party's over. On your feet. Back to the parade ground at the double."

"Looks like we've got ourselves a proper sadist," Stan mumbled as he winced when he put his feet to the ground.

"What was that?" The man wheeled around and stared straight at Stan. "Name?"

"Bradley, Private, 47653."

"And why are you frowning, Bradley?" The man poked Stan's chest with a baton.

"Because me bleedin' feet hurt... sir."

"It's Sergeant, not sir. And, trust me, when you've finished doing everything I want you to do, it won't just be your bleedin' feet that hurt, Private Bradley."

Billy sighed. Stan had already brought himself to the attention of a superior — there was a surprise. How did he know this was never going to end well?

They did another hour of drill before they were finally released for some free time. By then Billy was too tired to do anything other than find his bunk. He'd have slept fully clothed if he hadn't been worried it would have breached yet another regulation. He hoped Vi would forgive him for not writing, but he didn't think he could string a coherent sentence together. His last thought as he settled down was of Violet, somewhere a long way from there, curled up with Tommy in her arms.

With a four-year-old son at home, Billy was used to being woken early in the morning. What he wasn't used to was being marched outside for drill before breakfast.

"I'd be better doing this barefoot," Stan said as he hobbled toward the parade ground. "How long before they give us our bleedin' uniforms?"

"I think it's because there are so many of us," David said, walking alongside the two of them. "I guess they have to kit out loads of us. Some of the lads have been taken that way this morning."

"How d'you even know where they need to go?" Billy asked, fascinated by how much the young lad seemed to pick up.

"Davy boy has inside info, haven't you?" Stan's spirits couldn't be kept down for long, even if his feet did hurt. He was grinning again.

"I asked," David said.

"What, simple as that?" Billy laughed. He hadn't dared ask anything so far. He was just working on the basis that if he needed to know, then someone would tell him. As it turned out, they had. It was just that he hadn't been expecting it to be the lad.

Two hours of drill was followed by breakfast and yet more drill. They were already standing straighter, despite the fatigue, in the hope that they wouldn't have the drill sergeant barking directly into their faces. At least the afternoon didn't look quite as monotonous, with physical training and an introduction to the assault course.

"Bradley!"

Stan was hanging from a rope toward the top of an obstacle, laughing. He'd failed to make it to the top and Billy guessed a mixture of tiredness and the surreal nature of the situation was getting to him.

"You are not doing this for fun." Their sergeant was addressing Stan at full volume, but doing so in a manner they were all expected to take notice of. "Your lives will depend on being able to deal with difficult terrain. The obstacles you will face in the battlefield will be very real, and if you don't climb over them, you'll be dead. Now MOVE IT."

Billy was worried that Stan would continue to laugh. Laughing was the way Stan always dealt with difficult situations — that and incessant talking. It had landed him into more trouble than Billy cared to think about. This time, Stan was able to pull himself up and continue with the course.

They were quiet for most of the time as they made their way back to camp later. Stan collapsed onto his bunk with a sigh.

"The next time I have a good idea after a drink, Billy lad, don't let me sign my name to anything."

Billy only wished he hadn't been talked into it this time.

As Stan propped himself up on his elbow, so he could light a cigarette, Billy knew he had to find a pen and paper and write to Violet before he gave in to the exhaustion he was feeling for a second day. Which parts would he tell her about? He didn't want her worrying about him. Come to that, if the letters were opened before being sent, he didn't want the censors to know what he thought of the army either. He'd just keep to the basic stuff for now. They had arrived safely and, for the time being, the main enemy was the bloody drill sergeant.

CHAPTER 5

Noo ye a' ken my big brither Jock,
His richt name is Johnny Shaw,
We'll he's lately jined a fitba' club,
For he's daft aboot fitba'.'
The Dooley Fitba' Club - James Currin - 1880s

17th April 1915 - Many Men Enlist After Yesterday's Futile Air Raid - The Daily Mirror

"Like this, love." Dad kicked the ball toward their makeshift goal in the street.

Somehow, outside her parents' house Vi felt less conspicuous, even with her skirt hitched, than she did in the back yard of the Dobsons' house. Because these houses had no yards of their own, everyone spent time out in the street; it was either that or in front of the shared privies and wash house. There wasn't anywhere else the children could play, unless they went down onto the railway embankment. That had always seemed a better idea as a child than it did now. The thought took her back a few years to when she was growing up.

Being the eldest, Vi often had to help Mam. Ena, next in line, was four years younger and had been Vi's playmate until the younger ones arrived. There'd been another before Ena, but he died before his first birthday. It meant everyone spoiled Ena when she arrived a year later, but Vi didn't mind. The two of them were always close, until Ena took up with Percy Mayberry. Why Ena married Percy in such haste, when she wasn't even expecting, Vi had no idea. He'd seemed nice enough at first, but they all knew he came from a rum family.

She kicked the ball back toward her dad as he'd shown her.

Vi thought her dad was still surprisingly nimble when it came to kicking a football, but then he was only in his mid-forties. Vi reflected how easy it was to assume that parents were old and laughed, thinking Tommy must see her in the same way. She was just glad that her dad was too old to fight. She couldn't see him volunteering, not with four children still at home. Her mother would never want to see that happen. Vi smiled. Her parents were happy, despite having so little.

Violet's younger brothers and sisters, as well as half the kids in the street, wanted to join them playing, but Dad shooed them all away so he could spend a bit of time teaching Vi one or two things about the game. She'd worry about asking him to explain more of the rules another time.

"That's it, love. You're learning fast."

Seeing the ball sail between the brick on the one side and the old bucket the other, their makeshift goal, gave Violet a real thrill. She wished Billy was here to see her, he'd be so proud.

After about half an hour, Tommy could keep away no longer. "Go on, Mam, let us play? Please?" The children had come running over and were followed by John.

"Sorry, Dad, Vi, I done me best with 'em."

As John stood catching his breath, Vi smiled. He'd reached that gangly phase when a boy's arms and legs didn't seem to fit with the rest of him; he wouldn't be bad looking once he'd grown back into his body. Vi needed to sit down anyway, so went inside to have a cup of tea with Mam and left Dad to play with the others. Dad would stay in goal, while the boys, and probably half the street, tried to score against him. He'd let some in, he always did, but the children had no idea that was happening and celebrated their victories; except John of course, but then he'd no doubt slope off for a smoke now Tommy and Bobby were under Dad's watchful eye.

"How's Dad doing with the accordion?" Violet asked her mam when she sat down with her cuppa.

"Oh, Vi love, you should have heard Maisie thanking him after Ted's do. Frank did Ted proud; he's a natural. Mrs Godber next door says her Polly goes straight to sleep when she hears your dad playing. I was worried the neighbours would be complaining about the noise, but it's quite the opposite. Mrs Simpson at number five says it's like going to the music hall without having to pay."

"What does Ena think? She's always been the one for the music hall." Vi drank the rest of her tea and took the cup over to the sink. She turned around when she realised her mam hadn't answered. "Mam, are you all right?"

Mam was frowning. "Sorry, love, just a bit worried about Ena. Percy's first words when he saw the accordion were that we could get good money if we sold it. He wanted to take it with him, to see if he could find a buyer."

"But…" Vi shook her head, not knowing what to say.

"Oh, I know, love. You don't need to tell me. Anyway, when Ena asked Dad to play her a song and then began to sing, Percy soon changed his tune. He said they could have her up on stage and make a bob or two that way."

"Ena has such a beautiful voice. She's the best of all of us when it comes to singing." Violet wondered what scheme Percy would come up with next.

"I know, love. That poor girl works her fingers to the bone, what with Percy's dad and brother to look after, as well as her job at the mill. He'd have her working all hours if he could, would Percy. Only been married to him six months and that's how it is." Vi's mother shook her head.

With Percy, there was always something — like the time he'd got hold of a big box of Camp coffee but wouldn't say where it came from. Vi hoped Ena was happy; that was the most important thing.

The conversation finished when the boys came charging into the house.

"Granddad says if I keep practising, I could be in the papers one day," Tommy said, running straight into his mother.

"Well, we'll have to go out into the yard as much as possible then," Vi said, realising that she would enjoy kicking the ball about with him.

"And Grandpa Alf can play with me more too," Tommy said.

"Grandpa?" Violet thought she'd misunderstood.

"He plays when they aren't busy at work, but I'm not to tell Grandma. He said she'd be jealous."

"Oh, did he now?" Vi was smiling. Billy's dad was a dark horse. She wondered what Elsie would say if she knew.

Over the next three weeks, Violet wrote to Billy every day. She told him more of the day-to-day things about life that he might feel he was missing, but especially about Tommy. She also asked him more questions about football and Billingbrook United. It was a shame there were no games to go to now, she'd have liked to take Tommy; it would have made her feel that little bit closer to Billy. The season had finished and, by the looks of things, wouldn't be restarting for a while, but there was still plenty in the sports pages of the *Billingbrook Mercury* for her to tell Billy about when she wrote. She had never read the sports reports before; she was starting to enjoy them, although she had no idea where some of the places were that were mentioned.

Tommy loved the time he spent in the workshop with his Grandpa Alf. The secret football sessions probably had something to do with that. However, Vi suspected it was just as much because he didn't have to be at home with Elsie during those times. When Vi had a spare moment, Tommy loved to play football with her, and she was learning fast.

As Violet walked to work on Wednesday morning, she was glad to feel the warmth of the sun on her face. She preferred the summer months when it was easier to be outdoors and when there were fewer muddy boot marks to deal with at home. She felt a twinge of discomfort and rubbed her tummy; her skirt was feeling tight and was going to need letting out. She smiled. That was a job she would enjoy doing.

She clocked on and made her way to her bench. Work was a little slower, but some people were still in need of bowler hats, which is what she was working on. Violet was a couple of hours into the day, repeating the process of sticking the brims when she gasped and clutched her stomach.

"Are you all right?" Maud at the neighbouring bench whispered to her without getting up.

Vi knew she was going to be in trouble with Mrs Prendergast, but the pain she was feeling was unbearable.

Staggering away from the bench where she'd been sitting, Violet abandoned the half-glued brim.

A voice boomed from the doorway of Mrs Prendergast's office. "Mrs Dobson, it is not break time. Please return to your bench."

Violet was doubled over in pain. Maud jumped down from her bench and went to Violet.

"The old bag will just have to moan," Maud said as Mrs Prendergast once again shouted loudly enough for them to hear her over the factory din.

"I'm sure I'll be fine. I just…" Another wave of cramps went through Violet. "I just want to curl up somewhere. I…" But the pain was too much to leave her wanting to talk.

"We'd best take you home. Wait here and I'll go see the dragon." Maud helped Violet across to the wall, so she had something to lean against. She then walked briskly across to Mrs Prendergast's office; none of them would have dared to run on the factory floor and face the consequences of that transgression.

When Maud came back, Violet was still where she'd left her. "She says I can take you as far as the front gate, but you're on your own from there — sorry. Sid might be able to help you."

Sid was a kind man, but he'd be in as much trouble if he left his position on the gate as Maud was going to be for leaving her bench. Violet knew she'd have to manage on her own.

The walk home felt like miles to Violet, as she supported herself against walls or railings after each brief stretch. She had never been so pleased to see Ivy Terrace, and for once could only hope that Elsie was around.

"Is that you, Alf," Elsie called as Violet went in through

the back door.

Violet didn't have the strength to answer and as she staggered towards the stairs Elsie came out into the hall. Violet braced herself for the inevitable rebuke as Elsie put her hands on her hips and opened her mouth, but looking at Vi more closely, the older woman's manner changed.

"Dear God, what have they done to you? Come." She took Violet's arm and gave her support as she went up the stairs. "Let's get you into bed, you're as white as the sheets on wash day."

As Violet lay back on the bed, Elsie went out of the room and came back carrying some tea.

"Get this down you, girl."

Elsie sat beside her.

"Where's Tommy?" Violet asked.

"He's at work with his grandpa, don't you worry about him. Now tell me what the pain's like?"

Violet ran through the events of the morning and Elsie nodded sagely.

"It's my guess you're having a miscarriage. It can feel pretty rough." Elsie took her hand.

In all the years she'd known her, Violet had never experienced such kindness from Elsie, but was in too much discomfort to ask more about it now. She heard voices downstairs and presumed Dad and Tommy were back for dinner.

"I'll keep them downstairs and ask Alf to take Tommy back this afternoon too." Elsie patted Vi's hand and went out, closing the door.

Violet lay as still as she could, praying that the baby would be safe and that the pains would pass. Why couldn't Billy be here to take care of her? She felt the tears run down her cheek to the pillow and did nothing to stop them.

Mid-afternoon, Violet went out to the privy. She knew now that Elsie had been right and the baby had miscarried; she was out there some while and did her best to clean up. She felt weak and emotional when she returned to the house. Elsie was once again waiting for her with tea. Seeing her there, Violet felt guarded, expecting some comment about it being for the best.

"Come and sit down, love," Elsie said, pouring out a fresh cup.

Violet didn't feel strong enough to argue.

"I'm sorry." Elsie's hand was shaking as she took the cup over to her daughter-in-law. "Hopefully you'll be able to have more when Billy comes home. I couldn't."

Violet looked up in surprise. Had she just heard her mother-in-law correctly?

"Did you want more children?" From Elsie's attitude, that thought had never occurred to Violet.

Elsie nodded. "We did. We lost two even before I had Billy, and then three more afterwards."

They sat in silence for a while.

"You will recover from this, but it takes a little time." Elsie drank some of her tea, which must have gone cold.

There were so many questions Violet wanted to ask Elsie, but didn't know where to begin. "I didn't know."

Elsie snorted. "How could you? We didn't talk about it. We're just glad we have Billy."

When Violet tried to write to Billy that evening, she could find no words to say. She wanted so much to keep her letters to him light and cheerful, but all she could think of was their lost baby and the life that wouldn't be. She stared at the page and could write no more than his name. Tommy was already asleep and she sat and listened to him, losing herself in the gentle snuffles of childhood slumber. It had never occurred to her that the Dobsons hadn't intended for Billy to be an only child. That wasn't something she wanted for Tommy; it had been wonderful growing up as part of a large family. Oh, there'd been times she could have disowned every last one of her siblings, but she loved them all nonetheless. She realised now that jealousy probably fuelled some of Elsie's comments in the past.

She turned back to the letter. *'Tommy is having a great time with your dad at the workshop. At this rate, they'll be offering him an apprenticeship before he even goes to school.'* She paused and reflected. *'Your mam is being very kind to us...'* Would that make Billy wonder what was going on? No, she thought it might just make him happy and have Billy thinking that Vi had been worrying too much. Perhaps she had.

She scribbled a few more sentences, but left out the real news. Then signed off and went to bed, lying there in the darkness wondering how long it would be until she would see Billy again.

The following morning, Violet felt wretched.

"You'd best stay here the day, love," Elsie said when Violet took her coat off the peg.

Quite out of character, Violet kissed her mother-in-law's cheek. "Thanks, Mam, but if I do that there'll be no job for me to go back to."

Elsie said nothing about the kiss, but stood with her mouth set and nodded.

They needed the money Violet earned, that was certain.

"Tommy will be fine with me here today, won't you?" Elsie said to her grandson, who looked a little surprised, but just nodded. "We might do some baking together."

It was Violet's turn to be surprised, but she too nodded, then went out of the kitchen door and through the gate to the passageway.

Violet had to walk slowly that morning. She could still feel the cramping, or more the memory of the cramping through her abdomen. All she wanted was to curl up somewhere and wait for the discomfort to pass.

"Bother." She was eight minutes late clocking on. She should have left the house earlier, but she didn't realise it would take her more time than usual. Mrs Prendergast was waiting.

"Mrs Dobson, please come to my office," the ever-vigilant Mrs Prendergast called before Violet even had a chance to sit at her bench.

Vi sighed and made her way toward the office. She just wanted to sit down.

"Mrs Dobson, I don't need to tell you that here at Strywell & Sons we expect our employees to be reliable."

Violet opened her mouth to apologise, but Mrs Prendergast had not finished.

"Not only did you take unscheduled time off yesterday, but you were late arriving this morning. This is not something we can tolerate. You can collect your wages from the pay office. I'm sorry we no longer require your services. Take this form down to them."

Violet was incredulous. She presumed if she explained, then this could be resolved. "But Mrs Prendergast, I had a miscarriage yesterday."

"Then that's another reason that you're better not to continue working at Strywells. If you're looking to increase the size of your family, then you won't be able to commit the time we expect from our employees. Goodbye, Mrs Dobson — please close the door behind you."

Violet had no idea what else she could do. She knew there were going to be job losses, so it was unlikely Mrs Prendergast would change her mind. Vi felt too weak to argue, so picked up her bag and left the office. Though she was not rebellious by nature, she didn't close the door. She collected her things from her bench, being careful not to catch Maud's eye; the last thing she needed was for Maud to be sacked as well.

By the time Violet reached the pay office she was concerned that her tiny act of defiance, in leaving Mrs Prendergast's door open, might affect her reference, but it was too late to do anything about that now. She waited while the cashier finalised her money and put it into a small brown envelope. Violet put the envelope safely away in her bag and then began the long walk home.

CHAPTER 6

For Belgium put the kibosh on the Kaiser;
Europe took the stick and made him sore;
On his throne it hurts to sit,
And when John Bull starts to hit,
He will never sit upon it any more.
Belgium put the kibosh on the Kaiser - Mark Sheridan 1914

28th April 1915 - British Repel All German Attacks - The Daily Mirror

"Dobson, Private, 47671." Billy was getting the hang of introducing himself as he was expected to do by his seniors.

"Greatcoat one, socks two pairs, boots..."

Without a word, Billy took the pile of things he was being given and went to try on the boots.

"How do they feel?" One of the ubiquitous sergeants was working his way up and down the room, checking on the recruits as they discarded their civvy shoes for the army boots.

"Here, Sarge, watch my bleedin' blisters," Stan said as the sergeant squeezed the toe of his left boot.

"We need a size bigger here," he shouted, indicating that Stan needed larger boots to try. "Having the right size boots is vital when you're going to spend so much time in them."

"And don't I know it?" Stan muttered, discarding the pair that were too small and putting on the larger pair. He looked at them and a smile broke across his face. "I don't think I've ever had a new pair of boots, not even as a nipper. There wasn't much call for them at the mill either; I had clogs for work. I made do with what shoes I could get. This last pair came from me brother Harry. I don't know why he didn't want them anymore." Stan pulled hard and tied the laces of the boots, then walked a step or two, still smiling. "In fact, I've never had this many clothes." Stan picked up the large pile. "Good job I like the colour."

In all the time they'd been friends, Billy didn't think he'd seen Stan look so happy as he did just then.

"Private Bradley," the sergeant barked as they were heading to the door.

The smile slipped from Stan's face and they both turned to see what the problem was.

The sergeant was standing, with one eyebrow raised, holding up a pair of old shoes, the sole of one flapping away from the upper. "Private Bradley, these I think are yours."

The sergeant wasn't angry and Stan instantly looked relieved. "Sorry, Sarge. It was the excitement of the new boots that made me forget all about those." He went back and took them, adding them to the top of his pile, and then joined Billy going back to the bunkhouse.

Billy couldn't help but laugh watching Stan swaggering back. There were twenty bunks in their room, all allocated to men they'd travelled with. Some of the men Billy knew by sight, but there were others he didn't. By a stroke of luck David, or Davy as they now called him, had been given a bunk in the same room. Davy knew none of the local lads; he had been privately schooled from the beginning and had most recently been away in a boarding school. He'd only come back in order to join the local regiment.

"Mother wanted me to stay in a local school, but I'd always wanted to go to the same school my father went to," he told them, standing taller as he spoke. "If I'd joined up through the school, I could have gone for officer training, but I didn't want that. I wanted to do the same as everyone else from Billingbrook. I didn't really think about the fact that I wouldn't know any of my unit. Stupid, really."

Davy was an oddball by Stan and Billy's standards. He was unlike anyone that Billy had known before. He'd led a very different life to them, and Billy couldn't really understand why anyone would turn down the opportunities that being an officer could have given the lad. But Davy was well-meaning, and Billy liked him. He admired the way Davy always started off believing he could do anything if he tried hard enough. That had never been the way that he and Stan had worked, but it was easy to see how much more you could achieve when you did.

They might all have volunteered rather than been conscripted, but if Billy had been under any illusion that joining the army would be one jolly round of camaraderie, that was shattered pretty quickly.

"Let's be having you, you lazy sluggards." The voice more roared than shouted at them early the following morning.

Billy heard Stan mutter, "Five more minutes," and wrap the thin blanket more tightly around himself.

He prodded Stan hard. He guessed it was better coming from him than the sergeant, whose life's mission seemed to be to propel them from the bunkhouse faster than a round from a rifle.

Everything seemed to be completed 'at the double', from washing and dressing, to breakfast, cleaning up and getting out on parade, but not in that order. Two hours every morning on the parade ground before breakfast set the tone for the rest of the day.

"Left, right, left, right, left, right. Halt."

"Not a-bleedin-gain," Stan muttered as they turned to face the drill sergeant.

The drill sergeant didn't miss a trick and before they knew it, he was standing practically nose to nose with Stan.

"Did you have something to say, sonny boy?"

"No, Sergeant."

Billy felt relieved that Stan was at least making an effort to comply with some things, although it was funny to hear someone barely older than they were addressing Stan as 'sonny boy'.

They continued to left turn, right turn, about turn, for long enough for Billy's stomach to growl and his feet to feel sore, even in the army boots. The drill was bad enough, but in the constant rain his wool uniform was becoming decidedly heavier and developed a wet sheep smell that any ram could have been proud of. Billy wondered just how heavy the greatcoat might feel after a thorough downpour.

Once lunch had been slopped onto their plates, and they'd eaten the edible parts and cleared away, it was back to the next stage of training, this time on the rifle range. For the first couple of weeks, they'd had to imagine what it would feel like to have a weapon in their hands. Now, each of them had responsibility for a Short, Magazine Lee-

Enfield standard issue army rifle. Billy for one had never held any sort of gun before and it felt heavy and strange. He'd even been corrected when he'd called it a gun; that term seemed to be reserved for much larger weapons used by the artillery.

They'd never had those distinctions when they were kids. Every boy had fired imaginary guns and in the battles of childhood they never missed and rarely found themselves affected by the recoil. Now, they needed not only to be able to fire straight, but strip the rifle down to clean it, reload it ready for action and to make it safe when it was not needed.

Then there were the bayonets.

"Do you think you could do it?" Davy asked, blinking.

"Do what?" Stan asked, looking with admiration at the weapons.

"Run another man through with that." Davy indicated the blade of the bayonet. "I mean, shooting a man at a distance is one thing, but up close?"

Stan moved nearer to the lad. In a whisper that was loud enough to include Billy he said, "Davy boy, if you're up close then it's him or you, and I know which I'll be choosing."

The boy's face lost all colour.

"Come on now, Stan. Give him a break." Billy clapped the boy on the shoulder. "Let's hope we're never that close, hey?"

The platoon of men who lined up across the training ground roared as they ran onward to plunge their bayonets into the hanging sacks ahead of them.

"Thrust, disembowel, disengage," their instructor shouted.

The next line of men followed shortly afterwards, and

the next, until it was Billy's turn. With the noise of other men's shouting ringing in his ears and his own voice at full volume as he went forward, Billy felt the adrenaline surge as he charged the bayonet forward at full stretch until it was driven deep into the sandbag. He pulled it out and moved to join the others, his heart still pounding.

"And that, Davy boy, is how you will do it if you have to." Billy took a few deep breaths to calm his heart rate.

Davy still looked uncertain, but he made a good attempt at it, though he appeared somewhat shaky when he returned to the group.

Billy had always had good upper body strength, from all the lifting and carrying he did as a carpenter, but even after a couple of weeks he couldn't help but notice the improvement in the strength of both Stan and Davy. For Stan that was in part down to eating enough food every day, but the repeated calls to do ten push-ups for minor misdemeanours was doing him more good than harm, and he seemed to have started to quite enjoy them.

It was the classroom learning that both Billy and Stan struggled with the most. They'd never been good at sitting still or listening, and being expected to do both was a challenge. There was no bunking off as there had been in their school days; that had always been the easy option. What Billy found odd was that the more he worked on concentrating, the easier he was finding it. He was even beginning to enjoy some of the studies, although he wouldn't mention that to Stan. His mate was still as out of place in the classroom as the coal merchant would have been among the sheets on wash day; probably as unwelcome too, for some of the questions he asked. By contrast, it was clear that Davy's school experience had been a very different one. Davy was used to learning and he picked things up quickly in the classroom. Davy could find his way around the site too, remembering where everything was. There was so much to learn that Billy was grateful for having the lad around. He'd taken to asking Davy to explain things to him at mealtimes, rather than ask the corporal who addressed them in class. Davy always managed to put things in a way that made sense to him, even if he was oversimplifying things for Billy's benefit. Billy had never had the best of memories, but maybe that, like concentration, was about practice.

It would be hard to find a lad, other than Davy, amongst their platoon who was more different from Billy and Stan, without him being one of the officers. The strangeness of the situation apart, the three of them realised pretty quickly that it was to all their benefits to stick together and help each other out.

Davy looked far less out of place behind a desk than he did on the assault course. The lad didn't have especially sharp hand-eye coordination, stamina, or for that matter courage. Thinking about it, Billy wasn't sure courage was the right term. In his and Stan's case, it was more a willingness to act without thinking about it, which amounted to much the same thing.

The other reason Billy thought having Davy around would be useful, was that he needed someone to help him keep Stan out of trouble. For that particular objective, two were definitely better than one.

"Right then, Davy boy, where are we supposed to be?" Stan asked.

Billy guessed Stan hadn't so much forgotten, as had not been paying attention. Billy shook his head. He hoped his mate would take things a little more seriously if they ever came face to face with the enemy; it was unlikely that Davy was going to be on hand to help him then.

"You know," Billy said one day as he laid his things out for inspection, "I could quite like being in the army if it weren't for the damned war."

"How do you make that out?" Stan asked, giving a last minute buff to his boots.

"I like not having to think for myself. There's always someone telling me what to do."

"You have that at home from your mam and your missus. I knew there was someone that drill sergeant reminded me of." Stan punched his arm.

Billy laughed. He had to; he didn't want the others to know just how much he missed Vi and Tommy. At least being busy every day didn't give him endless time to think. He took what chances he could to write to them; he preferred not to be too obvious about it. When he did put pen to paper, he told them about the funny things that happened and the food, rather than the fact he was scared senseless of what it was going to be like when they went over to France, or the fact he'd stuck a bayonet through an imaginary person.

Recruits were arriving at the barracks almost every day and the existing buildings weren't large enough to accommodate them all. As the number of battalions being housed increased, Billy's carpentry skills were put to good use, helping to extend the camp.

"You'd do anything to avoid that bloody drill ground," Stan said when Billy finally returned to the bunkhouse an hour after Stan and the other lads had finished. "Mind you, you missed a great game of football earlier. One of the lads used to be in United's reserve team. He's a mean striker. I think we need to keep him as our secret weapon for when we play the officers."

Billy laughed. "I'm guessing they know who's joined up in the unit — they already had my carpentry skills down. He'll have to play in disguise. Here, give me a hand with these, seeing as you do so little real work around here." He threw one of his boots to Stan and began polishing the other.

For all the impressions of being as idle as possible, Stan never let him down and readily chipped in when it was just the two of them. He was a good mate. "How's young Davy doing?"

"He's never going to be famous for his footballing skills, but he might just bail us out on the legalities on the battlefield. I'd never really thought about the fact that there were any rules to war; I just thought you saw the enemy and shot them, and that was all there was to it. I suppose I wouldn't expect to be shot if I was in the middle of surrendering. I don't much fancy the idea of being taken prisoner, but I guess it's better than being left in pieces on the battlefield. It's not like when we all used to play war down near the allotments and still go home at teatime." Stan shook his head in apparent bewilderment.

"It helps to know who the enemy is first." Billy spat on his boot to remove some dirt.

"It's just like football — one team plays in the home colours and one wears the away strip. Except there's more than two strips and the score's a lot higher." Stan threw the boot back to Billy, now in a respectable state.

Billy put the boots neatly below his bunk. "We just need to make sure that Billingbrook comes home victorious."

"Comes home at all would be a start. Mind you, I don't much fancy being back working in the mill after this. I'm happier outdoors than I ever was there. Better fed too,"

Stan said wistfully. "Makes me wonder how me old mam's doing without me under 'er feet."

"Hasn't she written to you?"

"No…" Stan paused, as if reflecting on what to say. "Thing is, she never learned to read or write, so there's not much point. I'm not really sure she ever went to school 'erself."

Billy didn't know what to say. It had never occurred to him that Stan's mam was completely illiterate. Stan's dad hadn't been around in as long as Billy could remember, and Stan never mentioned him. He'd ask Vi to go round to see Mrs Bradley and check she was all right. Vi could tell her a bit about how Stan was doing while she was there. He was sure it would cheer the older woman to know her youngest was safe and well.

CHAPTER 7

It's a queer, queer world that we live in,
And Dame Fortune plays a funny game
Some get all sunshine,
Others get the shade
The Black Sheep of the Family - Fred Barnes 1907

*10th May 1915 - World's Grief and Rage at Lusitania Outrage -
The Daily Mirror*

After her miscarriage Violet was grateful to have a few days to recover. However, the loss of the baby brought Billy's absence more starkly into focus, and without the routine of going out to work she felt disorientated.

She was looking out of her bedroom window at nothing in particular when she heard Elsie shouting up the stairs to her.

"Where are those sheets, Violet? It's washday and no time for dawdling."

Violet smiled. It was the first time that Elsie had spoken to her sharply since she'd lost the baby. Vi guessed it was the older woman's way of telling her it was time to carry on with life; with the number of miscarriages that Elsie had suffered, she had probably earned the right to make that point. Vi stripped the bed and tried to return to some sort of normality. Over the next few days she was happy to go about the chores that needed doing at Ivy Terrace, and when there was time, she took Tommy to her parents' house for a couple of hours. That gave her a chance to see her family and play football with Tommy without feeling conspicuous. She loved those times and could, for a while, forget all their problems.

"It's not right, them sacking you like that," Dad said when she first went over.

Violet shrugged. "There's no good dwelling on that now, there's not much I can do about it. I just need to find another job."

"Let's hope you can find someone that realises what a gem they've got," Dad said as he left the table to go back to work himself.

"Isn't there enough money with what Billy's being paid?" Mam asked.

"I don't know. There might be if we didn't want a place of our own," Violet said, thinking through the costs. "We could just about manage, but we've been putting a bit by. There wouldn't be enough to do that." Her wages might have been much lower than Billy's, but they made a big difference to what they could afford.

It was not until a few days later that Violet began to think about looking for another job. No one had expected this war to drag on the way it was doing, and many businesses were laying women off; she supposed everyone was trying to economise. Wasn't the Government encouraging them all to do that, anyway? So much for the war being over by Christmas. She supposed it would be over by some Christmas or other, but it hadn't been the last one and it might not be the next.

Vi took the savings jar down off the shelf and counted what was there. She would have no choice but to put some of that toward the bills until she found another job.

Feeling a wave of determination, Violet picked up her bag and coat and headed downstairs. "I'm going to see what jobs there are. Tommy's gone to the workshop with Dad so I'll make the most of the time."

Elsie nodded. "Buy some potatoes while you're out. It'll save me a trip."

Violet was planning to call at the greengrocers to ask if anyone had mentioned any positions, but decided to do that on the way back so she didn't have a heavy load to carry.

After three hours of walking to every place she could think of — the newsagent, the noticeboards outside the main factories, even some of the shops in town — Violet felt thoroughly dejected. She'd bought a copy of the *Billingbrook Mercury* to check the situations vacant, but other than that she had no notion where else to look. Quite apart from the war meaning fewer suitable jobs, no one wanted to employ a married woman with a child. She'd even wondered about removing her wedding ring and not telling the truth, but if she secured a position on that basis they'd only fire her when they found out.

She read the news pages of the paper, as had become her custom since Billy went off for training. She had no idea where Ypres was, or what a salient was when it was at home, but she shuddered as she read the correspondent's words: 'shelling our trenches all of the morning, before bringing their gas cylinders into play'. She forced herself to read to the slightly happier conclusion that thanks to the masks being worn, the men were not killed, but fought back bravely and to the surprise of the enemy.

The weeks passed, and still Violet hadn't found work. Billy's letters didn't ask about the hat factory, so she didn't mention it to him; he had enough to worry about without adding that. The training sounded hard work, and he said he thought his battalion would travel to France soon. She shuddered. He sometimes included the funny stories of what Stan was doing, especially for her to read to Tommy, who loved to hear them.

In her turn, Vi had told Billy about losing the baby. She couldn't lie to him when he asked about their growing family. She treasured his response and carried it everywhere.

'My darling girl,

I'm so sorry that I wasn't there for you when you lost our baby. I wish you hadn't had to go through that on your own. I love you more than anything in the world and always will. I'm sure I'll be home soon, back with my girl. When I am, nothing will ever part us again.

Your ever loving

Billy.'

No one tried to guess when 'home soon' might be, but she clung to the thought nonetheless. Even more, she clung to the words that he loved her. This time, those words weren't addressed to Tommy, or to anyone else; they were for her and whilst he might not say it often, she knew he meant what he said.

In another of his letters Billy had asked her to visit Stan's mam, and whilst she had time on her hands she took the opportunity to go.

"Will Uncle Stan be there?" Tommy asked as they went.

"No, love. He's still away training with Dad."

"Why are we going then?" Tommy was all questions.

Why, indeed? Billy thought it would reassure Stan that his mam was all right, but as he'd never seemed overly fussed Vi wasn't so sure. As far as she knew, Billy had never been invited back to Stan's house. It didn't seem odd now that they were adults, as the house was his mam's; but when Vi came to think about it, even as kids, she didn't think Billy had ever mentioned going.

Stan's mam lived nearer to her parents than to Billy's. Turning into the street, she could see the railing of the railway embankment at the far end. These were back-to-back houses, like the ones her parents lived in, so only a front door and no garden front or back. She was used to all the kids being out in the street, that was the same in her day; but as she looked at the urchins on Lancaster Street, she held Tommy's hand a little tighter.

Hardly any of the steps had been scrubbed and there was filth in the gutters where the children were playing.

"Mam," Tommy said, frowning up at her, "I don't want to go to Stan's house."

Vi could well understand the sentiment, but as lightly as possible tried to reassure the child. "We won't be here long. Just say hello to his mam and check she's all right."

Stan's mam's house was only one away from the railway embankment and the brickwork was blackened with soot from the passing trains. Vi knocked tentatively on the dull and cracking paintwork of the door.

"Who's 'at?"

Vi heard shuffling from inside and waited.

"Can we go?" Tommy was tugging at her hand. "I don't like it."

"Not yet, love. We'll just say hello."

The woman who opened the door could have been any age from forty to eighty; her hair was unbrushed, and she smelled of alcohol and stale urine. Violet struggled to contain the gasp she felt and wished she'd left Tommy at home. Mercifully, the boy was struck dumb.

"Mrs Bradley?"

"Who's asking?" The woman hiccupped.

"I'm Mrs Dobson, Billy Dobson's wife."

Stan's mam stared at her blankly but said nothing.

"Stan's friend Billy. I'm Billy's wife."

"He's not home. He didn't come home last night neither."

Violet opened her mouth to explain, but realised that with the state of Mrs Bradley there was little point. She began to say, "Thank you," but Stan's mam had already closed the door and Vi could hear her shuffling away. She sighed, and keeping a firm hold of Tommy, turned and headed back along the street.

"She wasn't very nice, was she?" Tommy said. "She can't be Stan's mam."

Violet smiled at the simple view of children. Tommy worshipped Stan; in Tommy's mind, she guessed he'd think that meant Stan's mam would be a nice person too. Vi had no idea what she would write back to Billy. Perhaps it was best not to mention that she'd even come here.

When she arrived home, Violet went to the jar on the shelf. Their savings were reducing, and funds were starting to run low; if she didn't find work soon, she'd be out begging. Tommy was growing fast and needed some new clothes. She could patch the ones he had pretty well, but there was no growing room left. Her own mam couldn't help, as the clothes they'd all had were handed down so many times there was nothing left by the time Bobby needed them, let alone any spare to pass to Tommy. She thought again of where Stan's mam lived and shuddered. If the Dobsons hadn't taken her in when she was pregnant at eighteen, that could have been how her life would have gone. It didn't bear thinking about.

Then she pulled herself up. At least she kept Tommy clean and tidy, even if some things were patched here and there. She'd never end up like Stan's mam. That wasn't just about money; Mrs Bradley clearly had enough to find alcohol when she wanted it. Poor Stan. Why had he never said? She supposed he didn't want them to know. That thought made her feel guilty for going; it was as though she'd stumbled on a secret that she shouldn't have seen.

The weather was warmer now that it was July. Vi wondered what it would be like for Billy when he headed to France. He hadn't gone yet, but from what he said, he didn't think it would be long before they did. Would the moon and the stars look the same to him at night as they did to Vi? Would he see the same clouds as they passed across the sky? She sighed and went back to her early morning chores.

As she stripped the bed for wash day, Vi looked out of the window and saw Tessie from next door heading off along Victoria Street.

"It's early for Tessie to be going out, has she found work?" Violet asked Elsie when she went downstairs.

"There're no maids wanted, her mam said that last week. I don't know if she's found something else. Why don't you go round and ask?"

Violet nodded and went out of the gate and into the adjoining back yard. She knocked at the kitchen door. Mrs Brown was always cheerful.

"Come in, Violet love, I've just put the kettle on."

"Thank you, Mrs Brown, that's very kind of you. I just wanted to ask if Tessie had found work? I saw her setting off this morning, and I just wondered…"

"Oh, Violet love, we should have thought to tell you. She's found a place up at the factory making munitions. I think there're still vacancies. I could ask Tessie…"

"Thank you, Mrs Brown." Violet didn't stay to hear any more, but headed back out to her own kitchen.

"She's got a job in a factory. They're still taking people on," Violet called to Elsie as she put the sheets into the tub. "I'll just do these and then I'll go up there."

"You'd better take yourself there fast, girl. You can do the sheets when you get back."

Violet almost smiled to see the old Elsie returning. Clearly her mother-in-law wasn't planning to go soft on her indefinitely, but that was all right. Things would never feel quite as they had before her miscarriage, now that Violet had a little better understanding of what lay behind Elsie's hardness.

"Can you mind Tommy while I go?"

Elsie's lips were set once again as she said, "I've been minding him all this time, I don't suppose I'll be given the chance to say 'no' now."

Violet resisted the urge to kiss her mother-in-law's cheek again and simply said, "Thank you," before removing her apron and going to fetch her handbag.

Caulder and Harrison was a large brick-built factory on the edge of town. It had been an engineering works; Violet had no idea what they'd actually made before the war or whether they were still doing that, but she could see that on the gate was a large poster saying 'Munitions Workers Needed. Help the War Effort. Apply Within.'

She took a deep breath. While she was walking, she had been wondering what to say about why she'd left her previous role and had settled on there being less work due to the war. That was at least true, even if it hadn't been the reason they'd let her go.

After her enquiry at the gatehouse she was shown into a long corridor where others, mainly women, were sitting on chairs waiting. The men who were in the line were older, and she guessed that was because so many of the younger ones seemed to be signing up now. The line was quite long. If this many people were applying, then what chance did she have? Who wanted a married woman with a child to look after?

One by one, the line moved down. Violet had no idea about the success or otherwise of each of the people waiting, as they went out by a different door. It was almost as though one by one they just disappeared. That thought made her smile.

She was a good worker, she could tell them that. She had a reference from Strywells; it didn't say much, but there was nothing to suggest she wouldn't do a good job.

It was well over an hour before her turn came. By that time Violet had convinced herself there couldn't be enough jobs for all of them. She'd be polite and thank them and hope there would be other places to try; she might even ask them to keep her name on file in case any positions should fall vacant again.

She was shown into the office and offered a seat. A bespectacled man was sitting behind the desk writing notes into a large ledger. She waited for him to speak.

"Name?"

"Mrs Violet Dobson."

"Previous position?"

"I worked at the hat factory." Violet was nonplussed by the perfunctory nature of the questions. Each time she answered, he jotted down what she'd said.

"Reason for leaving?"

"They were over-staffed due to the war. Not so many…"

"Address?"

She continued to answer his questions and waited for him to write down her answers. Eventually, he looked up at her. "Mrs Johnson will show you where you'll be working. You will be working twelve-hour shifts. You will need to hand this in to the wages office." He handed her a slip of paper with her hours and rate of pay. "You can start at eight o'clock tomorrow. Don't be late."

"I won't, Mr…?"

"Next."

Violet was ushered out by Mrs Johnson and led along the corridor of the building. There were windows to a row of inner offices but the glass was distorted, making it impossible to see what went on inside. Each door had a little metal plate with either a name and job title or a department name. She tried to take them in as she went past: 'Cashiers'. 'Accounts'. 'Mr A. C. Parker, Accountant'.

"You'll come past the gatehouse and then to the B entrance in the morning. You will need to leave your bag in a locker out here." Mrs Johnson indicated a bank of grey lockers. "You will have to change into your overalls, so arrive in plenty of time. No jewellery, including wedding rings. No metal anywhere about your person." Mrs Johnson looked her up and down. "And that includes corsets if you wear one."

Violet blushed but shook her head. She'd managed to get her figure back after Tommy was born and hadn't resorted to a corset, which she found far too restrictive.

"You need to take a great deal of care around the explosives, Mrs Dobson, so we like our girls to be of a sober disposition and prepared to follow the rules to the letter. Do I make myself clear?"

"Yes, Mrs Johnson." Violet was starting to wonder if Mrs Johnson were in some way related to Mrs Prendergast and almost smiled. She decided she'd go next door to talk to Tessie when the younger girl came home from work, just to see if there was anything else it would help for her to know.

Violet checked the time before leaving the factory so she could see how long the walk would take. Maybe she could walk with Tessie in the morning; it would be better than going in alone.

As she washed the sheets and put them through the mangle that afternoon, Violet was singing as she worked. She couldn't wait to write to Billy to tell him the good news. She would be doing her bit for the war effort and helping to make sure he and others going to the Front had what they needed. It was better paid than the hat factory too; longer hours, but that would be all right. Maybe she could put the money back in the jar and build up their savings. Once Billy came home, they might still be able to rent a place of their own. That was something to look forward to.

CHAPTER 8

So we are at the benches,
and our pals are in the trenches.
And all our work serves the end,
And mere women too,
are here to help us throughout
In our efforts our world to defend.
Kathleen Bruckshaw - Munition Workers Song

*21st July 1915 - 'Theatredom' Mobilised For Charity - The Daily
Mirror*

By the time Tessie came home from her shift it was too late
for Violet to go round, so she decided to catch Tessie as she
set off for work the following day.

For the third time that morning, Violet checked that she'd
taken her jewellery off. She'd only ever worked at the hat
factory before and had started there when she left school
eleven years ago. Thankfully, when she had Tommy she
hadn't been working on Mrs Prendergast's section of the
factory, otherwise she'd have lost her job then.

Vi put her hand to her neck, checking for her necklace
again and then laughed at how silly she was being. She'd
be fine, but she'd be grateful for some company on the way
to work and the chance to ask all the things she'd forgotten
on the previous day.

"You be good, I'm going outside so I catch Tessie." Vi kissed Tommy and went to wait at the front of the house. She couldn't bear the disappointment on his face that she wouldn't be around during the daytime anymore; she wouldn't even be home by the time he went to bed, but that was something she hadn't explained. Her mother-in-law scowled when Violet told her the hours she'd be working, but said nothing, for which Violet was grateful.

"Good morning, Tessie," she said, as the girl closed the gate to the passage and came out into Victoria Street.

Tessie stopped and looked confused. "Hello, Mrs Dobson. Are you waiting for me?"

They fell into step together. "Yes, I am. Did your mam tell you I went to the factory yesterday to see if there were any jobs going? I'm going to be working there too, so you'd best get used to calling me Vi. Mrs Dobson makes me sound really old. I'm only twenty-three."

"That is old to me." Tessie grinned. "I suppose it is a lot younger than me mam. Vi it is then." Tessie seemed delighted and slipped her arm through Violet's as though they were close friends. "The work's ever so hard."

Violet thought she already knew a thing or two about hard work, so wasn't unduly worried.

"We have an hour break at lunchtime, but the rest of the day we have to keep our heads down. You need to concentrate on what you're doing. They've made ever so clear that it would be dangerous to make a mistake."

"How dangerous? What could happen?" There had been talk about some of the chemicals at the hat factory being risky, so that didn't worry Vi. Everyone knew the expression 'mad as a hatter'; it was one of the reasons they hadn't stayed working on one section too long at Strywell & Sons.

Tessie frowned. "Well, one man was saying that you could blow the whole place up, but I think he was just trying to scare us. I don't think you could, really. Oh, and make sure you push all your hair into your cap. It goes yellow otherwise. That's from the chemicals."

By the time they arrived at the factory Tessie had explained about packing the explosives into the shells and just how heavy the finished shells were. It was only then that Violet really thought about what they were making. She hadn't been given any explanation the day before and there'd been no chance to ask questions, even if she had known what to ask. These were weapons, designed to kill. She shuddered. As her mind wandered to what Billy and Stan had gone off to do, she had to take a deep breath and focus hard on where she was. In her mind she needed to separate the job she was doing from what others would do with the finished product. When she'd made hats, it was the opposite; she used to daydream about the people who would wear them and where they might go. She certainly couldn't let herself think like that about shells.

"I'm 'C' entrance," said Tessie as they approached the factory. "I'll see you at lunchtime. You'll be all right."

Despite Tessie being so young and nearly nine years younger than Violet, it was she who seemed like the adult as they parted. Violet only wished that she had the same level of confidence as the girl. She headed for 'B' entrance and the locker she'd been shown. By eight o'clock when the whistle sounded, she was at her bench and Mrs Simmons was already showing her what she needed to do to pack the shells.

The work was far more physical than hat making had been, but Vi was used to the smell of chemicals on the air and thought little of the risks, despite Tessie's warnings.

What was the danger she might be in compared to Billy facing the enemy? She was doing this for him. She was helping to keep him safe and bring him home all the sooner. As long as she focussed on that, she was sure it would seem all right.

By the end of the day she was more tired from the intense concentration than from the physical side of things. She knew that would be easier as she became more familiar with the tasks. For now, there seemed to be a lot to remember, and she wanted to do a good job.

Walking to and from work with Tessie soon became a normal routine. As the weeks passed Violet realised, from picking Tommy up, that she was getting stronger. Even though he was growing, she was finding him easier to lift than she had done in the past. The days were long, but Elsie seemed to complain less about caring for Tommy than she used to, so life fell into a more comfortable pattern. Violet's letters to Billy were now filled with news of the goings on at work as well as how Tommy was progressing. It was the people she worked with she wrote about; they'd been warned not to say anything about the factory workings, and Vi was very careful about this.

Some nights, after Tommy was asleep, Vi would take Billy's jacket out of the wardrobe and hold it to her. Even the smell of the Woodbines was fading, but she tried hard to remember as she held it. Then she'd put it away again and sit down to write.

'I don't know what you're going to think when you see me. I'm a proper canary now that the front of my hair has bleached. All the girls who work at the factory are so easy to recognise. It's like having a uniform, but without needing to wear my overalls at home.'

Violet looked across to the dressing-table mirror at the way her hair was now two-tone. It could almost be a fashion if it was something they chose, although what people would think if she'd done it deliberately, she couldn't imagine; they'd have said she was 'a girl with loose morals'. The very thought made her smile. She was proud of how it looked; it showed she was working for the war effort. She couldn't afford to be one of those women doing all the charitable work, but she was glad to be doing something.

She went back to finishing the letter to Billy and then climbed into bed beside their son.

Until recently, the factory had been staffed mainly by men. Some of the ones who were left, those who hadn't joined up due to age or family commitments, still played football in the yard at lunchtime. Tessie and some of the other younger girls would watch them and shout to the players; it was friendly enough banter and Violet would watch from a distance.

"What was that?" Florrie shouted. She was a girl about a year older than Tessie, from what Vi could gather. "We could do better than that, couldn't we girls?" The girls around her all laughed.

"Go on then, prove it." The men enjoyed the taunts as much as the girls and were happy to respond. "I'd like to see you try."

Violet gasped as Florrie jumped down from the bench she'd been sitting on and marched out into the yard in her overalls to join the game. "Here, Tessie, give us a hand."

Tessie broke into joyful laughter and went out to join Florrie.

"Tessie Brown, whatever would your mother say?"

called Violet, concerned about what Tessie was doing.

"Best not tell her," Tessie called as she rolled her sleeves back and laughed. "You could always come and play, too."

Violet gasped. Whatever would people have to say about that if she did? Playing with the children at home or at her parents was one thing, but playing against the men was most unseemly. She looked around to see if any of the overseers were around. They were tasked with managing the moral standards of the women employees, and Violet thought they might have something to say about their girls playing football - and against the men. She didn't want Tessie to lose her job. There was no sign of them, and Vi relaxed a little.

"Beattie, what's your dad going to say when he hears what you're doing?" one of the older men called to a girl as he walked past. "Someone's bound to tell him."

"Oh, go on, Uncle Walter, I'm not doing any harm. Don't you go saying a word to him. Please? Let me leave being grown up and respectable until I'm married. Besides, don't you know there's a war on? Everything's different now."

"Don't be cheeky to your Uncle Walter, now, young lady. I'll turn a blind eye, but don't you go making a habit of it. You'll never find yourself a husband at that rate."

Vi watched Beattie's Uncle Walter go back into the main building and shook her head. Even though she could see the point he was making, she couldn't tear herself away from watching. She found herself a place to sit a little distance from the makeshift pitch and was surprised to see that there were now about half a dozen of the girls out there ready to play. They were the younger ones, all still under twenty by the looks of them. Eva, who worked opposite her, was among them. How could they be so bold?

Violet laughed to herself, watching. The girls weren't much of a threat to the men, despite their bravado. She thought of all her dad had been teaching her and how much the others would benefit from his coaching.

"Why don't you join in?" Tessie called to Violet one lunchtime as she sat watching.

"Me? A married woman, Tessie Brown, whatever would people say?" Violet was laughing but felt genuinely shocked by the suggestion. The only married women who did things like that were ones whose morality would be questioned by everybody, especially her own mother-in-law.

"Go on, Vi, what harm can it do?" Eva joined in the encouragement. "You said yourself how much fun it looked."

"Eva Podmore, whatever are you suggesting?" Violet gasped, but felt wistful that she couldn't take part. "Can you imagine what Billy's mam would have to say about that, never mind what Mrs Johnson would say? She'd have my guts for garters."

Eva stopped on the sideline to do a quick impression of the overseer of the girls' welfare for their section of the factory. "Mrs Dobson, I don't want to see such unseemly behaviour from any of the married women in my section. Your husband would be horrified."

The others laughed, but Violet wondered what Billy would think if she joined in. He loved his football, but perhaps it was too big a stretch to think of his own wife playing. Then she thought that Stan would almost certainly encourage her, if only to cause trouble.

Tessie came over to her. "You know, it is 1915, it's not

like it's Victorian times or anything."

Violet shook her head. Had times changed? Maybe they had a little, but not as much as Tessie seemed to think.

Vi started feeling low, thinking about the boys and wondering where they were and whether they were safe. They were still at the training camp when Billy last wrote, but he thought they'd be heading off any day now. It was a way of thinking she couldn't allow herself to fall into, so she turned her full attention back to the game taking place in the yard.

Whatever the weather, that time in the fresh air was essential before going back into the chemical smell of the factory. She did allow herself to wonder if the boys were playing much football. Billy had mentioned early on that they played a lot of sport, but he'd said less about that in his last letters; he'd talked more of the route marches they'd done, carrying full kit, and of the work he'd been doing in helping to extend the camp.

When she sat down to write to Billy that night, Violet decided to tell him about the girls joining in the game, to see if he made any comment when he replied. Looking at the sheet of paper, she moved the pen from hand to hand. She wouldn't say she'd like to have a go; instead, she'd leave that until she knew what he thought. That couldn't do any harm.

'You should see the girls at break, some of them are getting quite good. They've even jokingly said they'll take on the men in a proper match. Most of the men seem to be my dad's age or older, or not old enough to join up yet.'

At the very least, a match like that was something she'd like to see.

Vi guessed if the match went ahead, they'd play on the field that Caulder and Harrison had recently bought in order to set up a sports club for the staff. They weren't a bad employer as far as Violet could tell. There were a lot of people working there now; the night shift arrived to pick up as the day shift finished. The benches were never idle. Two twelve-hour shifts meant work went on around the clock. They didn't routinely work Saturday and Sunday, but there was always overtime available if you wanted to keep working. Vi had done some extra Saturday mornings when the factory was busy, but she valued her time with Tommy, so she tried not to accept the extra hours all the time.

That Sunday Violet took Tommy over to see her parents.

"You look worn out, love. Are they working you hard?"

Mam was always keen to take care of her, even if only for an hour or two, and as Tommy had disappeared off with Bobby and Violet's youngest sisters, Lizzie and Kate, Violet had the opportunity to relax.

"I'm all right, Mam, but it's long hours and heavy work, lifting the shells. I just keep thinking of the boys. What I'm doing is nothing compared to them."

"That's as maybe, but you're my first concern, girl, and I don't like to see you looking so tired. Even your skin's looking a bit yellow. It's not natural."

Violet laughed. "I'm fine, Mam. We all look like that. I think it's trying to match my hair."

Queenie shook her head and put a plate of biscuits by her daughter. "Here, have a couple of those before the children come back in and we don't see them again."

Dad uncased the accordion and as quietly as was possible began to play a tune. Violet closed her eyes and let the sound wash over her. Just listening to the tune, she could feel the muscles in her neck and back starting to ease. It was a beautiful sound; he had so much natural musical ability. She presumed that was where Ena got her singing from.

By the time she and Tommy had to leave, Violet was feeling much better than she had and hummed one of the tunes as they walked.

"Bobby says we have to go to school soon. I don't want to," Tommy said.

"You won't have to go just yet. Not until next year."

Violet wondered if there would be a way for Tommy to go to the same school as Bobby when the time came. They lived in different areas of the town and the infant school near her parents' house didn't cover their area. When Billy had been a child, his parents had lived closer to that end of town; it was how he, Stan and Violet had all gone to the same school then.

"Lizzie says she's going next week, and Kate already goes." Tommy sounded worried.

"Lizzie has to go now because she's older than you and Bobby." Vi sighed.

"Well, I don't want to go. I want to work with Grandpa."

Violet didn't think that Billy would be much help on this particular issue if he'd been at home, but she'd have liked him there for support. From what she could remember, neither Billy nor Stan had been the best attendees at school, but she supposed it hadn't done them any real harm. "Maybe you could still spend time with Grandpa in the workshop during your holidays." Then she decided she'd be better to change the subject and likely as not Tommy would forget all about it before they reached home.

In the middle of August the newspapers were full of reports of the shells that had hit a coastal town in Cumbria, and the idea of war didn't seem so distant anymore.

"Do you think they could drop shells here?" Tessie asked as they walked to work the following day. "Mam says anything could happen."

"I don't know, the shells are awfully heavy. I guess we're too far from the sea for them to land here." Violet tried to imagine how scary it would be if you lived close to where the shells could reach when they were fired from the warships.

"Can't they sail up the rivers?" Tessie was clearly anxious.

"I suppose so. We must have soldiers there ready to stop them, or sailors more likely. Mind you, our river isn't big enough. You wouldn't sail those ships up here — they'd be stuck long before Billingbrook." Violet had never seen a warship except in the newspaper, and found it hard to imagine how big they were; but she did know a river she could wade across wasn't going to be big enough for more than a toy boat.

"Vi," Tessie said, but her voice faltered.

Vi looked at her. "What is it?"

"The shells that they fired on those people… are they like the ones we make?" Tessie was biting her bottom lip as she asked and looked very young.

Vi nodded. "I don't think they meant for them to hit people from what I read in the paper — but yes, they are like what we make. I try not to think about it. I just think about the job. It's easier that way." She put her arm around Tessie and gave her a little squeeze. They walked along in silence for a while.

There was always a long gap between any specific news being relayed in her letters and a response from Billy to what she'd written. When Billy did finally make a comment about the football being played at work, he did everything but give Violet an idea of what he'd think if she were to play.

'With Billingbrook United not back this season, I suppose there's interest in any games that take place. We have a match against the officers on Sunday. We lost the last one, so we're looking to even the score. I can't wait to be back on the terraces at Whittingham Road watching Billingbrook play, and be back home with you and Tommy.'

Violet sighed. For now she'd continue to watch from the sidelines when the others played at work. However, playing at home was different, and when she had the opportunity, she went out into the yard with Tommy, trying to fill Billy's shoes as best she could. The more she played, the more she found she enjoyed it. She wished she didn't have to be the goalie every time, but then Tommy was only four. It made it all the more enjoyable when they visited her parents and Dad would be in goal for a change. At those times, she could be out front kicking the ball. It provided a great release from the pressures of the rest of life.

CHAPTER 9

Pack up your troubles in your old kit bag,
And smile, smile, smile!
While you've a Lucifer to light your fag,
Smile, Boys, that's the style.
What's the use of worrying?
It never was worth while.
So, pack up your troubles in your old kit bag,
And smile, smile, smile!
*Pack Up Your Troubles In Your Old Kit Bag - George Asaf
(George Henry Powell) 1915*

*18th August 1915 - Soldiers March Suspected Spy To
Headquarters - The Daily Mirror*

"To recap — the front trench is the fire trench, this is the
support trench and behind that you have the
communications trench." The corporal was pointing,
showing the measurement and structure on a large trench
diagram in front of the class. "Any questions?"

Davy raised his hand.

"Yes, Private Moore?"

"Did you say we only dig dugouts in the reserve
trenches, Corporal?"

"That is correct. It is all covered in the Infantry
Manual."

Billy was glad to leave the classroom and go out for

physical training. He'd ask Davy to explain the things he hadn't understood when they sat down later in the canteen.

"I've got a question," Stan said, as they walked away from the building. "Can I dig half a hole?"

"Half a hole?" Davy said. "But you can't have half a hole. It would be…"

Before he went any further, Stan clapped him on the shoulder and burst out laughing. "Had you there, lad."

Davy looked confused, and Billy sighed. He was just glad Stan had resisted the temptation to ask the corporal.

The days passed, and they became more proficient in all aspects of trench warfare, the theory and the practice — as far as was possible without a real enemy to face. There were times some of their platoon had to pretend to be the enemy for their exercises and things did become competitive, but never enough to feel any edge of danger.

Two hours of physical training was a pleasure compared to sitting indoors. Davy would have rather stayed in the classroom, something that Billy would never understand. However, all three of them had better stamina now than they'd had a few months ago, and when they headed to the parade ground after their evening meal it no longer felt as though their bodies were heavy sacks being dragged along with difficulty. As a result, the drill sergeant no longer seemed like the malevolent man they'd thought him on their arrival. He was still an evil sadist, but just not as bad as they first thought. They only had to find him barking into their face at no more than a nose-length's distance to be reminded of that.

"Squad, halt! Right turn!"

Billy had now done so much drill that he was expecting to start doing it in his sleep. He could have cleaned and reloaded his rifle blindfolded and knew more about digging a trench than he'd ever thought necessary. He'd been surprised to find out that a trench wasn't just a hole in the ground; getting that right could be the difference between life and death.

He stood absolutely still and straight, his eyes forward.

The drill sergeant stepped aside and their commanding officer moved to the front to address them. "You will be leaving camp tomorrow at 0700 hours. You've done a sterling job and you are now ready to face the enemy. Your presence is required on the Western Front. Good luck, and I hope you will all make your battalion proud."

The words echoed around in Billy's head; Lieutenant Colonel Patterson made it sound more like a party invitation than battle orders. After nearly five months of training, the time had come. France awaited. At least he had a rough idea of where they were heading. He still hadn't fathomed exactly where Gallipoli was, though it was mentioned in the newspaper regularly; that and somewhere called the Dardanelles.

Billy had hoped he'd be given leave to go back and see Vi and Tommy before he had to face the fight. Now that he knew that wasn't happening, he felt a sudden feeling of panic. Would he ever see them again? He had to believe he would. They all had to believe they'd come home; that had been drummed into them day after day. He thought back to the ramshackle group of lads he'd boarded the train with back in Billingbrook. Even Stan now stood taller and followed commands without thinking — most of the time at least. To a man, they were fitter, stronger and about as prepared as they were likely to be. After a shaky start, Davy could now shoot straighter than any of them, but he'd already been singled out as a specialist signaller.

Many of the lads were excited about fighting; there was a pride in winning and a thirst for adventure. Not for Billy. Those thoughts had gone from his head by the time he arrived home on the day he'd enlisted. The look on Vi's face had brought him back to earth pretty sharpish. He still wanted his family to be proud of him, though; he wanted Tommy to be able to hold his head up and tell his mates that his dad had gone to fight for King and Country and all that.

As soon as the parade was over, Billy went in search of pen and paper. He wanted to write one last letter back to Vi before they shipped out. He sat on his bunk and tried to think what to say.

"You all right?" Stan asked, sitting on the neighbouring bed.

"'Course. Why?"

Stan shrugged. "I just thought... well, I knew you were wondering if we'd have some leave before we went." His voice trailed off.

Billy went back to his letter, but was conscious that Stan was still watching him. He looked up at his mate.

Stan waved his arm toward the doorway. "I might just... I was thinking... Where d'you find the paper? I might drop a line to Mam, what with... Someone can read it to her."

"Here." Billy passed him the spare sheet he'd put by, in case he needed to start again. "There's a pen with Davy's things. He won't mind you using it."

"Ta." Stan took the paper and went to find the pen. "Do you think if I sent it to Vi she might go round and take it to Mam?" He waved his hand around again as he spoke, as though filling in the gaps in what he was saying.

"Yes, she'd do that. I'm sure she'd be happy to." Billy

tried to remember what he was about to write to Vi.

A few of the men must have slept well that night. Billy lay on his bunk, listening to them snoring; if they snored like that in the trenches, the enemy would have no problem finding where they were. He reckoned he could always get some kip on the train; he guessed it was going to be a long journey, and there was only so much looking out of the window he wanted to do. He must have dozed at intervals, but for once it was a struggle to get out of bed that morning. Despite being a fine crisp day, not quite autumn but without the summer warmth, and already light, the parade ground had never seemed so uninviting.

They were used to packing their kit; they'd had enough practice. Everything had a place if you were going to carry it comfortably. It also meant you were more likely to notice if you'd left an item behind. That was something no man could afford to do, however dippy they were, and some of them most certainly were. Once you'd loaded up, you were more like a bloody packhorse than a soldier, but there was no point complaining.

Without conversation they formed up into their units and marched from parade ground to station. The only sound was the regular stamp of boot on ground and the instructions being issued to them all. Three months ago, the boot clomps on the ground had been like an echo repeating at uneven intervals as their feet came down out of time. Now it was a regular left, right, left, right... When they halted, the noise cut dead. It was as much a marker of the change in all of them as anything could be. Now they were more in tune with each other and with the orders they were given; a fighting force.

The train line had been extended through the camp.

With the number of men coming and going, it made sense. Billy wondered how many thousands of men had already left this camp on their way to the Front, and how many of them would come back. He'd never thought a lot about God, but that didn't stop him praying for a safe return.

The train rattled on across England, hour by hour, taking them closer to their Channel crossing. Despite his apprehension, Billy couldn't deny that a small part of him was excited. This is what the training had all been for. It was the same feeling of pent-up energy that he felt waiting for the whistle to start a Billingbrook United game. For others the game was already in progress, but for him, Stan, Davy and the other lads, the whistle was about to be blown, and that at least felt good. The difference was that normally he'd be on the terraces as a spectator, but now he would be out on the field.

"Blimey." Stan's eyes were wide.

Billy looked along the dockside at the motley array of ships waiting to take them across the Channel. There was everything from large fishing vessels to regular ferries, and even some river pleasure boats. Billy hoped they were all worthy of a sea crossing.

"They're a bit bigger than the rowing boat we take out fishing," Stan said as he lit up a cigarette.

"I should bloody well hope so, I don't much fancy going over in one of those. We had to bail out the last one we had. This is the sea, Stan, not some duck pond at the park."

"I've never been on a proper boat before," Davy said, looking a little anxious.

"Well, the good news," said Stan, clapping him on the back, "is that you don't have to do the rowing." He gave a hearty laugh while Davy looked confused.

"Don't mind him." Billy sighed. "His idea of a joke. I don't suppose there's many of us been on something like this. I hadn't really been more than a mile or two outside Billingbrook before we went to camp. I've certainly never seen the sea before. It's weird, all the stuff we're doing for the first time as a result of the war. It's like, whatever happens, life won't be the same again. The world was just Billingbrook before this started. Now I can see there's more than that."

He'd enjoy telling Tommy all about the train and the boat when he wrote to Violet later. He wished he could share it with them, but without the war part. It was like things you read about in the newspaper, or books, though he'd never really done much of that. It made him start wondering what it might be like to go to Blackpool for a day; there were trains from Billingbrook that offered a day return. Maybe when he went home, he'd take the rest of the family — even his mam might enjoy that.

"At least the weather's good. Don't much fancy a stormy crossing." Stan dropped his cigarette end and ground it out with his heel. "Come on then, lads." He straightened his shoulders and joined the line going up the gangplank onto their allotted vessel.

It wasn't one of the larger ships and was rocking a fair bit, even in the good conditions. Billy found a wall to lean against to give himself some stability. They kipped wherever they could; they'd already been warned there was a fair march to be done once they docked on the other side.

Billy had no idea how long he'd been asleep when he heard a shout.

"Land ahoy."

He looked around from where he was sitting on the deck. The night was thick with dark, and he could only assume there were lights along the shoreline as no one could have seen the land itself.

Rather than the thoughts of how their training had made them a united body which had gone through his mind on the parade ground that morning, suddenly he felt completely unprepared for what lay ahead. Did any of them have a real idea of what to expect?

Davy was the only one of them who spoke French, but they weren't likely to have much call for that most of the time. He'd stick with Davy if they ever had the chance to go anywhere outside their camp.

The welcoming party who met them on the dockside were British soldiers, just like themselves; except they weren't like Billy and Stan. They all looked older and as though their time here had etched itself deep into the contours of their faces. It was not just the fact that their uniforms were far from pristine, that went for all the lads. Nor was it dirt that had drawn those lines, although there was clearly plenty of that. Call it experience, call it hard graft and weariness, but it was obvious to Billy from their eyes that these were men who'd seen a lot more of life and death than he had done yet.

"Move along there. We need to fit you all in the carriages."

The men disembarking from the boats were herded toward the trains. At the back of the train were wagons stencilled 'Hommes 40 Cheval 8'. Billy, Stan and Davy managed to board one of the carriages further forward, which was already rammed with fellow arriving soldiers. This time the view from the window was not the rolling countryside of England but a flatter terrain, much as had been described to them in preparation. They had been warned about how wet the land would be and the risks that posed to the trenches. If the enemy didn't kill you, the mud would.

The first sign that they were getting closer to the Front itself was an area cordoned off by barbed wire. Billy felt his heart rate quicken.

The train stopped some distance short of their camp. By now it was growing light; the last few miles would be done on foot. This is what they'd practised for and now the route march was for real. They were carrying packs, which Billy guessed weighed about half as much as a coal sack. Before he'd joined the army, he'd never have thought of carrying half a sack of coal for a ten-mile stretch, not for anyone.

As they were marching six-abreast, even though the daylight was increasing, Billy could see little more than the man in front of him and the ones in the column to either side. He wondered what there was around, but kept his eyes forward. He guessed he'd find out soon enough.

Whenever he put his left boot down, Billy could feel a sore developing on his foot. He must have worn through the sock; it would need darning. That wasn't something he was good at, but maybe Stan could be persuaded to help. Stan had turned out to be a dab hand at mending clothes, something Billy was quite used to his mam or Vi doing for him when necessary. Stan was marching on the end of his line and was sure to have plenty to say later. Billy would have to wait to hear his thoughts.

It was a good couple of hours before they reached an encampment and were directed to their tents. What struck Billy wasn't that they would be under canvas for the night, or how well organised it seemed to be. It was that the men giving the directions were often on crutches or missing a limb. They were the walking wounded, still doing their bit. He shuddered to think what those men had been through.

"Rest up, men. Take what sleep you can. You'll be moving to the reserve trenches tonight." With that, they were dismissed. No time to find their way around or learn the names of those running the camp. In and out; a brief chance to make running repairs before the real stuff began. It was good to put down some of their load, even if for a short time.

"Get your mess tin." Stan was waiting for Billy and Davy outside the tent.

Billy had just removed his boot to check the state of his sock.

"Bloody hell, man. Let's have some grub before we worry about anything else." Stan winked at Davy.

Billy grimaced and put his boot back on. "That's all right for you. Your darning doesn't leave great lumps in your sock."

"That's because I've been doing it so long. If I didn't do it, I'd have had no socks to wear. You're just soft and spoiled."

Billy hobbled after the other two toward the line collecting food. Stan was right; the way his stomach was grumbling, food was definitely the first thing he needed. He was probably right about him being spoiled too, but Billy wasn't going to confess to that one.

"You'd best get used to it." One of the men serving the food gave an unnerving leer. "Tomorrow's will look much the same as today's." He seemed to take a cheerful satisfaction about the pronouncement as he slopped the food into the mess tin.

"Bully beef, my favourite." Stan always gave as good as he got, and Billy admired him for it.

"This is it then," Davy said when they found somewhere to perch while they ate.

Billy nodded, but was too busy chewing to reply.

"We're certainly not here to paint the landscape. Not from what I saw, anyway." Stan shook his head.

"Well, don't just leave it at that. What did you see?" By now Billy had almost finished, and wished there was some of Vi's bread pudding to follow.

Stan went quiet and Billy waited.

"Not much, really." Stan looked away into the distance. He shook his head. "Nothing to worry us. It was just... oh, I don't know — a feeling. If I believed in ghosts, I'd have said there were more of them out there than I'd want to meet on my own on a dark night."

Billy watched Stan as he looked down and shrugged.

"You're starting to sound more like Vi's mam." He expected Stan to laugh, but he didn't, and a shiver ran through Billy.

CHAPTER 10

Do you think my dress is a little bit
Just a little bit — Well not too much of it,
Though it shows my shape just a little bit
That's the little bit the boys admire
*When I take My Morning Promenade - A. J. Mills and Bennett
Scott 1908*

*24th September 1915 - Heavy Fighting on Whole of Western
Front - The Daily Mirror*

"Oh my days." Elsie had picked up the *Billingbrook
Mercury* from where Alf had put it on the sideboard.

She sat down heavily and was continuing to read.
Violet wondered what the item was that had caught her
eye. She waited in the doorway, presuming that Elsie
would tell her when she was ready.

"They're turning the big house into a military
hospital," Elsie said finally, looking into space ahead of
her. "There must be a lot of injured boys if they need to do
that. You wouldn't think…" Her voice trailed off.

Of course the newspapers had held reports of the
fighting, but most of the time it seemed distant and a little
unreal. Violet had been given the distinct impression that
our boys were winning every battle, and that Billy would
soon be home safe and well.

"You mean Billingbrook Hall?" Violet asked, wishing

she could take the paper from Elsie and read it for herself. She'd never actually been in the hall, or the grounds come to that. She had looked over one of the garden walls to see what was on the other side and it was a terribly grand affair. There were even supposed to be deer in the grounds, although she hadn't seen them.

"You don't suppose…" Elsie didn't finish her sentence.

Vi could see from the worried look on Elsie's face that she was thinking about the possibility of Billy coming home injured. "No, Mam, I don't think it would do to suppose, at all. We had a letter on Tuesday. He's still our Billy." At least he had been when the letter was written. Despite her own private fears, she had to stay strong. "He hasn't even been near the fighting yet."

She hoped it would stay that way. As always she'd opened the letter with trepidation, and from its contents knew he was now heading to France; he would be nearer to where the action was happening. He hadn't given them any indication that he was in more risk, for now. She'd loved his suggestion that they could all go to Blackpool when he came home, Tommy had talked about nothing else since she'd read it to him; even Elsie had smiled at the thought he wanted to take them all. Vi had to believe those days would come. Thinking about it reminded Vi that she needed to go over to see Stan's mother to read the letter he'd included; she was bracing herself to do that on Saturday. She'd take Tommy to her parents' house and then go without him.

Eventually Elsie passed the paper to her, and Violet read the report. Her eyes widened when she saw the number of beds the hospital would have. The paper was appealing for volunteers to work there, alongside the nursing staff. She wondered whether it was something her sister, Ena, would want to do. Her current position at the mill was looking increasingly precarious, but Ena would need a paid position and these all looked to be unpaid. Ena couldn't afford to volunteer.

Violet wished there were some way she could help at the hospital, but she was already putting in long hours and was hardly at home. What little time she had she needed to spend with Tommy.

"I suppose the Hall's a good place for them to use, as it's so near to the barracks. Where do you think Sir Danvers will go?" Violet had known a girl who worked up at the hall, and Sir Danvers Hamilton was supposed to be a lovely old gentleman, though he must have rattled around in that house.

"I dare say he'd have enough space in one of the estate cottages." Elsie seemed to be trying to pull herself back together and was busying herself tidying the ornaments, which in Violet's view were in no need of attention. "He probably doesn't need more than a housekeeper these days. He never seems to entertain anymore." Elsie stopped and looked wistful. "When I was younger, I used to love to hear of the big dances they had and what the ladies wore." She sighed. "Oh, there were such stories. I used to know a girl who was a scullery maid. She wasn't given much time off, but when she was she used to have us all in stitches, telling us some of what went on during the house parties there."

Violet couldn't remember the last time she'd even seen Elsie laugh, and wondered just how different she had been when she was younger. However hard life was, she hoped that she never lost the ability to be happy.

On Saturday, Violet decided it was best to go to Stan's mam in the morning; she thought that would give the best chance of her being sober. She wished Billy hadn't asked her to go, but then she hadn't told him about her first visit.

She would wait to open Stan's letter. It felt wrong to know its contents before she read it to his mam. Even Billy's mam had now accepted that Vi should see letters addressed to her before Elsie read them. She should treat Mrs Bradley the same way she expected to be treated, even if she wouldn't be able to read it for herself.

"I don't have to come, do I?" Tommy looked as though he was about to cry when Violet said where she was going.

"No, silly. You're going to play with Bobby." Violet could see Tommy's shoulders relax and his face brightened.

"I'm sure it'll be fine, love," Violet's mam said when Vi left Tommy with her. "She'll be pleased to hear from her son. What mother wouldn't be?"

"She didn't even know he'd gone when I was there before." Vi refastened her coat and put her hat on.

"That was the drink," her mam said in a soothing voice. "I'm sure when she's sober it's a different matter."

As she walked, Vi wondered whether there were ever times that Stan's mam was sober. She'd seemed in a pretty bad way.

Lancaster Street was just as bad as she'd remembered, as Vi walked along toward Stan's house. She looked up at the terrace as she approached to knock on the door. She frowned; something was different. The windows were clean, and the step had been polished. Maybe Stan's mam had stopped drinking. Vi smiled and knocked with more enthusiasm than she had been feeling.

A head poked out of an upstairs window next door. "Who are you looking for?"

Violet looked up at the woman, who blew out a ring of

smoke as she waited for a reply. "I'm here to see Mrs Bradley."

"You'll have a job, love."

"Oh?" Violet was torn between knocking again or continuing to talk to the neighbour. "Why's that? I have a letter for her."

"Bit late for that, love. She died. My Horace found her. There's new people in there now, but they're out."

Before Vi had the opportunity to ask anything further, the woman shook the ash off the end of her cigarette and closed the window. Violet's visit was clearly no longer of interest.

Violet stood on the doorstep, not knowing what to do. She presumed from the changed appearance of the house that the neighbour was telling her the truth. There'd be no benefit in waiting to see the new tenant. She started back along the pavement away from the house. After about fifty yards, she turned and looked at the terrace. She was surprised that none of Stan's older brothers or sisters had written to him to let him know. One of them must have cleared their mother's things, or what would have happened to Stan's belongings? She would have to write to Billy and ask him to tell Stan.

"Have you heard?" Eva asked her at break on the Monday. "Management are asking for ways to raise money to help the soldiers' hospital. There's this big appeal, Mr Giffard has asked for ideas."

"Not much we can do, stuck in here." Violet had been thinking about it, but couldn't see a way to do anything. Making shells was doing her bit.

"'Ere, you're never going to believe this." Tessie was out of breath as she hurried up to them. "Mr Wood has suggested we play them at football as a way to raise money. What do you think?"

"What?" Eva jumped down from the bench and clapped her hands together. "You mean a real game? Us girls against the men? That would be a lovely idea."

Tessie nodded.

"You can't do that." Violet was horrified. "What would your mam say?"

"Don't talk daft." Tessie was standing with her hands on her hips. "If I tell her it's to raise money for the hospital, she'll be all in favour."

"How will it raise money?" Violet couldn't quite see what Tessie was getting at.

"By selling tickets, silly." Tessie was bouncing with the excitement of the idea.

Violet gasped. "You're going to let people watch you play? You mean you'll be parading around in public?"

Tessie rolled her eyes in an exaggerated fashion, teasing Vi. "Why else would we make it a proper game? Oh, do say you'll play."

"Me? I can't do that. I'm a married woman." Violet was dumbfounded by the idea. "Billy's mam would have my guts for garters if I did something like that."

"Don't tell her." Eva laughed.

"It may have escaped your notice, Eva Podmore, but Tessie Brown lives next to me — her mam's bound to say something. Besides, I'm not starting to lie to Billy's mother. Where would it end? You know as well as I do that women who do things like playing football are seen as having loose morals. I can't play, and that's all there is to it." Violet was surprised by the disappointment she felt as she said it. For the first time she realised she would quite like to join in. She had a sudden thought. "What if you're in the papers?"

"Hey, Tessie," Eva said, "we could be famous."

The younger girls laughed, and Violet didn't know what else to say to make them understand how serious this was. No respectable woman went parading themselves in public like that, not even if they played in their overalls.

"Will you coach us, Vi?" Eva was looking at her earnestly. "Tessie says your dad's been teaching you, and, well, we could do with some help."

Violet was shocked. "How did you know that?" She turned to Tessie.

Tessie grinned, unabashed. "I heard you in the yard with Tommy, showing him how to do it and saying it was like Granddad had shown you."

"Right." Vi didn't know what to say. Showing the others how to do things wouldn't be the same as playing, would it? And it was for a good cause. No, maybe it would be just as bad. "I'll think about it. I could ask my dad if he has time to help."

"It needs to be lunchtimes while we're all here," Eva said, looking at Vi with big soulful eyes. "Please say you'll help?"

"I said I'll think about it." She turned away, feeling confused.

In reality, she did nothing but think about it as she packed the shells that afternoon. It really couldn't do any harm. She wished she could ask Billy what he thought. Maybe she should go over to see her mam and dad and see what they said. She couldn't very well ask Billy's parents; Elsie already thought she was from a very common family, and Vi didn't want to hear her make even more comments about the Tunnicliffes. It was a shame her dad couldn't train the team. He'd be much better at it than she would, and he'd enjoy it.

As they walked home that evening, Tessie slipped her arm through Vi's. "You aren't cross with me, are you?" Tessie turned and looked at Vi. "Go on, say you will."

Violet knew immediately what she was talking about. Oh, she wanted to, but whatever would people think? She was a respectable married woman, and she didn't want people saying otherwise. Most important of all, what would Billy think? Vi thought about what he was doing, facing the enemy. In a moment of clarity it occurred to her that if Billy or Stan were to come back injured, she'd want them to have the very best of medical care. She wouldn't want the hospital to be short of anything they needed.

What point was worrying about how people might see her, if, as a result, she didn't help men who were in desperate need; men who had had the courage to fight for their country? If there was anything Violet could do to help, then she had to do it.

Violet stopped walking and turned to face Tessie. "I'll do it. We start tomorrow. I won't play, mind — that would be going too far."

Tessie hugged her and began skipping along the road.

Violet shook her head in despair at Tessie's unladylike behaviour, but smiled anyway. How she still had the energy after a day at work was anyone's guess. Oh, to be fourteen again.

The following lunchtime the hard work began.

"Now, I don't know a great deal, but I'll see my dad on Saturday and ask for some more advice," Vi said as they all got together.

Tessie was looking around to see which of the girls had come down for the practice session. "She's pretty good from what I've seen." Tessie gave a conspiratorial wink to the other girls.

Vi felt herself blushing. "You've only seen me play with Tommy in the yard. Anyway, from watching you all have knockabouts at break, I've been thinking about where on the field you should each play. Florrie, I think you should play up front with Clara. Tessie, you play well in defence. Edith, can you be goalkeeper?"

Edith nodded, with a broad grin on her face. "That suits me, there's less running."

The other girls laughed.

Violet, although she'd never done anything like this before, found she was enjoying working out how to give some structure to the girls' game. "You need to pass more. If they come toward you, don't be afraid. They just want to wind you up. Don't let them intimidate you — you know what they're like."

For the rest of the lunchtime the girls practised passing the ball back and forth between them, to a chorus of whistles from some of the lads. Violet watched earnestly and began to shout encouragement and instructions to them.

"I'll tell Mr Giffard it's on then, shall I?" said Joe Wood, who'd made the original suggestion, as he came across to watch.

Violet had only gone as far as opening her mouth to give a cautious reply when it was Eva who answered for them.

"Yes, you do that. You'll need some practice, mind."

Violet gulped. There was no backing out now.

She was still thinking about which of the girls would be best in each of the positions as she went back to her bench after lunch. They were going to need one or two more girls to join the team too.

"Mrs Dobson."

Vi jumped and was surprised to see Mrs Johnson waiting for her.

"May I have a word?"

Vi let out a heavy breath. This was all she needed.

"Yes, Mrs Johnson." She followed the overseer across the floor to her office.

Mrs Johnson waited until she was inside and then closed the door. She did not indicate for Violet to sit, so Vi stood in front of the desk, trying not to fidget.

"Mrs Dobson, Mr Reynolds has made it known to me that you are encouraging the younger girls to play football."

Vi tried to think who Mr Reynolds was. She thought he might be one of the older men at the other end of their floor.

Mrs Johnson continued. "May I remind you that it is my responsibility to look after the moral welfare of the girls and the women on our section, and I do not expect to find any of my girls behaving in such an inappropriate manner."

Violet closed her eyes. This was exactly the sort of reaction she'd been afraid of. She supposed if they carried on, Mrs Johnson would just be the first of many. Perhaps she should bow out now, before this went any further. Opening her mouth to speak, an image of Billy came to mind and a picture of wounded soldiers, though in her head Billy wasn't wounded; she couldn't think of anything happening to him. In any case, she was doing this on behalf of the company to help raise money in their name.

Violet squared her shoulders and looked Mrs Johnson in the eye. "I'm very sorry, Mrs Johnson, I thought Mr Giffard would have spoken to you. He's asked us to form a company team." That last bit was bending the truth a little, but she wanted it to sound official.

Mrs Johnson's eyes widened. For a moment, she didn't seem to know what to say. "Please return to your bench, Mrs Dobson."

"Yes, Mrs Johnson." Violet left the office as quickly and quietly as she could. Eva caught her eye, but other than raising an eyebrow, Violet said nothing.

CHAPTER 11

I don't know where he's going
But when he gets there, I'll be glad
I'm following in father's footsteps
Yes, I'm following the dear old dad
Following in Father's Footsteps - E. W. Rogers - 1904

27th September 1915 - Victorious British and French Advance on 20 Mile Front - The Daily Mirror

Violet decided that as she was coaching the team, she would mention it to Billy when she wrote to him later. When she was just a spectator, she wasn't sure he'd been that interested; now she was involved, it would be something different to tell him. He would probably think it was funny, given that when he went away she knew nothing at all about the game. The war was forcing lots of people to learn new skills. In some cases, Vi thought, that was a good thing. Then she thought of some of what Billy was having to learn. She couldn't picture him darning his own socks, as hard as she tried to. It made her smile.

The girls now ate the bread and cheese they took for their lunches during morning break, so that the whole of lunchtime was free for practice. Vi did the same, although she learned after the first day to save something for the afternoon, otherwise her stomach was growling long before home time.

None of the girls had trained in any sport before. Most of them hadn't kicked a ball, unless they had brothers they'd played with as children. To begin with they reminded Violet of Tommy, but thankfully their coordination developed more rapidly than that of a small child. There were times that Violet wondered if the team would ever make any progress, but little by little their game improved.

"Agnes, try to kick the ball like this." Vi went over to Agnes and kicked the ball across to Clara. "Can you see the difference? Clara, send it back so that Agnes can have another go."

Agnes kicked the ball and it veered away off the pitch. "It's easier with my other foot." Agnes looked despondent.

"Then why don't you use your left foot when you have time to choose?" Violet said.

"Am I allowed to?" Agnes asked. "Mam never let me use my left hand for things. She said it was bad to do that."

Violet groaned. It was actually harder than teaching Tommy. He at least didn't start with ideas of what was right and wrong; he just tried.

"Yes," Vi said, "you can use your left foot if that's better. To control the ball, you will need to use both feet, just not at the same time."

Agnes tried again with the inside edge of her left foot, and this time the ball went more or less in the direction she'd intended, and the practice picked up again.

"Have you seen this?" Edith was clutching a handbill. "It's official, we're playing in three weeks. The tickets have gone on sale." They all gathered around to read the small piece of paper. 'All proceeds to Billingbrook Hall Hospital'.

"Do you really think anyone will pay to watch us?" Florrie asked.

"I shouldn't think there'll be many." Edith sighed. "Although I did hear some of the other girls saying they'd come to cheer us on. Mr Giffard says we can use the recreation ground to practise on Saturday afternoon if we want to." She looked pleadingly at Violet.

"Have you girls told your families that you're playing?" Violet asked, wondering how she could explain where she would be going on Saturday.

"I have," Florrie said. "I even wrote to Frank and told him. He's my eldest brother. He's fighting, so I want to do my bit."

Violet could understand how Florrie felt. She looked around at the others.

"They'll find out sooner or later," Clara said, "so I told them. Mam asked if she could play. You should have heard what Gran said, Mam and her didn't half have an argument. Gran said Mam shouldn't be letting me do it. Honestly, as if they could stop me." Clara laughed. "Anyway, Mam wants to come and watch. I don't suppose Gran will want to."

Violet chewed her lip. "I'd need to bring Tommy, but maybe I could go over and see if Dad would come too. That way I could learn more as well."

The other girls were so excited about playing that they would have agreed to anything. The Saturday practice was decided. Many of them had younger siblings at home, so they wouldn't mind a four-year-old getting under their feet.

If there was any hope of her dad being able to join them, Violet would have to walk over to see him that evening on her way home. It would mean being even later back at the

Dobsons' house, but there was no other time she could go. Tommy would already be asleep, so that wouldn't be a problem. She set off as soon as the klaxon sounded.

"Oh, Vi, is everything all right?" Her mam was up like a shot when Violet went in through the door. "It's not Billy, is it? Tell me it's not Billy."

Violet hugged her mam. "No, nothing like that. It's nothing bad at all."

"Thank God." Mam sat down in her chair, her hand to her chest as she regained her composure.

"I wanted to ask Dad a favour," Vi said, but there was only Mam and John in the downstairs room. The younger ones would already have gone to bed, and Dad was nowhere about.

"At this time of night? That's not like you. He's only gone for a pint, he'll be back in half an hour. Mind you, I don't blame him — Bobby can be quite a handful. I wouldn't have minded going out for some peace." She chuckled to herself. "Now what's the favour?"

John sat quietly in the corner of the room, but said nothing.

Violet explained to her mother all about the football and her mother listened, her eyebrows slightly raised.

"I'm not sure I know what to say, love. You do need some fun, but are you sure about this?" Mam was shaking her head in apparent bewilderment.

"My sister playing football." Unlike her mam, John sounded impressed.

"I'm only coaching them, I'm not playing." Violet fidgeted as she replied.

Mam nodded. "You get off, I'll explain to Dad. I'm sure he'll come, but I might make him bring Bobby with him so I have some peace. You be off. It's late enough already."

Violet kissed her mam's cheek. "Thanks, Mam."

Hurrying home, Vi realised she was quite looking forward to Saturday.

"Where's Edith?" Violet asked.

"She'll be here as soon as she can. She had to do her granddad's cleaning first," Eva said.

Violet sighed. It was going to be difficult getting the team together when they had so many other responsibilities. Even the youngest of them seemed to have someone they needed to look after.

It was strange to be in the open field of the recreation ground after being used to the enclosed yard in the factory. Violet gasped when she looked around. Most of the girls wore their overalls, but Florrie was wearing long shorts and socks to her knees.

"You look the proper picture. Where did you find them?" Tessie seemed impressed.

"They're me brother's. He don't need them as he's gone off to fight. Mam said I may as well use them."

"That's what you all need." Violet's dad walked briskly over the grass to greet them. "I'm Frank Tunnicliffe, Violet's dad." He shook hands with each of the girls. "Can't management help you with the kit? It would be much easier than you having to play in those overalls. Although I daresay that's easier than the skirts Vi's been playing in."

Vi could feel herself colouring. "It would cost a lot just for one game. And besides, what will people think if the girls' legs are showing?"

"Violet, love, if you're going to do this, you're going to have to stop worrying about what people will say. If you keep that up, you'll get nowhere."

Violet knew he was right, but it was easier said than done.

"Now," her dad continued, "how many of you have brothers who might have something you could borrow?" He turned to Vi. "Would any of our John's stuff fit you, lass?"

"But I'm not playing." She thought she'd already made that clear.

"You're going to be doing a lot of running up and down with the girls, whether you're playing or not. Why don't you come over and talk to John tomorrow?"

Violet nodded but said nothing.

Her dad turned back to the others. "What about the rest of you?"

Tessie pulled the leg of her overall up and danced around as though she were on the stage, showing her ankle and calf. "If it's good enough for that Marie Lloyd in the music hall, it's good enough for me."

They all laughed.

Tommy and Bobby wandered onto the pitch to join them.

"Here, Tommy, you and Bobby go over there with this ball." Dad kicked a ball to the two young boys so they would be off the pitch where the women were practising. Then turning back to the others he said, "Let's see what you can all do."

The girls spread out across the field and started kicking the ball to each other. Edith had arrived and positioned herself in the makeshift goal.

"I'm sorry, I don't know all your names yet," Vi's dad shouted, "but I want to see the goalkeeper taking part for now, so I can see your footballing skills."

"I'm Edith," she shouted. "I'm only any good in goal."

"I'll be the judge of that," Frank shouted and stood watching them moving about the field. After letting them chase the ball for a few minutes he said, "You know, love, you really should be out there."

Violet hesitated a long time before turning to her dad. "You know I can't. I'm a married woman."

"Give over, love. You're the best player they haven't got, that's plain for anyone to realise who's seen you with a ball at your feet." He turned back to the girls. "No, Tessie, you need to keep it moving. If you keep the ball like that, you'll be tackled before you know it." He went over to demonstrate what he wanted. "Here, Vi, come over so I can pass the ball to you and show Tessie."

Violet went over and kicked the ball back to her dad. He returned the ball to her and began to work his way down the pitch. The rest of the girls were watching what he and Violet were doing. Violet felt herself smiling as she kicked the ball back again. It was only after the second or third pass that Violet realised what her dad was up to; this was his way of bringing her onto the pitch. She stopped where she was with her hands on her hips and didn't kick the ball.

"Go on, Vi," Tessie shouted over to her and started clapping. The other girls joined in.

Violet was just wondering whether to carry on when an older man walking a dog paused alongside the pitch. "You girls should be ashamed of yourselves, parading around like that. You," he pointed his stick at Florrie, "the one in the shorts. Put some clothes on, young lady, before I have you arrested."

Violet gasped, but Florrie was unfazed.

"Do you want to join in?" Florrie called to the man, who was smartly dressed and standing very upright for a man of advanced years.

He waved his stick at her and marched away from the ground.

Violet shook her head sadly; that was exactly the sort of thing she was afraid of. Her dad knew she'd have loved to play if things were different. She walked back to the sideline, her head down. She shouldn't have said she'd do this, even if it was a good cause.

Tommy came running up to her. He took her hand. "That man wasn't very nice. Are you going to play, Mam? I think you're good."

Violet smiled at the innocence of childhood and picked him up.

Tessie came over to them. "Please don't give up, Vi. We need you. We can't do this without you."

Violet looked at Tessie's bright, innocent face. Had times changed enough for her to ignore the prejudice that surrounded them? "I'll think about it."

"Vi love," Dad spoke to her softly. "I'm going to stay on and give the girls some training. Why don't you take the boys back home and have a cuppa with Mam? Tell her I'll be back in an hour."

Violet nodded. Then, taking Bobby and Tommy's hands, walked away from the pitch toward the road.

The boys went running into the house ahead of her.

"You're back early," Mam said, sounding a little disappointed.

"Yes, sorry. Dad says he'll be about an hour." Violet slumped into a chair.

Her mam said nothing to her, but went and put the kettle on. She turned to John who was whittling a piece of wood. "Take the boys out into the yard, John, and keep them out of mischief for a bit."

The boys sloped off out of the house, leaving Violet and her mother on their own.

"Ena's taken the girls over to her house for the afternoon, so we have some quiet. Now, will you tell me what's going on?" Her mam brewed the tea as she spoke and then brought it over. She frowned at Vi. "You've not fallen out with Dad, have you? He can be a bit of a slave driver when he has it in his head to do something." Mam laughed.

"No, Mam, it's nothing like that." Vi explained to her mother the events of the afternoon and her mam listened and nodded.

When Vi had finished telling her mother the whole story, and had even told her some of the things that Billy's mam had said in the past about the Tunnicliffe family, Queenie Tunnicliffe looked intently at her daughter.

"Now you listen to me, girl. I'll admit when you first told me about the football, I was very unsure. When you'd gone I asked Dad what he thought and he saw things differently. He said it seemed unfair and just plain wrong that men do so many things for enjoyment and women are just left with all the work. I'd never really thought about it like that. I'm not a big thinker, but I realised he was right. All we do is work at home and go out to work as well. Oh, I know some of those swanky women with money do other things, though I don't rightly know what, but the likes of you and me don't. And don't you mind the things Elsie Dobson says; she hasn't been lucky enough to have daughters and watch them growing up. That's not her fault. There's nothing she can say that can take away all the happiness I've had in bringing up my family. They might have been able to afford a bigger house with fewer mouths to feed, but I wouldn't have swapped with her.

Anyway, what I'm trying to say is, if you enjoy playing football and you're doing it for the right reasons, then don't listen to anybody else except your Billy. If your Billy doesn't mind, then do what makes you happy. You spend long enough dead, lass. Just look at that Stanley's mother." Queenie patted her daughter's hand and then went to put the kettle back on.

Violet sat thinking about what her mother had said. Was it as easy as that? She wished that Billy was there so she could talk it through with him. She wondered what he'd say.

The boys came running into the house and the silence was broken. "Can I stay with Bobby tonight, Mam?" Tommy asked, out of breath from running.

Vi looked across to her mam. "You'd better ask Nanna?" she said to Tommy.

"Can I?" he asked, running over to his grandmother.

Queenie scooped him up and swung him around with the practised care of someone used to tight spaces. "I don't see why not."

"Thanks, Nanna," he said when she put him down, and the boys ran back out into the street.

"It will give you a bit of time to think," Queenie said to her daughter.

Violet hugged her mam. "I'm going to get off and write to Billy. The only way I shall find out what he'd say is if I ask him. Tell Dad I'll see him tomorrow." She hesitated. "And tell him, I'm sorry for walking out today." Then Vi headed off back toward Victoria Street, thinking about everything her mother had said.

CHAPTER 12

"…hold your hand out naughty boy
Hold your hand out naughty boy
Last night in the pale moonlight
I saw you
With a nice girl in the park you were strolling full of joy
And you told her you'd never kissed a girl before
Hold your hand out naughty boy!"
Hold Your Hand Out Naughty Boy - David Worton 1913

4th October 1915 - More Pictures of the Great Advance - The Daily Mirror

"Is that you, Vi?" Elsie called, as Vi closed the back door.

Violet forced herself to smile and put her head around the sitting room door. "Yes, Mam. Tommy's staying with his Nanna and Granddad for the night, so I'm going to write a letter to Billy then I'll come down and prepare tea."

Elsie let out her usual harrumph and Violet withdrew before her mother-in-law could ask her where she'd been. She hoped that with Tommy staying with her parents, it might leave the impression she'd been there all afternoon.

Vi settled herself down with a pen and paper and thought about what she wanted to write. She dealt with all the regular news and then tried to word what she wanted to say about the football.

'I know I already told you that some of the girls at work are

playing football in their breaks. Well, the Company has asked if they could play a game against the men as a way to help raise money for the new Billingbrook Hall Hospital, the one that wounded soldiers will be brought to…'

Vi hated talking about things like that to anyone and felt awkward raising them with Billy.

'*… I think I also told you that the girls have asked if I will coach the team and I've been doing that, although I don't suppose I'm very good…'*

There was no getting around it, she wanted to know what Billy would think if she were to play. The only way she was going to find out was by asking him outright.

'*… The thing is, they want me to play too. Of course, if you don't want me to, I won't. I'd never want to do anything that would upset you. It's just that I've really enjoyed playing with Tommy and I think I'd like to try. Please will you write back as soon as you can and tell me what you think?'*

Violet signed off the letter with a little more about Tommy and then sent Billy all their love. She folded the paper and placed it in the envelope. She'd walk down the road and put it into the box before she started cooking tea. Her mind made up, she put on her coat and went downstairs as quietly as she could, so that she didn't have to answer any awkward questions about the urgency of the letter.

Once she came back from the postbox, Violet went back to the sitting room to pick up the used teacups for washing.

"Have you seen this?"

The outrage in Elsie Dobson's voice gave Violet a start.

"Your factory, your factory…"

Violet's heart sank. Elsie had said it with such vehemence that Violet was expecting her to say they were involved in working for the enemy.

"Your factory is advertising tickets for a football match in which a women's team is playing. Women, playing football. Can you imagine it?"

Violet realised how unwise it had been to take Tommy with her to the practice session, and was even more grateful that he'd stayed the night at her parents' house. The last thing she needed was Tommy blurting out what she'd been doing. Thank goodness she'd written to Billy and told him everything, before he heard something from his mother. She wondered how long it would take for him to reply. Perhaps she would be better not to coach the team again until she heard, but that didn't seem fair to them now; besides, she'd already told him about the coaching.

She racked her brain for an appropriate response to her mother-in-law, who was still looking as dark as the chimney before it was swept. Vi tried to keep the wobble out of her voice. "It's to raise money for the new hospital — you know, the one you were telling me about. It's doing such important work that the girls thought it would be a good way they could make a contribution. We all want any soldiers who are wounded to have the very best treatment. The girls'll raise a lot more that way than they would baking cakes." She wasn't sure where that last bit had come from, and thinking about it, it seemed ruder than she'd intended. At least it was no comparison to Elsie, as Vi couldn't remember her ever baking a cake for anyone other than herself.

"Well, I never did. I'm glad no daughter-in-law of mine would take part in something like that. Aren't you, Alfred?" The seriousness of the matter was emphasised by using Dad's full name.

Alf looked up from the sports pages of the previous day's paper and puffed slowly on his pipe. He looked across at Vi with a slight frown, and for a moment she felt as though he could see everything she was thinking. He narrowed his eyes as though piecing it together; he must have guessed. Vi bit her lip, waiting for what he was going to say. There was a long pause and he took another puff of his pipe.

"How much are the tickets? Perhaps we should be supporting it. Besides, there's no other football to watch. Do you think you could find out for us, Vi?"

Violet could have sworn he winked at her from behind the paper.

"Alfred Dobson, you'll do no such thing. Watching young women parading themselves in public — well, it's not proper. Whatever are their mothers thinking letting them do something like that?" Elsie slapped the newspaper down on the side.

It was clear to Violet that Elsie hadn't even thought there might be any married women involved. What would she say if she knew where Violet had been that afternoon, never mind the fact that Violet's dad had been helping? As soon as she could do so politely, she picked up the empty cups and went out to the kitchen. Should she say something to Tessie to make sure Mrs Brown didn't tell Elsie the whole story? It was perhaps best to wait until she saw her on Monday; if she went round now, there'd be more questions asked by Elsie. Then of course there was Tommy. She'd better leave him and Bobby with her Mam if they had practice again next Saturday. She might get away with him not mentioning it this time, but she'd be unlikely to if it happened every week.

Dad brought the last of the cups out to her. "I don't suppose you already know anything about this football, do you, love?" His voice was barely more than a whisper.

Violet's mouth opened and closed, but she had no idea what to say.

Alf continued. "I was just thinking… if I could help in any way…" His voice trailed off as Elsie came out to the hall.

Violet turned back to the sink, blinking in surprise at what Alf had said. She poured some hot water from the kettle into the bowl and added some cold. She tried to think through the events of the afternoon and make some sense of them. Perhaps she'd go for a walk after tea. She sometimes went and sat down by the stream; she felt close to Billy there. She looked out of the window at the already gathering gloom. It was too late today; she'd go tomorrow on the way to her parents' house.

"Look, love," Vi's Dad said after he'd given her his thoughts on the practice the previous day. "There's going to be folks who don't like what you're doing, there always are. It doesn't mean you shouldn't do something, though. That bloke yesterday, what does he know? Would he have been so dismissive if he'd known why you were doing it? He looked as though he might have been in the army once himself — if he'd known more about it, he would have seen it was a good idea. None of you are doing anything wrong."

"You should be more like our Ena," Mam said, a resigned expression on her face. "You only have to tell her she can't do something and she'll go and do it before you've finished talking. Just look at her marrying Percy and you can see that."

Vi hadn't realised her parents had told Ena not to marry Percy. "How is Ena? I've not seen much of her since she married." Vi was happy to change the subject. If she was going to keep to her resolve to be involved with the football, as long as Billy didn't object, then she couldn't think too much about those who would be against it.

"None of us have seen her, not unless she wants to borrow something. Borrow is probably the wrong word when we never see anything come back." Mam shook her head.

Dad shrugged. "I don't suppose they're having an easy time of it." He didn't elaborate, and Vi didn't like to ask.

Vi knew they had Percy's dad to look after; he wasn't fit to work anymore. Then there was Percy's no-good brother, when he wasn't behind bars for some brawl or petty theft. She should give Ena more support. Vi sighed. She missed her sister; Ena used to be the one person Vi could confide in, before Percy came along.

There were still two weeks until the match against the men was going to be played. Every day, the girls practised at lunchtime and, while she worked, Violet tried to think about ways they needed to improve. The girls with brothers, or other close relatives who played football, had been asking what they could borrow to wear. By the following Saturday they'd cobbled together enough suitable clothing not to have to play in overalls. They were hardly the height of fashion, and for some of the girls the fit was better than for others; as the things they wore were different colours, they didn't look much like a team. Despite that, the opposition and the crowd would easily recognise them, as they'd be the only women on the field.

"What are we going to do with our hair?" Clara asked as they admired each other's appearances.

"Your work mob caps," Violet said with complete certainty. "That'll be the most appropriate. You can put all your hair up into those quite well."

Violet's Dad had been offered an extra shift at the mill that Saturday and couldn't afford to turn it down, which left Violet coaching the team on her own. She wished she could have asked Billy's dad to help after what he'd said, but she really couldn't face incurring Elsie's wrath.

If she was honest, Vi was enjoying herself; but it would have been more fun with her Dad there too and the girls did learn more from him than she could teach them. Not having anyone else to help her meant Vi spending more time on the pitch during their practice, but she was still adamant that she would not be playing without Billy's permission. As yet, there had been no reply to her letter, but it had only been a week.

"They've sold ever so many tickets," Tessie said as they walked home from work on the Tuesday before the match. "I heard from Beattie that the newspaper's coming and everything."

"How did Beattie know?" Violet never ceased to be amazed at how the other girls seemed to find out so much of what was going on.

"Her mam cleans down at the newspaper office, she heard them saying. Mind you..." Tessie paused. "She heard the man say that he didn't think it was right, girls playing. We'll show him."

The house was quiet when Violet went in and she almost wondered if anyone was home. Billy's mam and dad were sitting in the back room, and despite there being very little light Dad was reading and Mam was mending a shirt.

"There's a letter on the side," Mam said in an accusing tone. "From our Billy."

Vi stiffened. For a moment she thought Mam had opened her post again, but the envelope was still sealed. "Thanks." She took it upstairs when she went to take her bag up. Tommy was tucked up as usual, and Vi sat on the edge of the bed and kissed his forehead. She stayed there and opened the letter.

'Dear Vi,

I broke the news to Stan about his mother. Other than to ask me to thank you for going, he's not said a word about it. He said there's no point in sending the letter back to him so you can throw it away.

Yes, post still reaches me just the same, even though we're now in the trenches. You would be amazed to see how well organised things are. I guess they have to be. I think it's because it helps to keep us going. Mind you, the food parcels help. There never seems to be as much to eat as we'd like. What I'd give for a Sunday roast and some of your bread pudding. I've seen enough bully beef to last me a lifetime, but when you're hungry, you'll eat anything.

I think it's great you're coaching the football. Of course I don't mind. You should ask my dad to help you, I've heard he was a good player when he was young. I don't know what happened that made him stop playing. I think it was when he and Mam started courting. Uncle Ted said not to ask, so I haven't.

Tell Tommy his Dad thinks about him every day.

Billy.'

Violet sat back and shook her head; there was a lot about Billy's parents that she didn't know. She realised her immediate problem was what she was going to say when Billy's mam asked to read the letter. She didn't suppose Billy had thought about that when he wrote about his dad and the football. She tucked it into the side pocket of her bag. It was clear that as he'd replied about Stan's mam and the coaching, his replies were a letter or two behind. At least she could coach the team with a clear conscience; she would certainly give that her very best effort. She wished he was here now so she could give him a hug.

"You girls don't stand a hope." It was the following lunchtime, and the taunt came from one of the men that the girls would be playing against on the Saturday.

"Don't they?" Vi answered, standing her ground for once. "They may not have been playing all their lives, but they're younger and fitter than most of your team." She gasped and covered her mouth, realising she was becoming as cheeky as the others.

"Three cheers for Vi," Clara shouted. "Hip, hip…"

"Hooray," they all cheered.

Violet felt herself blushing.

"What are you so jolly about?" Eva asked her.

"Billy's happy for me to coach you, so now I want to make the most of it. I shouldn't have said what I did though." She felt ashamed of her behaviour, but oddly felt more confident in herself than she had for a long time, and was excited about the match.

"You know they've brought in two or three of the lads who are Tessie's age, don't you?" Eva said.

"Oh dear, have they? I thought the whole team was older." Violet felt disappointed. She thought the girls might have had a chance.

"They don't let the younger ones work on the same section as the girls. I think they're worried what might happen." Eva laughed.

Violet broke into a grin, thinking about Tessie, Florrie and Clara. "They're probably right. Goodness knows what effect that's going to have on the girls when they play on

Saturday."

"Have we found anyone to be our substitutes?" Beattie asked.

Vi had tried asking around, but it was only the younger ones who were even prepared to consider it. There were some who would have liked to take part, but they had family duties, which meant they couldn't play. "Only Maggie, but as she's never kicked a football before it would be a shame to have to use her. I was hoping she'd join today's practice, but she had to go home for lunch."

Violet just hoped they wouldn't have to resort to using Maggie on the pitch.

CHAPTER 13

Mademoiselle from Armentieres, parlez-vous,
Mademoiselle from Armentieres, parlez-vous,
Mademoiselle from Armentieres,
She hasn't been kissed in forty years,
Inky, pinky, parlez-vous.

You might forget the gas and shells, parlez-vous,
You might forget the gas and shells, parlez-vous,
You might forget the groans and yells,
But you'll never forget the Mademoiselles!
Inky, pinky, parlez-vous
(Traditional 1st World War song with several possible authors and based on an earlier work)

1st October 1915 - 'Advance without respite, Conquer or Die.'
General Joffe - The Daily Mirror

"Jesus Christ, Billy, are you sure this is safe?" Stan was talking at barely more than a whisper, as he manoeuvred himself out of the trench and into the open expanse of no man's land.

Billy could see that Stan's hand was trembling as they heard another shell land somewhere in the distance and felt the shockwave through the ground. "I think the C.O.'s definition of safe might be different to ours. Just keep your head down and let's get this done as quickly as possible."

There'd been no fighting along this stretch of the Front for a few weeks, and it had given time for some of the men to undertake repairs along some of the barbed wire separating them from the enemy lines. This was Stan and Billy's second night of work, and if things went well they'd be moving back to the reserve trench the following day. The distance between the Allied and the enemy trenches seemed a long way, until you were above the parapet and felt exposed. Then, the thought of a sniper, or of soldiers manning a machine gun post on the enemy side, was a chilling prospect. Never light three cigarettes from one match might sound like a crazy superstition, until you learned how long it took for a sniper to locate you in his sights.

Billy and Stan began to inch forward across no man's land. They had a pretty good idea of where they were heading, but the directions they'd been given were not for the faint-hearted. 'Keep left of the corpse impaled on the first post' was not something Billy wanted to think about for too long. What trees there had been were now nothing but splintered stumps of trunks, stark sentinels of the overwhelming destruction. They'd been unarmed innocents in a battle with humanity, and they had lost. Billy shivered. He couldn't help thinking there were no victors in war.

The lads carried on across the mud, taking care to keep away from the craters formed where previous shells had landed. Stumbling into one of those would mean almost certain death in the quagmire of mud, with the other rotting corpses who'd died there ahead of them.

Every sense was heightened as they made their way from the comparative safety of the trench to the rolls of barbed wire stretched out for miles, protecting them from the advancing enemy.

"I'll swear they're getting nearer." Stan dropped to the ground next to Billy as another shell exploded somewhere to their left in the night sky.

On high alert, Billy would have taken some convincing that the minutes they were experiencing were only the same length as they used to be back home. Some hours seemed to go on forever. That night's cloud cover was good, but occasionally there was a threat of silver light and they would both drop to the ground until the moon passed behind another cloud. A moonlit silhouette was more than they could risk presenting to the enemy. On one such occasion Billy dropped behind a slight mound, only to realise it was the rotting carcass of a horse. He vomited what was left of that night's stew and inched away. To Billy, the animals that died seemed worse than the men. They'd had no say in being there, no way to defend themselves — no way to fight back. He took a deep breath and put thoughts of death from his mind.

Scrambling to the barbed wire from the trench took an eternity. The actual repair they needed to do took comparatively little time, even allowing for their shaking hands and the darkness they were working in.

Painstakingly they made their way back again and when they dropped back down into the trench the relief was overwhelming. Billy began to breathe more deeply again.

The trenches were not built in straight lines but turned back and forth at regular intervals, to offer the men greater protection. It meant Billy and Stan had to zigzag their way back along the trench until they came to their own section. A few weeks earlier, Stan had adopted a little dog, Chip, and as they arrived back, he was waiting for Stan, a look of delight on his little face.

Billy could have slept on his feet once the adrenaline had worn off. Someone had dug funk holes in this stretch of the trench's wall, small hollows to rest in when the opportunity arose, and, as long as there was no shelling in their area they provided modest comfort and security for an hour or two. Billy wouldn't want to be trapped there if a shell came down, but for the time being it was better than sleeping in the mud of the trench itself. Chip did a good job of keeping the rats at bay, for which he was exceedingly thankful.

The slow journey back from the front line trench for their platoon was no easy process as they worked their way around men who were getting what kip they could, and others, blanket covered, who would never wake again. Billy's tension eased as they moved into the cross trench, heading back toward the greater safety of the communication trenches and reserve trenches behind. Two or four days on the front line was a long enough stint for any man; for others, including Billy, it felt far too long. Every once in a while the relief platoons didn't appear when expected and the men being relieved would be there longer; but generally it was only a short stint on permanent high alert, with precious little sleep.

Now Billy's section was back to lighter duties for a few days, if digging trenches, graves and latrines could be considered lighter.

It was never a difficult decision, what you should do first, when you reached base camp. Sleep, eat and make yourself dry and clean were always the highest priorities; sheer exhaustion overrode all other concerns. Once that need was addressed, you could start to think about other things. Without some sleep, you couldn't think at all.

"Night off tonight," Stan said as they went to breakfast the following day. "Are you coming with me?"

Billy knew exactly what his mate meant. Stan wanted to go into the local town. In Billy's case, the main attraction was eating some decent grub and keeping Stan out of trouble. In Stan's case it was trouble he was going looking for — or at least one of the local girls, which would amount to much the same thing. Billy nodded.

"Wonder if Davy's back?" They'd been on different missions over the last few days. Billy wanted to be sure the lad was all right, but apart from that, if Davy could go into town with them, then at least Billy would have someone to talk to if Stan was waylaid with female company.

"You haven't seen Private Moore, have you?" Stan asked one of the soldiers they passed on their way to breakfast.

"Yes, heading for triage. Walking wounded," the medical orderly replied.

"Bloody hell, at least he's walking. Wonder if it's a Blighty one. Lucky bugger if it is," Stan said. Stan's fascination with the war had dimmed; hardly a surprise given what they'd seen.

"We can go over after we've eaten. I shouldn't think he'll have been dealt with that quickly. I'll take him some food if I can." Billy was still very protective of the lad, even though they saw rather less of him now.

"It's only a graze," Davy said cheerily, looking down at the red which had seeped through his jacket sleeve. "I managed to drop down before any real harm was done. I just need a bit of patching up and I'll be back to duties within hours."

"There goes the mademoiselles being interested in me tonight," Stan said. "Nothing like a bit of sympathy to make a man attractive."

Davy blushed.

"Leave it out, Stan." As far as Billy knew Davy had no experience with girls and was very shy in their company. The last thing he was ready for was any of Stan's antics.

Days off were precious, and few and far between. Billy took the opportunity to write a longer letter to Vi and then had another nap; catching up on sleep was a wonderful feeling. Some of the lads were playing football when he ventured out, and he was more than happy to join in. He smiled at the thought of Vi and Tommy playing at home. He couldn't wait for them all to be together again. Then he remembered he hadn't answered Vi's question. Of course he was happy for her to play football. He wondered if she'd be any good; maybe one day he could see her play.

There were married lads amongst their unit who were as keen to meet the local girls as Stan was, but that wasn't Billy's way. Egg and chips and a glass of beer was all he was after.

The nearby town was a strange place; it was much smaller than Billingbrook. Some buildings had been damaged earlier in the war and were derelict reminders of how close they still were to the Front Line. Billy wondered what the town had been like before all this started; fifteen months in, the residents must have been wondering if it would ever return to normal. Some people from the town were making the best of the bad situation, others he guessed were keeping their heads down and just trying to survive. What a life. He couldn't begin to imagine what it must be like to try to continue with regular life in the middle of all this. Did any of them understand what it was about? He certainly didn't. He was fighting for King and

Country, but when he thought about it, except for the pride of the nation, he had no idea what that meant. It was something like football, but more dangerous. You supported your own side, no matter what.

"Usual?" Stan called across to Billy as they arrived on the edge of the town.

"Where else?" Billy had no wish to change to a different café. Stan always said that the waitresses were prettiest there, but the reality was the food portions were larger and, whilst it wasn't the cheapest, the thought of a hearty meal was a big attraction.

"I'll sit up against the wall," said Davy, taking the furthest chair where his left arm in its bandage sling could be protected from anyone passing.

Davy had said he wasn't in pain, but Billy could tell by his occasional grimace that that wasn't the truth. Davy was no shirker, and he'd already said he didn't want to be pulled off duties any longer than necessary. Billy couldn't help but admire the lad; he and Stan would have bunked off at a moment's notice. He supposed it was through a better work ethic that Davy's family had come to be well off. Billy grinned. Maybe he could learn a thing or two from the lad. It made him think.

Billy had never drunk wine before he came to France. He wasn't sure he liked it now, but the bottle came with the meal and they wouldn't be letting it go to waste; they could wash it down with beer afterwards. Most of Billy's pay went back to Violet and Tommy, but he had a little to spend on himself and precious few opportunities to use it, other than on cigarettes and to supplement his meagre army diet.

By the time the three of them had finished eating, Stan had made arrangements to meet one of the waitresses when her shift finished.

"Just time for a beer or two first. What do you say, Davy lad?" Stan winked at the waitress and stood away from the table.

"I'm not sure." Davy raised his bandaged arm and winced.

Billy fancied a beer before returning to camp, but could see it was going to be hard for Davy in a busy bar. "How about you wait outside and I'll bring one out to you?"

"In this weather? I know it's drier, but it's not exactly warm." Stan turned up the collar of his greatcoat.

"Thanks, but I'll be heading back." Davy turned to go.

"Wait up." Billy sighed. "I'll go with the lad. You'll never miss us given the promise you're on."

Stan waved them off and swaggered toward the bar, whistling.

"I just hope he doesn't overstay his pass again." Billy wouldn't have been hanging around in the town until Stan had finished all his activities, so there was precious little he could do to save Stan from yet another loss of pay. How many charges had Stan been on? Billy had lost count. He was starting to think his mate enjoyed being dressed down, judging by the frequency with which it seemed to happen. Billy shook his head. "How's the arm?" he asked Davy.

"Not so bad. I'm on light duties for a day or two, but I'll be fit as a fiddle in no time." Davy's smile didn't reach the rest of his face.

Billy wondered just how bad the wound was, but if the lad insisted he carried on there was not much Billy could do there either. When had he become a surrogate father to the lad? He shook his head and laughed to himself. The things you did when you missed your kid.

The distant sky lit up as a loud explosion made them both jump.

"Jesus, that was a big one. I'll swear it was closer. Maybe our stretch of the line isn't going to be quite such a picnic as it has been." Billy straightened himself up.

"Picnic?" Davy snorted. "If I get this on a picnic..." he was clutching his arm, "then I don't fancy joining them for dinner."

"We may have no choice, Davy boy. We may have no choice." Billy shivered.

CHAPTER 14

Now, Father's sticking in the pub through treading in the paste
And all the family's so upset they've all gone pasty faced
While Pa says, now that Ma has spread the news from North to South
He wishes he had dropped a blob of paste in Mother's mouth.
When Father Papered the Parlour - Robert P. Weston & Fred J. Barnes - 1909

11th October 1915 - The Road to Victory: Sir John French Reports Another Fine Advance By the British - The Daily Mirror

"What's the matter, Vi love?" Alf Dobson had come into the kitchen where Violet was staring out of the window.

"It's nothing, Dad. I just…" She stopped what she had been about to say. Although Alf had offered to help if he could with the football, they'd said no more about it. Vi was still worried about how Elsie saw things.

Her father-in-law put his hands onto her shoulders and gently turned her around. "Today's your big day. Are you sorry that Billy won't be here to watch?"

Violet glanced toward the door, worried that Elsie would hear what they were saying.

"Don't you go worrying about Mam, she was still

snoring when I came down to take some tea up. You know I'd come and watch the game myself if it wouldn't upset her. What's wrong, Vi?"

Violet let out a heavy sigh. "I wrote to Billy and asked what he'd think if I were to play, rather than just coach the team. I was hoping he might have answered by now." She looked up at her father-in-law. "I'm not playing, I wouldn't without his say so. It's just, we only have one substitute and she's hopeless. I'm sure she'll be all right once she's had some practice, but she's only just joined in and she'd never so much as kicked a ball until a couple of weeks ago."

"Alf, are you down there?" Mam shouted from upstairs.

Vi's shoulders slumped and she turned away.

"I'm just coming, love," Alf shouted back and made a point of rattling some cups and saucers so that she could hear. Then he turned back to Vi.

"Vi love, I can't speak for Billy, but I think I know him pretty well. You're not to mind what Elsie says and thinks. She grew up in a different time, and sometimes doesn't realise how much things have changed. I think Billy would be happy for you to play. I think he'd want you to enjoy yourself, and what you girls are doing to help the hospital is very important."

Violet heard the stairs creak and she stiffened.

Alf put his finger to his lips and took the kettle off the stove. He made a show of pouring the water into the waiting teapot while Violet went back to peeling the potatoes she was leaving ready for later.

"Here you are, my love," Alf said, lifting the tea tray up and going toward the open kitchen door. "I'm on my way."

He waited while Elsie turned around and then followed her, leaving Violet on her own in the kitchen.

Violet's stomach was churning. She began to think through the last-minute preparations for the game as she finished preparing the vegetables. She knew she'd done everything she could, but she was still worried.

There was a quiet tap and Tessie poked her head around the back door. "Is it safe?"

Vi smiled. "You daft lass. Come in, I'll put some more tea on."

"I just wanted to make sure you were all right, and check what time we're going." Tessie scooped some tea from the caddy into the pot as she spoke. "Have you borrowed anything to wear from your John, like your dad said?"

Vi shook her head. "I'll be all right in my overalls on the sideline. I don't want my legs showing in public."

"It's only my knees — the shorts I've borrowed come down to the tops of them. You should have seen Mam's face when I showed her, she reckons I'll have all the lads queuing up at the door. Chance would be a fine thing." Tessie giggled.

Once Tessie had gone, Vi got Tommy ready to take him to her parents. She'd then meet Tessie on the way back. Elsie wasn't stupid, she'd probably work out where Tessie was that afternoon, but at least she wouldn't see the girls leaving together.

They arrived at the Caulder and Harrison recreation ground in time for the girls to change and have a warm-up session before the game. From the level of chatter, the girls were as nervous and excited as Vi was. She hoped they'd settle down enough to play their best.

The entrance to the sports field had been roped off and

there were stewards positioned at the entrances; only ticket holders would be allowed access that afternoon. Vi thought they might be being over-optimistic about the size of the area that would be needed. However, to her surprise, there were already people starting to gather along the sidelines. Some, who Vi recognised from work, seemed to have brought their entire families.

As the girls warmed up, there was a steady stream of arrivals. There were men whistling at the girls, and despite Vi's best efforts the girls were shouting back saucy responses to some of them.

With thirty minutes to kick-off, Clara came running over carrying a bag. "Doris can't get away, her mam's sick. She said you can use these." She presented the bag to Violet, who looked at it open-mouthed.

"Maggie, you're on," Vi shouted to their one and only substitute. She turned to look for Maggie.

Maggie was already in full kit and grinning. "I came prepared. I promise I'll do my best."

Vi didn't have time to say anything further because a boy of no more than ten or eleven years of age came running over to them all. "Excuse me, is one of you Mrs Dobson?" he asked, looking around at them all.

Vi frowned and stepped forward.

The boy thrust a piece of paper into her hand. "I have to give you this."

Before Vi had the opportunity to say anything else, the boy had run back away from the girls. Vi unfolded the paper.

'Dear Mrs Dobson,

I will not be permitting my daughter Agnes Fairbrother to do something as immoral as play football. I have only just become aware of this moral turpitude. Such behaviour is the work of the devil.

May the good Lord save your souls and pluck you from the fires of damnation.

Yours sincerely

Reverend C. T. Fairbrother'

Vi was standing with her mouth open. She had no idea what turpitude meant, but she didn't think it sounded very good.

Tessie came over to her. "What was that about?"

Vi was still looking across at where the boy had gone.

"Vi? Anybody home?" Tessie waved a hand in front of Vi's face.

Vi shook her head and brought herself back to what Tessie was saying. "That was about us only having ten players, even with Maggie in the team. Did you know that Agnes's father was a vicar?"

"Agnes? Give over."

"There's no time now to explain. We have a game to play." Tessie looked around at the other girls. "Eva, are all the men's team here?"

"Yes, they have substitutes too. We can't play without a full team. We'll be the laughing stock." Eva was biting her lip.

Clara picked Doris's bag up and handed it to Vi. "Put these on. We need you."

"I can't. I just can't." Violet's heart was pounding.

"You bloody well can. We're your team and we need you." Eva was standing with her hands on her hips. "Besides, when have you ever taken any notice of some vicar?"

Vi gasped. "Eva Podmore, that's a dreadful thing to say."

"Are you girls about ready?" Joe Wood, who was

captaining the men's team, had come over to them, grinning.

"We will be," Florrie said with confidence. "I just need to find my uncle." She ran away from where Vi was toward the large crowds who were gathering to watch.

Violet stood there frowning. What should she do next? There were hundreds of spectators — no, more like thousands. They couldn't let them down, but what on earth was she going to do?

After only a few minutes, Florrie came back arm in arm with a kindly-looking gentleman wearing a dog collar. Vi recognised him from All Saints, their local parish church.

"Vi, this is my uncle Anthony," Florrie said proudly. "Uncle Anthony, this is Violet Dobson, she's our coach."

"Good afternoon, Mrs Dobson. It's a pleasure to see you again. How is Mr Dobson?"

Violet felt the whole situation was surreal, standing at the side of the football pitch talking to the local vicar as though she was outside of church. "He was well the last time I heard. He's away at the Western Front." Vi bit her lip.

Florrie's uncle nodded sagely. "What you're all doing today is a wonderful thing. It is the work of the Lord to be raising money for our injured soldiers. I'm delighted I could buy a ticket to come and watch."

"But... but..." Vi pulled the letter from her pocket and handed it to the vicar. "Reverend Fairbrother says it's the work of the devil." She handed the note to the vicar.

"Indeed," he said, having read the note. "I do believe he thinks I'm going to hell as well." He gave out a deep chuckle. "He's the minister of the Baptist church on Elm Street. He has some strongly held views. You girls should play today and play with God's blessing. Mind you, it would do no harm to see you in my congregation a little more often, Mrs Dobson." He winked at her. Then he held out his hand to shake hers. "Good luck, Mrs Dobson. I'm sure your husband is very proud of you." He handed the letter to her and turned to go back to the crowds, waving to the girls as he went.

"Now will you play?" Florrie asked.

Violet looked down at the bag of Doris's kit. She nodded and sighed. "I do hope I'm doing the right thing — but yes, I'll play. Now, if anyone asks, my name's Tunnicliffe. Make sure the men's team knows that and can someone tell Mr Giffard. The last thing I need is my married name appearing anywhere, and I do mean anywhere."

The girls were all chattering with excitement as Violet marched off to the new changing rooms carrying the bag. Doris wasn't far off her size so if the clothes were a good fit on Doris they shouldn't be too bad. It depended who Doris had borrowed them from.

Once Vi had changed, she looked in the mirror with a mixture of pride and dread. Thankfully, Doris's kit was not too revealing, and being a bit on the big side, came down further than she'd feared. She took a deep breath and headed for the door. Her stomach was flipping like a pancake toss and she hoped she wasn't going to be sick. She was still tucking the last strands of her hair into the mob cap as she came out. The other girls cheered and Vi looked up, startled.

"You'd be best as a forward," Clara said. "I don't mind being in defence. I wasn't really looking forward to having to push through the line of men, anyway."

Violet's mind was racing. She hadn't even thought about needing to change the team around. Doris was a great defender and they were going to miss her. She nodded slowly. "Right, so it's me and Florrie up front." She ran through the entire team and each girl nodded.

Violet had thought it would only be those who worked at the factory who came to watch — and her dad, of course, he'd promised to support them — but there were still men and women streaming into the ground to watch. A crowd surrounded every side of the pitch, several deep. There were also children sitting on shoulders and others who seemed to have climbed onto any posts they could find. There were even a couple sitting on some lower tree branches. At this rate, if they ever played again, they'd need a bigger stadium. The works ground wouldn't hold many more than were already there.

She gasped as her dad came over to wish the team luck. Running behind him were Bobby and Tommy.

"I thought you were leaving the boys with Mam? What am I going to do if Tommy says anything to Billy's mam?" Vi was starting to panic.

"I couldn't leave them out, love. It will be all right, I'm sure it will. Besides…" he was grinning broadly, "… your Mam's had a word with them, and they have promised faithfully to keep it a secret."

Vi shook her head. That was all she needed; she was trying to teach Tommy to be honest. This would never end well. It was done now, and they'd already seen her in football kit, so it was going to be hard to pretend she wasn't playing.

She'd have to rely on the fact that Tommy had a vivid imagination and laugh it off. She would at least say she'd watched it with the boys and her Dad, maybe she could get away with that. Oh, but she didn't want to have to start lying. That was no example to set to her son.

The referee had been brought in from outside, to ensure it was a fair match. Violet thought it was possibly the first time he'd had to deal with a situation in which, as he waited to blow the whistle, half the players of one of the teams were busy giggling. Most of the girls were still little more than fifteen or sixteen, and before going onto the pitch their main concern was which of the local lads would be watching them. One or two of them even had their eye on some of the younger ones in the men's team, which Vi doubted was likely to make them play their best.

Violet wished she hadn't eaten anything. It hadn't seemed a problem when she thought she'd only be watching; now it felt as though there was a football being kicked around inside her as well as the one on the pitch. She tried to keep her eyes focussed just on the rest of the team. When she looked up and saw the crowd, her heart began to race.

She was surprised to see, even now, there were still people arriving, and given the basic nature of the Company ground she hoped they'd all be able to see.

The men were to kick-off. As they came forward, Vi realised they had found five younger lads to play. She'd thought almost all the men's team were going to be older and that the girls might have had an advantage as a result. As long as the girls didn't show themselves up completely, she'd be happy.

When the whistle blew, the men made the most of the fact the girls weren't ready. They set off with the ball, going past Vi and Florrie and were well down the pitch heading for the other end. It was when Sidney Shepherd struck the ball in the direction of the goal that the girls' laughter finally died down. Violet's heart sank, but to her relief Edith was prepared and stopped the ball going into the back of the net.

There was cheering from some of the crowd, but from others Vi could hear other comments being shouted.

"Show us your legs."

"She's a cracker."

Violet frowned. As soon as there was an opportunity, she gathered the girls around her. "Come on, let's show them what our football skills are like." A couple of the younger ones started giggling again and Vi wondered if it was worth it. She didn't want to be cross with them; she wanted them to enjoy playing, but she also wanted them to take it seriously. She tried to sound authoritative without being sharp. "We're doing this to help the war effort. If we make a good game of it, we'll be doing our own men proud. I know it's a bit of fun and you're enjoying the attention, but let's make all our practice worthwhile." She hoped she'd had some effect, but until they restarted she'd have no way of knowing.

As the game got underway again, Vi and Florrie, together with Tessie, Eva and Clara started playing more as a team and Vi breathed a sigh of relief. However, it was thanks to Edith's goalkeeping skills that the girls were only one goal down at half-time. Edith shied away from nothing, and however fast the ball looked to be travelling, she blocked its way if she possibly could. Vi felt very proud of her.

"Is that it then?" Sarah shouted as the teams moved to the sides of the pitch.

"No, it bloody isn't," Tessie shouted back. "We have half a match to beat them in yet."

"My feet are killing me." Sarah reached down to unlace her boot.

"Don't do that, you'll never want to put it on again."

Tessie squatted down in front of the girl and retied her boot before she had a chance to do anything further.

Violet was feeling more exhilarated than tired. When the whistle blew and the second half started, she just hoped the other girls had listened to the things she'd said to them.

It took until halfway through the second half for their team to get a break. By now, the men's team were winning three goals to nil. Florrie, who was being marked by one of the older members of the men's team, managed to outrun him and make her way down the pitch. As one of the other men came toward her, Florrie passed the ball to Vi, who passed it back as soon as Florrie had dodged her opponent. Florrie had enough time to go a little further down the pitch before kicking the ball past the keeper to score the very first goal for the girls' team. The cheers from both the players and the crowd rang in Vi's ears. Even the men's team were applauding, and for a moment the girls lost concentration as a result. Unfortunately, that was long enough for the men's team to regain the upper hand, and before Vi knew it the ball had gone over the line to the right of Edith. The men were winning four goals to one. Joe Wood seemed to positively swagger after scoring his team's goal. Vi clenched her fists. She wouldn't give up; maybe not today, but one day she'd wipe that smile off his face.

The game was nearly over when Tessie passed the ball to Vi. There was nothing Vi wanted to do more than score a goal. She began running forward, dribbling the ball, but there was Joe Wood again — he seemed to be everywhere. She wanted to keep going, but there was no way she'd manage to pass him. Hadn't she always told the girls to pass the ball? She looked around and saw Sarah coming up the field. Vi knew how tired Sarah was and wondered if she could be trusted. She had to try. Florrie had space on the far side, but Vi couldn't kick the ball to her directly. She kicked the ball to Sarah and prayed.

Vi could hardly bring herself to watch what happened next. She kept moving to find a clear space in case Sarah passed the ball back to her. Then she looked and almost cheered when she realised that Sarah had not only received the ball safely, but had passed it straight out to Florrie. The girl might moan about her feet, but she was clearly taking it seriously. Vi could feel her heart racing. It must be almost full-time. Just after Florrie kicked the ball toward the goal, for a moment silence fell. As the ball sailed over the line, the whistle sounded for the end of the game. Vi couldn't hear the crowds cheering for the sound of her own excited scream. They hadn't won, but at least they'd scored two goals against the men and given them a good game. That was good enough for her - for now.

Vi could feel the adrenaline pumping as she searched for her dad after the match.

"You were great, love. The best on the pitch."

Vi laughed. "You have to say that, that's what dads say." She paused for a moment. "Although usually about their sons." She looked at him ruefully.

"You know," he said, "I think your Billy would be proud of you too."

Violet went quiet. She wondered if he would. She'd write and tell him about the game when she went home; if there was anything in the *Billingbrook Mercury* she could send him a copy. If there was something in, she just hoped that Elsie wouldn't see it. She felt sure Alf would keep it to himself if he read anything, and she didn't think that Elsie normally read the sports pages. Then she had a horrible thought; because of the fundraising, would the match be in amongst the news?

CHAPTER 15

Oh! Mr Porter, what shall I do?
I want to go to Birmingham
And they're taking me on to Crewe,
Take me back to London, as quickly as you can,
Oh! Mr Porter, what a silly girl I am.
Oh! Mr Porter - George Le Brunn (and his brother Thomas)
1892

18th October 1915 - Allies Reprisal Raid for Bombardment of
London - The Daily Mirror

Vi walked home with her dad and the boys after the match. She couldn't stop herself smiling.

"You were great, love," her dad said.

"Could you see much from where you were standing?" she asked him.

"That was the good thing about having this pair with me — people are very good about letting children move through to the front so they can see. I just had to stay with them."

Her father gave a very boy-like shrug, which made Vi laugh.

"Can I stay with Bobby again?" Tommy asked.

"Well, that depends on what Nanna and Granddad say. If they say it's all right then yes, but it will be lunchtime before I can pick you up." Vi looked across at her dad.

"We'll ask Nanna," her dad said. Then he looked at Vi. "You could stay for a spot of lunch, I'm sure Mam will make it stretch."

Whilst Vi loved staying with her family for meals, she felt a pang knowing how hard it was for them to make ends meet. She wondered if there was anything at home she could use to make a pie. Yes, there were some apples in the pantry if she remembered rightly — she could replace them on Monday. If she made two pies, there'd be one for Elsie and Alf as well. "That would be lovely, I'll talk to Mam when we go in."

Violet's mam was delighted when they all arrived. "Now, are you going to tell me all about the game?"

Queenie was looking at Vi as she asked the question, but it was Bobby and Tommy who replied.

"She was ever so good," Bobby said.

"And who's she?" Queenie said to her youngest child.

"Sorry, Mam. Sorry, Vi. Vi was good. We were right at the front, weren't we Tommy?"

The boys started acting out the football match and Queenie stood shaking her head and watching them. Then she looked at Vi. "And what did you think, love?"

"I really enjoyed playing. Thank you for the things you said last week — they helped." Vi gave her mam a kiss.

"We'll have less of that," Queenie replied, a little flustered.

"Nanna," Tommy interrupted them. "Can I stay here tonight?"

"I said that Vi could stay for Sunday lunch when she comes for him," Frank said.

"I'll bring a pie for pudding if I do," Vi said.

"That would be lovely." Mam looked at her daughter.

"And what are you doing in the morning?"

Vi couldn't get anything past her mother. "I'm going to church."

"Well, I'll go to the foot of our stairs. What brought that on all of a sudden? Are you worrying about Billy?" Mam asked.

"It's funny, I probably should be, but it wasn't that. It's a long story, but it was because of Reverend Smith from All Saints that I played today." Then Vi explained to her parents about Florrie's uncle Anthony and how he'd helped her make the decision. "I suppose I just thought attending the service tomorrow was the least I could do."

Her mother burst out laughing. "Well, I've heard of many reasons why people go to church in my time, but that's a new one. Say one for me while you're there, love — God knows we could do with it." She patted Frank's arm and then went to put more tea on to brew.

Vi had never been to church on her own. They'd been in the weeks when the banns were read for their wedding, and once or twice with Billy's parents just before Tommy's christening, but she thought that was the last time, other than weddings and funerals. She had talked to Billy about sending Tommy to Sunday school, but that had been a short conversation. She'd thought it might be good for him, but she could see Billy's point about having to go to school being bad enough without Sundays as well. It was as well Tommy had asked to stay with Bobby the previous night, as she couldn't imagine him sitting still through a service.

Vi didn't want to tell Billy's parents where she was going. She hoped they would just think she was going straight over to her own family, but Elsie saw her as she came downstairs in her best dress and hat.

"Going somewhere special?" Elsie asked, looking at Vi from under an arched eyebrow.

"All Saints. I was just…" Vi scrambled for an explanation.

Elsie's face softened and she patted Vi's hand. "We worry about him too. If I'd known, I might have come with you. Maybe another time."

Vi blinked. It hadn't occurred to her that Elsie would just assume Vi was worrying about Billy; she thought Billy would have laughed if he'd thought they were attending church because of him. In her eyes, it certainly couldn't hurt. She wished now that she had asked Elsie to go.

Vi sat toward the back of the church so she could see what was going on. She recognised a few of the people there and then spotted Florrie much closer to the front and wished she'd gone to sit with her. She struggled following the service; it felt like some secret club where everyone else knew the rituals and she didn't, but she enjoyed most of the hymns. They were clearly listed on a board at the front and she could find their numbers in the hymn book.

When they sang 'Onward Christian Soldiers', Vi wondered if the same hymn was sung in churches in other countries. Did all the soldiers think they had God on their side? Was He on anyone's side when it came to war? Vi shuddered and didn't want to think about it.

When the service was over she joined the rest of the congregation, filing out and shaking the vicar's hand.

"It's good to see you again, Mrs Dobson. That was a fine performance yesterday. I hope I shall have the opportunity to watch you play again."

Vi felt herself blushing. "Thank you, Reverend Smith." She wanted to say so much more than that, but there were rumblings of impatience from behind her as others wanted to shake the vicar's hand, so Vi left it at that and continued down the steps of the church.

"Vi."

Violet turned to see Florrie coming down the steps to her. With her hair in a long tidy plait and the neat white collar to her dress, Florrie looked much younger than she did either at work or football.

"How lovely to see you here. Uncle Anthony will be ever so pleased that you came. Come on, come and meet my mam and dad." Florrie led her over to a small group of people talking on the pavement. "Mam, Dad, this is Mrs Dobson, the one who's been teaching us to play football."

For a moment, Vi was horrified and wondered what sort of reception she was going to receive. But she relaxed when both of Florrie's parents seemed genuinely pleased and thought it was doing their daughter good. How varied people's opinions seemed to be.

When Vi eventually arrived at her mam and dad's house, the table had already been pulled out into the middle of the room and extended to its full length.

"It's set for ten," Vi said. "Who else is coming? I only have the one pie."

"Our Ena's coming and Percy, of course. It's a rare chance for her to get away of a Sunday, but Percy's dad has gone to stay with his brother's family for a day or two." Mam was working to prepare lunch in the tight confines of the corner of the room where the stove was. "Can you give me a hand, love?"

Vi took off her coat and hat. "Can I put these upstairs out of the way, Mam? They're my best."

"Of course you can, love. Put them on our bed, they'll be safest there." Mam blew a stray strand of hair away from her face where it had tumbled out of the pins which held it up.

The house was three storeys high, with her mam and dad's room on the first up from downstairs and the children all sharing the room at the top of the house. When Vi came down she found an apron out of the drawer and went to help her mam.

"That's what I like to see," Percy said as he came into the room, "a woman who knows her place." He slapped Vi's bottom by way of a greeting to his sister-in-law and Vi bristled.

She gritted her teeth before replying, "Hello, Percy," then gave a genuine smile to her sister. "It's lovely to see you. It's been ages."

Ena looked nervously across to Percy before answering. "It's not always easy, what with Dad Mayberry."

"How is he?" Mam asked.

"He'll outlive all of us," Percy said and laughed.

Violet saw the look on Ena's face and thought her sister probably hoped otherwise.

Vi was quiet over lunch; Percy always dominated the conversation, and she had no wish to be involved with most of it. Her mam had managed to put together a wonderful meal. It was easier at this time of year with root vegetables being plentiful; her dad would have grown most of them on the allotment. There were big Yorkshire puddings too, her mam had always been good at those, and all soaked with plenty of gravy. What was more surprising was that there was even enough for all of them to have some meat, although she couldn't see if there was any on her mother's plate. With John working, things must be a little easier for them.

Violet wondered if there might be an opportunity to suggest that she and Ena went for a walk after lunch, so they could have a proper catch up. However, as soon as the meal was over and before he could be called on to do anything useful, Percy left the table.

"Well, we must be going, mustn't we Ena?" Percy gave no explanation for their rapid departure.

Ena looked surprised. She wiped her mouth on her serviette and began to gather up the dishes from pudding.

Mam rested a hand on Ena's arm. "Don't worry, lass, I'll do them."

Ena looked flustered and didn't seem to know what to do with her hands. They seemed to want to automatically continue with the clearing up.

Vi could see her distress and reached over, taking the plates from Ena. Vi forced a smile. "I'll take these. You fetch your coat." As Ena looked at her sister, Vi could have sworn there was bruising on her cheek, but said nothing.

Mam must have seen what Vi was thinking as they waved Ena and Percy off. She looked at Vi and said, "I'm sure she'll be fine," but her tone of voice sounded as though she was anything but sure.

"Thanks for washing Doris's kit for me." Violet took the bag from Tessie to carry it as they walked to work on Monday. "You didn't tell your mam, did you?"

"You funny thing. You were the star and you still don't want people to know."

Violet felt a sense of rising panic.

"It's all right, I know what Billy's mam's like — I won't say a word. Mind you, they might find out from someone else. You did enjoy it though, didn't you?" Tessie linked her arm through Violet's.

Violet felt herself smiling. She'd loved it, but she tempered her enthusiasm in her reply. "Yes, it was all right."

"Mr Giffard wants to see you in his office, miss." The gatekeeper was looking serious as he said it. Then he broke into a smile. "It was good to see the football on Saturday. Well done, girls."

Tessie giggled.

"What do you think Mr Giffard wants? I've never been to the management offices. Do you think I should go straight there?" Violet's heart was beating hard.

Tessie put her head on one side and put her hand to her face in a mock gesture of deep thought. "Should you go up in your respectable civvies or change into your grubby overalls first? I do believe that's a difficult decision, Violet Dobson."

Violet laughed, seeing the sense in what Tessie was saying.

"Tell me what he wants at break," Tessie shouted after her, as Violet turned toward the management part of the building.

Vi could hear her heels echoing as she walked along the corridor and tried to walk more quietly.

"Morning, Mr Wood."

Joe Wood was also waiting outside Mr Giffard's office. "Good morning. You did a good…" Joe didn't finish his sentence, as the secretary came out at the same moment.

"Mr Giffard will see you both now. Follow me." She led them back through the open door and across her own small office into a neighbouring much larger office. Vi was amazed by the plush carpet, and a Chesterfield armchair and settee on the other side of the room.

Mr Giffard had been sitting behind a grand wooden

desk in a high-backed leather chair. He stood up as they entered. "Mr Wood, Mrs Dobson, do sit down."

They took the chairs which were placed in front of his desk and Violet held her bag tightly on her knee.

Returning to his chair, Mr Giffard began. "As the two team captains, I thought you might like to be the first to know how much the football match raised for the hospital. We shall be releasing a statement to the *Mercury* later, but I thought you would like to hear direct from me." He glanced down at a note on his desk as though he needed reminding. "I'm pleased to say a cheque for 25 pounds, 2 shillings and 6 pence will be handed over to Major Tomlinson this evening."

Violet gasped. "How much? But that's…"

Mr Giffard smiled. "Yes, a large sum of money. You heard me correctly, Mrs Dobson. Our little football match raised over 25 pounds. Well done to both your teams and thank you."

Violet couldn't wait to write to Billy. "Can you believe that?" she said to Joe as they walked back along the corridor. Violet felt as though she was floating and no longer cared two hoots if her shoes were making a lot of noise. "I wonder what it'll say in the *Mercury*."

Although the report on the fundraising wouldn't be in the paper until the following day, by lunchtime one of the girls had obtained a copy of that day's paper.

"Have you seen this? There's a report of the match," Clara said, laying the newspaper out on the table.

"What does it say?" Eva tried to look over Clara's shoulder.

By the time Violet read the report, it was with some trepidation. The other girls had already called enough snippets out for her to know it said more about how the girls looked and what they wore than it did about the football they'd played. She also knew they'd given out the players' names and ages, so whilst she might be listed as Miss Violet Tunnicliffe, the fact that she was twenty-three made it pretty easy to work out who it was. Even if that were not enough for her mother-in-law, she was very likely to talk to their neighbour, mother of 'Miss Tessie Brown (14) and one of the stars of the team'. Violet sighed heavily. She could only hope that being in the sports pages there might be some chance her mother-in-law wouldn't see this. She wondered what the Reverend Smith thought of the reporter saying 'Miss Florence Smith (15)' was one of his personal favourites for her looks.

If Elsie Dobson didn't see the report of the match, she'd almost certainly see the news report on the amount the match had raised, but hopefully that would not include the names of those who played.

Vi was barely through the door that evening when she heard Elsie's voice.

"Is that you, Violet?"

Who else would it be letting themselves in at this time of night? Violet painted on a smile and poked her head around the door. "Yes, it's me, Mam. Is there any post?"

"Well, that's a fine thing to be asking when you've been parading yourself wearing next to nothing and using your maiden name."

Well, that answered that one. The *Billingbrook Mercury* was neatly folded in front of Elsie.

"What do you have to say for yourself? If it weren't for you being married to our Billy, I'd have a good mind to tell you to move out and live somewhere else."

Despite the situation, Violet almost smiled at the

woman's absurd logic. If she weren't married to Billy, she wouldn't be living here anyway.

"I've told Alfred to write to our Billy to make him aware of his wife's behaviour. You're writing tonight, aren't you Alf?"

In an uncharacteristic move, Alf lowered his newspaper and looked earnestly at his wife. "Yes, my love, I'm writing to Billy to appraise him of the... er... situation." Then he raised his paper slightly to the side so it blocked Elsie's view, but not Violet's, and he winked at Violet.

Violet could have laughed. He was on her side, although not prepared to openly disagree with his wife. Vi coughed to clear the smile that had been threatening to erupt. "When you write, please do tell him we raised over 25 pounds for the new soldiers' hospital."

Alf raised an eyebrow to acknowledge what she'd said and nodded a 'well done' to Vi.

As Vi went out of the room, Elsie was still chuntering. "That's as maybe, but however much you raised doesn't take away from the fact that you're a married woman."

Violet was glad that although Billy hadn't yet replied, she had written the whole story to him when she arrived home on Saturday night and posted the letter on her way to church. She only hoped he received the letter from her, before the one his mam intended to send.

CHAPTER 16

In the Daily Mirror, no matter what your age
If you've done anything that's queer
They'll put you on their title page
Now, I know lots of people that they seem to have missed
For instance, I've a lady friend of thirty-five
And she says she's never been kissed
So I said to her, darling, if that's true
That you're five and thirty quite
And you've never had a bite
Front page, Daily Mirror, for you.
Daily Mirror, Front Page - H Lonsdale

20th October 1915 - Lord Derby's Great Recruiting Scheme - The Daily Mirror

Violet was surprised on Wednesday when she was called to Mr Giffard's office for the second time that week. On this occasion Joe Wood wasn't waiting outside the office, and Violet was shown in on her own. She wondered if she'd done something wrong and began to fidget with the cuff of her coat.

"As you know, Mrs Dobson, the football match on Saturday proved surprisingly popular, not just with other employees from our factory but with the general public as well."

Violet sat listening, wondering where this speech was

leading to. Mr Giffard seemed in a good mood, so she presumed she wasn't in trouble and began to relax a little.

"The thing is, I'll come straight to the point — we've received a letter from the manager of a munitions factory over near Blackburn asking if we'd consider a ladies' football match against their factory to raise money for the war effort. Half the money would go to their local Voluntary Aid Detachment for the work they are doing with the wounded, and half to Billingbrook Hall Hospital. Now, before you answer, I've been giving some thought to what you might need in order to play. If you and the girls are amenable, shall we say, the factory could provide suitable clothing for the team as well as a couple of hours a week paid time in order to practise. We'd see it as part of our contribution to the war effort, so that the team could raise money. I was rather thinking," he coughed nervously, "that perhaps Mr Wood might be willing to take on the coaching of the team — there may well be other games to be played after this. We'd need to find a more suitable ground for the match, of course, somewhere we could sell a few more tickets for. If you could perhaps talk to the girls, then we can make a start?"

Violet was left unsure of whether she'd been asked a question she was expected to answer, or if it was being presented to her simply for confirmation. Being paid to practise sounded good, but the thought of even bigger crowds was probably more of a surprise. She wanted to ask why the company would be so generous; she couldn't see why they'd do it. Wouldn't it be easier just to make a donation? Then when she thought about it, Vi realised they had raised a lot of money on Saturday, so maybe this gave the company a way of donating more, while it cost them less. "I'll talk to the girls at lunchtime."

"That's the spirit. If you can see Mrs Simpson with what sizes will be needed for the team strip, she'll order them."

As Mrs Simpson showed Violet out of Mr Giffard's office, she gave no acknowledgment that she was aware of the plan, although as she was the one who no doubt opened the post she must have seen the incoming letter. Violet wondered if she didn't approve, or whether she was always so unreadable.

"Well, that's what Mr Giffard said," Violet finished as she explained it to the others at lunch.

"That's good news, isn't it?" Tessie was clearly excited. "We'll be a real team."

"The thing is," Violet was choosing her words carefully, "I don't think I'll be able to take part." She pictured Elsie's face after Saturday's match and shuddered. "It's different for me."

"Don't talk wet," said Eva. "We need you."

"I only filled in for Doris. Now she's back, you'll be fine."

"She might be back, but Agnes isn't. Her father's told her that if she so much as watches us, he'll see to it that she leaves working here," Florrie said. "Honestly, the poor girl must have no fun at all."

Vi suspected Florrie was right. She could understand now why Agnes had never talked about her family.

Clara crossed her arms and looked at Violet defiantly. "If you don't play, we don't play. That's right, isn't it girls?" She looked around at the others, who nodded in turn.

"It's not that I don't want to." As she said it, Violet realised just how much that was true. "It's just that my in-laws don't approve, and I could be out on my ear if I upset them too much. In Billy's mam's eyes, married women just don't do things like that. Why don't I tell Mr Giffard we have a team, and we'll worry about the details later?"

Clara uncrossed her arms and pouted. "You'd better play, Violet Dobson. Don't let us down."

Violet had Clara's words ringing in her ears as she worked that afternoon. She was torn between the fact she wanted to play and just how much it had upset Billy's mother. She'd write to Billy again that night and ask what he really thought; if he agreed with his mother, then there was no more to be said on the subject. She sighed heavily, and then realising she wasn't thinking about what she was doing, pulled herself together and went back to concentrating. She certainly didn't want to send them all up in smoke.

The air in the Dobson residence was still decidedly frosty, with Elsie making snide remarks at every opportunity. By contrast, Mrs Brown next door was obviously proud of Tessie, and Violet was pleased for the girl. Vi kept herself to herself as much as she could, and although she told Mr Giffard that the girls would play, she didn't outline her own predicament. When she gave Mrs Simpson the measurements for the kit, she did include her own, assuming that as she was not as slim as some of the younger girls, if the clothes fitted her than they should be plenty big enough for someone else to take her place. Thankfully, after the success of their first match, they now had enough girls coming forward to make a complete team and substitutes.

It was a little over a week before Violet received the letter she'd been waiting for. She read Billy's words carefully.

'We are still relatively safe doing repairs by night and getting what kip we can during the day. Stan's adopted a Jack Russell Terrier. His last owner didn't come back, poor bugger. He's called the dog Chip, don't ask me why. He had been called Frank, but Stan was adamant about the name change. Chip's said to be the best ratter in our division, so we're lucky to have him. It's made sleeping a little easier. Stan dotes on him. It's made me think we should have a little dog for Tommy, if times are better in the future. I've never seen Stan so happy. When his mam died, it was a long time before he said anything about it. When he did, he quite took me by surprise. He said he thought it was all his fault for signing up. He thought with him away, it might stop her drinking, though what made him think of that, I have no idea. Turns out his brothers and sisters gave up on their mam years ago. Stan was all she had. When she died, he said there was no point him coming home now. I had no idea he felt like that. Anyway, Chip seems to have put a spring in his step again, for which we're all grateful. I just hope he doesn't have to leave the dog here when we come home.

It's funny to think of you playing football. I should think Tommy loves it. I hope he saw the match. If the money you raise for the hospital can save the life of one of the poor sods being shipped back to Blighty, then play as Violet Dobson, or Tunnicliffe, or the bloody Queen of Sheba and do it with my blessing. Don't worry about the taunts that I can't keep my wife in her place. They usually come from men who can't find a wife in the first place. I shall tell Mam the same when I write to her. When you've seen some of what we see here, you start to realise that life will never be the same again. I'm proud of you, Vi. Maybe I'll be able to see you play one day.'

Violet pulled her handkerchief from her pocket and dabbed her eyes. She didn't think she'd ever loved Billy more than she did at that moment. She wanted to run downstairs and show the letter to her mother-in-law, but knew that would only make matters worse. She'd let Billy tell his mam in his own way. Vi couldn't wait to tell the girls the good news.

Being able to practise on a Wednesday afternoon was a big help. Weekends were precious, and although the girls still fitted in some training then, they kept the sessions shorter now they had the midweek time. The elderly gentleman who'd told them it was wrong for them to play when he saw them at the early training session still walked his dog across the recreation ground. The girls had taken to waving at him, and calling 'Cooeee', to attract his attention. He now chose to ignore them all and would quicken his pace as he passed. It gave the girls something to laugh about; if only Billy's mother could be so easily put off.

Violet was standing in the hallway, holding her bag and waiting for her mother-in-law to finish speaking.

"You're never at home these days. It's all very well you gallivanting about, but who's going to scrub the step and clean out the grate? You know I can't get down there." Elsie Dobson was in full flow. "And another thing, you expect me to look after Tommy when that's your job."

Violet longed to point out the flaws in what Elsie was saying, but instead ran through them in her own head and remained quiet. 'Firstly, you sad old woman, you offered to look after Tommy — he could have gone to his nanna. Secondly, the longer hours mean more money, and you depend on me bringing in some extra; with Billy's dad's job uncertain, the money's more important than ever. Thirdly, you are perfectly capable of getting down to floor level to do the cleaning. I've seen you on your hands and knees at the box under the sideboard when you don't think anyone's around. Something is clearly important enough for you to get down there, and you didn't have any difficulty getting back up then.' She tried to keep the smile on her face and not show what was going on underneath.

Vi realised Elsie had finished talking, and from the look on her face, she had ended with a question. She was now expecting a reply. Violet breathed a sigh of relief when Tommy chipped in.

"She's ever so good, you should come and watch her."

The question must have been something about going to the football practice. She was taking Tommy with her, so it wasn't about looking after him on a Saturday afternoon.

"You might have our Billy's blessing in this ridiculous business, but you most certainly don't have mine. It's not proper." Elsie shook her head as though to emphasise her point.

Violet sighed. Was that what was at the bottom of this, feeling like she'd lost control of those around her? Maybe Elsie should find a life of her own and see what was important. Violet knew she was pushing her luck, but she said, "You know we're only doing it to help the war effort. You could always become involved and maybe help out at the hospital. They're appealing for volunteers."

Elsie harrumphed and Violet took that as her cue to grab hold of Tommy's hand and leave. "Bye then. I'll do tea when I come in." She didn't wait for the reply.

They met Tessie outside.

"I wondered where you were. I was about to knock," Tessie said, taking Tommy's other hand.

"It's probably a good job you didn't." Violet gave Tessie a meaningful look, but had no intention of discussing her mother-in-law with Tommy able to hear every word.

November was always a dismal month. Walking along between the rows of terraced housing to work, Vi wished the grey of the sky would lift and the sun peek through; the dank, murky days did little to lift her mood. Every day the newspapers reported more about the war, and every day Vi was grateful that most of the main stories seemed to be about countries she knew nothing about, and not where Billy was. She worried whenever she saw any news from the Western Front. She had no way of knowing where he was exactly, or what he might be involved in.

As Vi packed the explosives, she couldn't help thinking about the sheer number of shells they were producing. She knew there were factories like this all over the country producing armaments; just the thought of it was shocking.

More and more of the men seemed to be leaving their regular jobs to join the army. It was still voluntary to join up, but Vi had seen women pressing white feathers into the hands of men in the street, or tucking them into the pocket of their jackets. There was even a big cartoon on the front page of the newspaper; it was from years ago about conscription by press gang when there weren't enough volunteers. Everywhere you turned, there was the same message: it was the right thing to do to fight for King and Country, and every man who was able should go. Her brother, John, was still only fifteen, but she knew of others his age who'd joined up without question. She hoped John didn't get it into his head to see if they would take him. Maybe it would all be over before he was called up, if they did bring in conscription. She had to take her mind off the war and think about something else.

When she used to make hats, she would dream up new styles as she worked; even if she was doing a monotonous task like sticking brims, the thought kept her going. She didn't suppose there was much demand for new hats at the moment, at least not the more extravagant ones. Thinking about hats was a lot more likely to make her smile than munitions were. She sighed.

Although Mr Wood was officially coaching their football team, Vi's dad continued to attend the training sessions when he wasn't working; even Mr Giffard had been along to see how they were doing and offer his encouragement. The girls practised in their new Caulder and Harrison team strip, which made playing much more comfortable than it was before. Their shorts came down to their knees and almost met their socks. Although the shorts were plain white, their shirts had broad black and white stripes and the company crest on the right-hand side. They also had brand new white mob caps to keep all their hair out of the way.

"Don't we look a picture?" Clara said when they first tried them on.

"It would be better if our shorts weren't so long," Beattie said with a broad grin.

"Beattie Collins, what are you like?" Violet shook her head in despair. She at least was glad that very little of their legs was showing.

Mr Giffard arranged for a photographer to come and take a team photograph and the *Billingbrook Mercury* included it in the paper with a story about the plan for them to play more games. The girls had all decided that Violet should be team captain and she was in the centre of the photograph, although still as Miss Violet Tunnicliffe.

She'd decided to continue to play under her maiden name as, despite Billy's blessing, she didn't want to cause even more upset with her mother-in-law than was necessary.

There were another four weeks until the football match against Blackburn. They were booked to play on Monday 27th of December and the girls needed all the practice they could get.

"Now girls," Mr Giffard said, when he addressed them all that afternoon before their training session. "I have some big news for you this week."

Despite the blustery November day, they all fell silent, waiting to hear. Mr Giffard was grinning, something which Vi didn't think she'd ever seen before.

"We have managed to reach an agreement for the match to be played at the ground of Billingbrook United."

Vi gasped. She looked across at her dad, whose eyes were wide.

"It means we can sell more tickets and raise a considerable sum of money for the hospitals." Mr Giffard looked very pleased with himself and the girls all cheered. He gave a nod to Joe Wood, who blew his whistle. The girls immediately took up their positions on the field for a practice match between themselves; they'd managed to rope in a few more to be substitutes and reserves, so they could easily play with eight on each side. Violet loved the times she was playing football.

Whilst she and the girls played, her dad supervised Tommy and Bobby. The boys, together with one or two of the siblings of other players, had their own little game which they seemed to enjoy as much as the girls did.

On the pitch, Violet could forget all about the war and how much she missed Billy; for that brief time there was just her, the team and a leather ball. Afterwards, she would always write to Billy and tell him how they were progressing and what she'd learned. It was more interesting than telling him about his mother's latest complaints. Better still were the days when she received letters from Billy; her heart leaped at the sight of those.

On rare occasions Billy would give more information of what his life was like, but never in any great detail.

'I'll never look at mud in the same way again after spending so much time close to it. I've forgotten what it's like to be clean. You would be horrified, but Stan and I just remember back to what we were like as kids, playing in the fields down by the river. We were lucky if it was only mud we came back covered in when the cows were in the bottom field. Mam used to shout blue murder at the state of my clothes.'

He never talked about the battles themselves, and never once gave Violet the idea he might be in any danger. She wondered how much he was careful not to say.

CHAPTER 17

Knees up Mother Brown
Knees up Mother Brown
Under the table you must go
Ee-aye, Ee-aye, Ee-aye-oh
If I catch you bending
I'll saw your legs right off
Knees up, knees up
don't get the breeze up
Knees up Mother Brown
Originally a pub song in the late 1800s - alternative words were
added later to bring it up to date.

26th November 1915 - British Troops Cheerfully Face a Second
Winter Campaign - The Daily Mirror

Violet found it impossible to believe that Billy had already been away for over seven months, and yet it seemed another lifetime since she'd worked at the hat factory. Sorting out odds and ends to make Christmas presents for her family, she came across the sketches she'd drawn of hats she'd like to make. She laughed; whoever would want to wear a hat that she'd designed? She tucked the pages at the back of the drawer, away from prying eyes.

She'd already put together a parcel for Billy of things for Christmas. She sent it early as he needed the warm woolly hat she'd knitted for him and the socks. She'd spent more than she should have done by the time she'd made a fruit cake, included some Woodbines and other bits she thought he would appreciate; she wished she could send more, but she'd done her best. On the top of the pile she included a photograph. It was not just the cutting from the *Billingbrook Mercury* this time; it was a copy of the photograph of the Caulder and Harrison women's football team with Violet right in the middle. When Mr Giffard had presented one to each of the girls, Violet was overwhelmed. She'd known immediately that she wanted to send hers to Billy. She hoped he'd like it.

In the box, Vi also included a beautiful smooth pebble which Tommy found when they were all together at the river before Billy left. It had been Tommy's treasure since then, but when he knew his mam was sending Christmas presents to his dad, he'd taken it out of his pocket and asked her to send it to him. Vi had tears in her eyes as she explained to Billy in the letter that she'd included with the parcel. He'd be very happy to know that Tommy hadn't forgotten him.

Searching through her sewing pile, Violet was pleased to find she had enough material to make new aprons for her mam and Ena and a scarf for Billy's mam. What she didn't have was time. She would need to spend every spare waking hour on making the gifts if she was to have them all ready by Christmas Day. She'd saved enough money for some shoes for Tommy, which was a good job as his old ones were already too small. She still needed something for her other brothers and sisters, and both hers and Billy's fathers. Billy had said to take some out of their savings and buy things, but she'd rather make things if she could, quite apart from not wanting to eat into the precious pot for them to move into their own home.

The next few weeks flew past and Violet tried hard to make sure she did her best for everyone. She knew the time she spent playing football should probably be devoted to other things, but she loved those times and didn't want to stop. The *Billingbrook Mercury* carried a couple of news pieces in the build-up to the game, focussing on the fact that the girls would be raising money for such an important cause, as well as a piece talking about their new football strip. The latter resulted in quite a few letters to the editor, suggesting that men should keep their wives and daughters under better control.

"They're happy enough for us to do the jobs there's no one else to do," Eva said, after Tessie read one of the letters out to them all.

"I don't think they're really happy about that either." Clara sighed. "My dad said when the war's over we'll have to go back into service or stay at home. He says we can't expect to carry on in men's jobs then."

Eva gasped. "He never? What did you say?"

Clara looked sad. "To my father? I didn't bloody say anything, he'd have taken his belt to me for cheek."

Vi shuddered. It reminded her that she hadn't seen anything of Ena since the Sunday lunch with her parents. She wondered if it was Percy who'd caused the bruising to her sister's face. She should go over to see her, but had no idea how she could find the time for that as well as everything else.

They'd been told by Mr Giffard that tickets were selling fast, and by the week before the match there were rumours twenty thousand spectators were due to attend.

"Can you imagine?" Tessie said. "You and me being watched by all those people."

Violet had imagined it, and she was excited about the

whole idea. How she would feel when she was finally out in front of them was an altogether different matter.

The atmosphere at Ivy Terrace was frosty. Violet presumed it was just because her mother-in-law disapproved of her playing, until one evening when she came in from work. As Violet stepped into the hall, Billy's parents clearly hadn't heard her come in. She could hear their raised voices coming from the back room.

"Elsie, love, will you stop this nonsense? If I want to watch the match our Violet's playing in, there's nothing wrong with it at all. It's not as though there are any other matches for me to go to."

"You want to watch all those nubile young girls cavorting around a football pitch whilst I sit here." It sounded as though Elsie was close to tears.

Vi heard Alf sigh. "No, love. I want you to come with me to watch a game of football. I don't care who's playing, although I for one am proud of what Violet is doing."

"You know as well as I do that it's not right, Alfred. Violet shouldn't be playing." Elsie's tone was unbending.

"This isn't just about Violet, love. It's…" He was clearly struggling to choose words that wouldn't cause more upset. "… it's about the football."

Violet decided her best move was to go out and come in again more loudly, so they knew she was there. This time as she slammed the back door behind her, she shouted, "Hello," to be certain.

She took her things upstairs and was pleased to see that Tommy was still asleep and hadn't heard his grandparents arguing or her coming in. By the time Vi went down again, everything appeared peaceful. She liked the thought that Alf wanted to attend the match, and wondered whether he would; she wished she could say something to him, but that was out of the question.

With a couple of days to go until Christmas, Eva had no colour in her face at all when she arrived at their bench.

The bell hadn't sounded yet, so Violet risked talking to her. "Whatever's the matter?"

Eva's chin trembled as she tried to reply. "Uncle Ted's been reported missing in action. Aunty Mabel heard yesterday — Mabel's Mam's sister. She's been round at our house all night with my cousins, she doesn't know what to do with herself. Oh, Vi, what if something's happened to him?"

Vi could see Eva was fighting back tears, but didn't dare go around to her side of the bench. Of course, they'd heard of others in the factory who had lost relatives in the war, but Eva was the closest person to Vi who'd had a telegram so far.

"Maybe he'll turn up. He could just be hiding out somewhere until it's safe to return." Even as she said the words, Violet's mind was thinking through all the other possibilities. Instead of Eva's uncle Ted, in her head she kept seeing Billy and felt sick.

"And just before Christmas, too. What if he's…"

Before Eva could finish, Mrs Johnson shouted across that they should have started work. For once, Violet was grateful; she hadn't wanted to hear the word that would follow, spoken out loud. She gave Eva a sympathetic smile and began packing the first shell casing of the day. Vi took a few deep breaths; handling explosives while thinking of missing soldiers didn't feel right. She wondered if Eva was having the same thoughts. She tried to think about the process of what she was doing, and not the specifics of what she was doing it with. Damn this bloody war.

Christmas Day itself was very odd without Billy there. Vi felt sick thinking about where he might be. After Eva's news, she felt more anxious than she had before. She'd read in the papers that there'd been a truce on the Western Front the previous Christmas, and the British troops played against the German troops in a game of football. That was a thought to cling to; she hoped that maybe the same thing had happened this year. She took a deep breath and wrapped her dressing gown a little tighter. There was no time to waste feeling sorry for herself. Vi wanted to make this a good Christmas for all of them, even without Billy being here.

Tommy was staring with wonder at the few bits she'd managed to find for his Christmas stocking. She pulled him into a hug. "Happy Christmas. There are two more presents downstairs, but you need to wait until later for those."

"Oh, Mam, can't I have them now?" Tommy looked at her pleading.

"Don't you 'oh, Mam' me. And no, you can wait until we've all had dinner."

They would have Christmas dinner with the Dobsons, but then go over to her family for teatime. She'd made a few bits of food to take with them, so there should be enough for the entire family.

"When can we see Daddy?" Tommy's eyes were glistening as he asked.

Violet chided herself, realising her own sadness was rubbing off on their child. "Soon, my darling boy, soon." She hoped that was true, but how could she explain to him that she had no idea? She drew Tommy to her and held him tightly.

It was still early in the morning. Vi wouldn't need to do

very much toward dinner for a while. "Come on, let's take a ball out into the garden. But we'll have to be very quiet."

Tommy's face lit up and he scrambled out of bed. Once Vi was dressed, they went downstairs. She groaned. "Oh, what a silly mam I am. I didn't really think about the fact it would still be dark. We wouldn't be able to see the ball."

"We could still play." Tommy's face was downcast, and his lip was wobbling as he said it.

Vi could have kicked herself. Instead of cheering him up, she'd just made matters worse. "You'll be able to play with Bobby later on."

"But I wanted you to play." He looked up at her, his eyes wide and now brimming with tears.

Vi wondered what she could do, and then had an idea. Maybe if she gave him one of his two presents now and saved the other for later, it would be all right. She didn't want Billy's parents to feel left out, but neither did she want to deal with Tommy blubbering at not long after six o'clock in the morning on Christmas Day. She put her finger to her lips and winked at him. "Close your eyes and I'll bring one of your presents through." Violet went into the parlour. Which should she give him now, the shoes or the spinning top? She decided the shoes would be the quietest option, and at least Alf and Elsie would see him play with the new spinning top.

She took the paper-wrapped parcel through to where Tommy was still sitting with his eyes screwed shut.

Violet helped Tommy to open the paper. He looked at the shoes, then he stared up at her with his mouth wide open.

"Are these really new?" Tommy asked, looking from his mam to the shoes and back.

Violet nodded.

"No one else has ever worn them? Not ever?"

Violet broke into a wide smile. "No, my darling boy, you are the very first person to wear them."

He stroked the sole of the shoe with tenderness, as though it were a small animal. Then wrapped his arms around his mam.

Once Violet had helped Tommy to put on his new shoes, she went back to the parlour to light the fire. As she came back through the hall to the kitchen for the kettle, Tommy was walking slowly up and down and saying, "I have new shoes. I have my very own shoes."

Christmas dinner felt very strange with Billy's place at the table empty. At regular intervals, Vi's mind wandered to where he might be and what he would be doing. She was feeling it more keenly than she did most days. From the strained look on Elsie's face, she guessed Billy's mam was feeling it too.

Alf had whittled a small dog from a block of wood as a present for Tommy and he loved it. He tied a piece of string around its neck and began to drag it along behind him, heading out into the hall.

"He's called Spot," Tommy said to them all when he arrived back in the parlour with the little dog now clutched in his arms. "Can I bring him to show Nanna?"

Violet sighed. She was going to have quite a lot to carry with the food she was taking and the little gifts she'd made. She couldn't refuse him, though. "I think you'll have to carry him. His little legs seem tired, I don't think he'll be able to walk."

Tommy tucked Spot under his arm.

Even though Elsie seemed pleased with her new scarf and Alf with his pipe, Vi was glad when everything was cleared away and she and Tommy could set off for her parents' house. She knew the mood there would be much lighter, and she was looking forward to that.

Violet sang Christmas carols quietly as they walked. Tommy seemed tired and she didn't need him wanting to be carried, so she tried to sound jolly and lively, even though she didn't feel it herself.

Before they even reached the front door of the Tunnicliffe home, Violet could hear the sound of her father playing the accordion. She broke into a broad grin and looked down at Tommy. His pace quickened.

He looked down at Spot still clutched under his arm and said to the little wooden dog, "That's Granddad. He's ever so good."

It was standing room only when Violet opened the door. Some of the neighbours were there, as well as Ena and Percy and Vi's other brothers and sisters. Dad was in the corner of the room nearest the window, which was slightly open, but still he looked warm as he played. He was lost in the music and oblivious to how many people were squeezed into the house to listen. Vi was sure that if there'd been room everyone would have been dancing, but they were tapping their feet and singing when they knew the words.

After a while, the children escaped outdoors and there was a little more space to move around the room. Violet went over to where her mother was sitting. "Merry Christmas." She kissed her mam's cheek and then tried to move toward the kitchen to put her basket of food out of the way. She would have tried to make her way to Ena, but her sister was standing close to Percy and Violet decided to wait until there was more space.

Eventually, Frank stopped playing and looked up with a very pink and happy face. "That's it for now. I need a cup of tea before I can do anything else."

Shouting cheery Christmas greetings as they went, the neighbours started to drift away, leaving just Violet's family.

Mam went to call the children in, and they finally exchanged their gifts. Mam had made a small pin cushion for Vi, and for Tommy she'd knitted a little woolly hat. "It's like the one your Mam knitted and sent to your Dad. I thought you might like to look just like him."

Tommy put it on, even though they were indoors, and refused to take it off again.

When Vi gave Ena the apron she'd made for her, Ena looked embarrassed. She shot a look to Percy and then back at the gift, fidgeting with her hands. "I ain't got you anything… I…"

From the look between Ena and Percy, Vi realised there was something more to this. She laid her hand on Ena's and smiled. "It's fine. I didn't expect anything, really."

She glanced at Mam, who was behind Ena and Percy. Mam was shaking her head. She seemed to be wordlessly telling Vi to leave it, so Vi said no more.

"Right," Dad said, as the room had gone very quiet. "Who's for a game of charades?"

It wasn't long before the children were either yawning or already asleep where they were. Vi's mam looked at Tommy. "He may as well stay here tonight, save you having to carry him back."

"Thanks, Mam. I had hoped he might stay here tomorrow night so I could go to the football ground early on Monday, but it's too much to ask you to have him two nights."

Queenie Tunnicliffe laughed. "We have a houseful, love. We don't notice one more little one. He's no trouble."

Vi wasn't sure that last comment was true, but she was grateful.

"I can bring him to the match on Monday and he can come home with you from there," Dad said as Violet put her coat on to go home.

"Thanks, Dad." Violet realised that she'd have a complete day to herself the following day, and wondered what on earth she was going to do with it.

CHAPTER 18

If you get stuck on the wire,
Never mind!
If you get stuck on the wire,
Never mind!
They'll leave you hanging there all day,
When you die they'll stop your pay,
If you get stuck on the wire,
Never mind!
If the Sergeant Steals Your Rum, Never Mind! - traditional
WW1 (numerous versions)

24th December 1915 - 'The Soldiers' and Sailors' Christmas:
Scenes in London and at the Front' - The Daily Mirror

"Football's really not your thing, is it, Davy boy?" Stan was laughing as Davy ducked when the ball came his way.

"I'm getting too used to dodging bullets to want something to hit me." Davy laughed as he picked himself up off the ground. "Besides, there's enough of you for the team to play against the officers without me having to join in."

"Shame it's not like last year. We could have been playing against the German troops." Stan picked the ball up and came over to the others.

"If the war depended on the result of a football match, I think we'd need more practice," Billy said. "As it is, we're going to have enough trouble beating the officers."

"We should put your Vi on the team, that would soon stop them. I wouldn't want to tackle her, that's for sure." Stan pretended to cower, but Billy knew he was only joking.

It didn't feel like Christmas; even the parcel from Vi hadn't changed that. He'd saved some fruitcake to eat today and he'd been wearing the hat since it first arrived, but other than that the day was just strange. The lads had sung some carols that morning, led by the chaplain, but that just made Billy feel more homesick. What he'd give to be back in Ivy Terrace watching Tommy try out the spinning top Vi had told him about.

The game against the officers turned out to be more a mud bath than a football match. By the end, it was almost impossible to tell who was on which side. The one thing they all knew was where the goal posts were, and as far as anyone could tell the officers won the match by three goals to two.

"Bleedin' cheek," Stan was fuming as he tried to dry off later. "It should have been a penalty."

"It's funny how they always seem to beat us by one goal. I wonder if the men have ever won." Billy was scraping off caked mud, but it was hopeless. "At least while we're playing football we're not having to fight. Back to work tomorrow."

Until now, they had been some of the lucky ones, but every time they moved forward, Billy could feel the odds shortening. They'd witnessed odd skirmishes, but most of what they'd done was maintenance and repair of the trenches and barbed wire; neither side had tried to engage their enemy along this stretch for a while. The stalemate couldn't last, not if anyone was going to win.

None of their exercises were without risk; there were always snipers on the lookout for movement by the other side. Billy had an almighty fright only the previous week; the sniper's bullet lodged in a tree stump six inches from where he'd dropped down; exactly where he'd been until a fraction of a second before. He'd sent up a silent prayer and used all the army taught him to return to safety. He wouldn't have been surprised if the sniper could have heard his heartbeat as he zigzagged his way back to the trench, as low to the ground as he could stay. Never had a trench seemed such an attractive place to be as it was when he scrambled over the parapet and dropped to safety that night.

"Here we go." Stan sounded remarkably cheerful as he packed up his kit the following morning, ready for their next stint in the front line trenches.

Billy put the last of his kit together and made sure he had tightly strapped his webbing. Davy wasn't with them; he and some of the others were being despatched on a separate mission, and Billy wondered whether they would meet up again or not. Of course, you became close to the other lads. In the trenches your lives depended on each other, but there was more to it with Davy. When they came back to base, they still fell into a grouping of the three of them. It felt odd to be back to just him and Stan.

As they marched there was a lot of singing in the line. It kept them going; the steady rhythm of the songs helped keep the marching regular and they stayed in perfect step, at least while they were above ground. It was impossible to march once you were in the trenches themselves. The first priority was staying on the duckboards and out of the mud. The mud was so thick it was hard to escape from; if you were lucky all you'd lose was a boot, but with the depth of the mud it could be far worse than that.

The difference in the demeanour of the platoon walking past Billy in the opposite direction was pronounced. The men that Billy was with stood tall, proud, and had an energy to them. The men coming back from the Front were covered in mud and carried an air of fatigue. Billy knew he and Stan would look much the same as them in another four days, but wondered what sights they'd endured on their current duty.

"Bleedin' hell." Stan's words were echoed by others of the men when they arrived at the trench.

There was work to do to repair the damage caused by a shell from the previous night. Billy wondered if they were going to find any poor sods underneath the debris, or at least parts of them. The dark red-brown patches on the earth were clue enough that the trench hadn't been empty at the time.

As Stan, Billy and some of the other lads worked to rebuild the trench wall and make it safe, Chip set to work on the rats, which Billy thought looked better fed than the men were. Working amongst the destruction probably should have been a sombre affair, but when you knew it could just as easily be you blown apart, somehow the only way to handle it was very dark humour, however inappropriate.

"He's not going to be wiping his own bum anytime soon," Stan said as he moved a hand to one side, still holding a tin mug.

They continued to work until that section of the trench was back in place and as much of the debris cleared away as was possible. Bodies and body parts were taken away for identification and burial; the grave digging was a continuous task, and a constant reminder of what they were facing.

Billy would have thought after that he wouldn't have felt much like sleeping, but he'd learned to get kip where he could and at any opportunity. You never knew when you'd have the next chance. Even Chip took breaks from his rat duties so he could nap. The next day could very well be worse than the one they were leaving behind; no man wanted to be asleep on his feet when the guns were firing.

The only battle action Billy heard that night was at a considerable distance from their position, far enough away to rest easy. The snipers remained in place along the Allied trenches, but there was little of interest to keep them busy. As he drifted off to sleep, Billy hoped that maybe the initial trench rebuilding work would be the worst of this stint at the Front.

"Private Dobson and Private Bradley, please report to Major Shaw."

"Yes, sir." Billy wasn't used to receiving orders from a Lieutenant on an individual basis. He felt a jolt which seemed oddly like excitement.

"Best be on our way," Stan said, raising an eyebrow.

They worked their way along the trench, stepping around men who were still trying to sleep and being careful not to go off the duckboards. There had been a few days of drier weather so the mud had eased, but with the ground being low-lying and largely flat there were never times when mud wasn't a problem. Once you dug down, there was water whatever the time of year. He'd been warned to expect worse to come. The best respite they could hope for in winter was temperatures being cold enough for the ground to harden, but that brought a whole different set of problems when you spent all hours outdoors.

The major was working on some papers in a surprisingly spacious room, dug deep into the side of the trench. Other than the absence of windows, he could be in any normal office. Well, give or take the mud floor, walls and roof which were supported by wooden struts. He had a regular desk and chairs. Billy was struck by the incongruity of it all and smiled.

They stood to attention. "Sir."

"Ah, Bradley and Dobson, stand easy."

They stopped standing to attention, but Billy felt anything but easy.

"We need to find out how far along the line the Germans are working. I want you two to go over to the enemy trenches to see if this stretch is occupied."

Billy wondered if he'd heard correctly. The major made it sound as though he was asking them to go to the corner shop.

The major continued, "You're to come straight back once you've established the coast is clear. Our intelligence suggests there shouldn't be any problem, but be careful. If they start shooting, then head for cover immediately."

"Yes, sir." Stan saluted and Billy followed suit.

"Lieutenant Croft will be managing the operation." The major nodded to them in dismissal and went back to some papers on his desk.

They made their way out of the dugout behind the lieutenant. Billy was no longer smiling.

"This is it, Billy lad. Time for a bit of action."

Whilst Billy felt some of Stan's excitement, he sincerely hoped this would not be 'it'. The shell damage suggested to him that the Germans were active, but he supposed there may not be snipers positioned on this stretch and the enemy trench might be empty. He presumed Major Shaw had better information than he did. At least, he hoped that was the case.

"We have men positioned to give you cover." The lieutenant led them along to the ladder he wanted them to use to go over the trench wall. "You have about five hours until the moon rises. There should be good cloud cover, but the moon is still three quarters full. It's a shame we couldn't have waited another week or so, but can't be helped."

Billy thought that might be easy for him to say; he wasn't the one risking life and limb.

They were briefed on the route to take to avoid the many hazards which lay ahead. Billy had never listened so intently to any instructions in his life.

"Before you go," the lieutenant said, "jump up and down and make sure nothing rattles."

They did as instructed. No man wanted his kit to give his position away.

"Head straight back as soon as you know the coast is clear. Don't hang about, but we do need to know if they are still operational along this stretch."

Billy and Stan acknowledged the command and made sure they had their rifles at the ready and their bayonets in position.

"All right, lads. Good luck."

"After you," Stan said, indicating the ladder.

Billy could have laughed; now was not the time for his mate to be chivalrous. He took a deep breath and climbed the short ladder out of the trench.

Billy had never felt so alive or so alert as he did moving forward across the area in front of the trench toward no man's land. He was overwhelmed by the feeling that any moment could be his last. He'd been up here many times, but only ever as far as the barbed wire. Beyond that was completely new to him; there was no cover, and what trees there had been were broken, ragged stumps — the greenery had gone. There were shell holes and craters, which were deep enough for a man to go across below ground level. Those provided some cover, as long as soldiers stayed below their rim but didn't venture further down, where the mud could be their undoing.

Driven by danger, Billy was amazed how much more he consciously registered what his senses were telling him. He felt as though he could have heard the blades of grass blowing in the breeze, if there'd been grass left to blow. He and Stan stayed close together, but remained silent. Billy's eyes strained to see in the near pitch dark. When the clouds parted there was a little starlight, but not enough to see more than the barest of shades. He continued to move forward, hunched, feeling his way, smelling the air. He was little different to any wild animal in an alien landscape.

They were approaching the enemy trench. Billy realised this might be the last thing he ever did, but there was no sound, so maybe the Major's intelligence was right. All they were instructed to do was to check the immediate line of the trench for life and then make their way straight back before dawn. Moonlight would be bad enough to risk, but daylight was far too dangerous. He wondered how long they'd taken so far.

Billy's heart was thudding as they reached the edge of the enemy trench; he had his bayonet ready, but prayed he wouldn't need it. There was silence. It didn't mean there were no enemy soldiers, but it meant it wasn't fully occupied. Now all they had to do was to go down and check the length as instructed. 'All', Billy shook his head at the thought. This task was not one he could dismiss that easily. He marked their point of entry to the trench; he wanted to be able to find it again later. Then he and Stan made their way along the trench, alert and terrified.

Apart from the fact the major had been right and the trench was deserted, what struck Billy was how well constructed it was. It had a much greater feeling of permanence than their own trenches. To him, that made it all the more unlikely that they'd abandon the position.

Making their way along the trench was slow. At every step they needed to take in their surroundings and be certain there were no current signs of life; no cigarette butts, no recent debris, no men. This had not been a hurried exit by the enemy, but an organised and thorough departure. Somehow that made Billy more uneasy. This wasn't an army on the run.

The moon was up a while before they reached the end of the section they were checking. As long as they made their way back in no more time than they'd taken so far, they should still return before early dawn. If the moon was out when they were in the open, it would slow their progress, but for the times they were safely hidden from view it would help.

Stan gave Billy a thumbs up sign. The trench was clear. They turned to make their way back. Although this should be a little faster, they needed to stay on the alert and be ready for action. There was still the possibility this was a trap.

They eventually arrived back at their starting point in the trench and Billy let out a long breath. It had taken them longer than they expected, partly down to a wrong turn, but they'd realised after a short distance and retraced their steps. Now all they had to do was go back over the top and cross over no man's land to the safety of their own trench.

Safety was of course a relative term — nowhere here was safe. He glanced at Stan and nodded. Time was short now if they were to complete their mission in darkness. Stan gave Billy a leg up over the parapet and then Billy reached down to help his mate. The two hundred yards they needed to cross didn't sound far, until you realised how dangerous the terrain was to navigate. This was no straight run, but a carefully negotiated field of hell. They needed to stick to the precise route that had been described to them, without any deviation. For one thing, finding the gap in the barbed wire was essential.

They set off together, Stan just ahead. Billy didn't like to think his mate was a coward, but he was aware that being in front gave Stan a little more protection from enemy fire.

Dawn wasn't far away, and as it approached a sniper would be able to find them in his sights — if he saw them and they were stationary long enough. They worked their way forward, crouching as they went, using the benefit of craters as they had before. They reached the enemy barbed wire. On the way out they'd cut a section in order to climb through; now they needed to go back through the gap they'd made.

Stan was ahead by a pace or two. They couldn't move fast; it would be too easy to miss their footing. Billy was looking to the ground and ahead of him, all in one continuous cycle.

"Jesus!" Stan said, loud enough for Billy to hear.

Billy looked up. He could make out Stan just ahead. That was bad news for two reasons. It meant that daybreak was approaching, and Stan was caught on the wire; he'd misjudged the gap. Billy's mind raced. He needed to get Stan clear of danger. His best option would be to cut him free. First, he needed his wire cutters. It would be safer for him to work from the other side of the barbed wire — not that there was much in it — but any lengthening of the odds was worthwhile. Billy tried to keep his breathing even as he made his way through the gap.

"Sorry, mate," he said to Stan as he had to be as close to him as possible to squeeze through.

Once on the other side Billy dropped down and found his wire cutters. He was going to have to cut the barbed wire in several places to release Stan. If he started with the highest level, then at least Stan would present less of a profile to a sniper. Billy's hand was shaking. He was conscious of biting on his tongue as he worked.

He made the first cut and Stan's shoulder was freed. There were two other cuts needed. Billy made another cut. Only one left to go. As Billy assessed the final place that Stan was caught, he heard the sound of a single shot.

Stan jerked forward and tried to stifle a moan.

Billy dropped down onto the mud. There were still about a hundred yards to go. Stan had been hit. Billy wasn't going to leave his mate; not here, not anywhere. He needed to cut the last piece of wire, but he also needed to find out how badly injured his mate was. It had to be the wire first. If he could put Stan on the ground, he stood more chance of saving him. With expert fingers, Billy made the last cut. Stan buckled forward.

CHAPTER 19

A football match last Saturday I went to see,
To have some fun was exactly what I meant, you see;
So off I goes like a sporting man so dutiful,
To see this game, which I reckined would be beautiful.
The Football Match - James Curran & Ed. Johngmanns - 1891

*27th December 1915 - Peer's Soldier Heir Married to a Chorus
Girl - The Daily Mirror*

Even though a day to herself was a luxury, Violet kept
busy; she needed to do things to take her mind off both the
following day's match and Billy. Being a Sunday, she
couldn't very well pass her time with the household
chores, and nor did she want to spend the day sitting with
Elsie and Alf. She wondered about going to church, but in
the quiet times of the service her mind would have strayed
to the very things she wanted to avoid.

After breakfast, she went back up to her room and took
the hat drawings from the back of the drawer. She hadn't
done any new sketches for a while. She smoothed out the
paper she'd wrapped around Tommy's shoes. It wasn't too
creased; if she cut it into squares, she could use that for
new ideas. For the next couple of hours Vi lost herself
drawing some designs, inspired as much as anything by
hats being worn by some French women whose picture
had been in the paper.

"Violet." Elsie's strident voice broke into her quiet. "Are you cooking this dinner?"

Violet started. She had been so lost in what she was doing she hadn't given dinner a moment's thought. "Sorry, is that the time? Coming," she shouted down to Elsie. Vi gave her drawings a wistful look, folded them and put them away.

Once dinner was finished Violet decided to walk over to see if Ena was at home. She would love an hour to sit down with her sister and talk as they used to when they were younger. She couldn't remember the last time they'd done that. Not since Ena had been with Percy, that was certain; maybe not since she and Billy had wed. Ena would only have been fourteen then. Maybe her sister wouldn't welcome her in the same way now.

She should have felt excited walking to Ena's. Instead, she felt apprehensive about the reaction she might receive from Percy or his family. He'd never made any pretence of liking Billy, and she presumed that meant he didn't like her either.

Violet gave a sharp rap with the knocker. She saw the net curtain in the front room move aside and then fall back into place.

Ena opened the front door, but stayed in its shadow.

"Hello, I thought we could catch up if you have an hour?" Violet began in a rush, but stopped as she saw Ena's strained and haunted face. "Ena, is everything all right?"

Ena glanced behind her and then back to Vi. She picked her coat up off the peg in the hall and took a step toward the door. "I'll just…" Then she hesitated and looked up and down the street. "No, I'd best not. They might be back soon. I…"

"Can I come in?" Vi asked, not knowing what else to say.

Ena shook her head vigorously. "He won't like it. I can't." Then it was as though she remembered who it was on the doorstep. "Thanks for coming, but I just can't." Ena gave her sister a weak smile and moved back a step into the hall, closing the door behind her.

"Ena." Violet rapped on the door again. "What's wrong? Who won't like it? I'm your sister, talk to me — please."

She could hear Ena on the other side of the door breathing heavily, but she made no move to open it again.

Violet stood on the doorstep dumbfounded. Whatever was going on that Ena couldn't see her own sister?

When Violet arrived back at Ivy Terrace, she couldn't face going inside. When she reached the end of the passageway, she turned right instead and knocked on Tessie's back door.

Vi had a lovely afternoon with the Browns before heading back to her own home. It was strange without either Billy or Tommy there; she felt as though she was trespassing in someone else's home. In bed that night she found it hard to warm up, and even harder to sleep. Some of that was nerves about the following day's match, she knew that, but there were all sorts of unwelcome thoughts there too. Would she stay living with Elsie and Alf if anything happened to Billy? Would they even want her? If it felt strange now, it would be a whole lot worse then. She was cross with herself and tried to think about some of the happy times they'd all had instead.

Although the men's Football League had been cancelled, there were still local games taking place. There'd been one in Manchester on Christmas Day itself, but nothing planned for Billingbrook. This was to be the one major fixture of the Christmas season.

The girls had arranged to arrive at the football ground early. Having never been inside Billingbrook United's stadium, Vi wanted to see what it was like before the whistle blew to start the match.

As Vi looked out of the window first thing that morning, her heart sank. She stared at the leaden sky; there would be little chance of any sunshine. She was glad they were due to kick off at noon. Maybe it would clear up by then, but the forecast was for high winds and heavy rain.

When she went down to the kitchen, she heard knocking on the back door. It was still only seven o'clock, but Tessie was there carrying her kit.

"Are you ready?"

Violet was still in her dressing gown, making the most of the opportunity of a later start. Her excitement and anxiety overflowed and she burst into fits of giggles. "Does it look like I am? Here, sit down and I'll make you a brew. Have you had any breakfast?"

The young girl shook her head. "I couldn't eat if I tried."

Violet brought out the loaf and started cutting some slices to toast. "You'd be best with something inside you." She realised she was starting to sound like her mother and smiled. She also realised she needed to follow her own advice; the way her stomach was churning she didn't much feel like eating, but they'd both need the energy, today of all days.

"Who's that I can hear in the kitchen?" Elsie's voice came booming from the hall.

"It's only me, Mrs Dobson," Tessie called in her

sweetest voice and winked at Violet.

Vi wished she had as much… what was that word? Audacity, yes, that was it. No one would ever believe Tessie's age.

Elsie was in the kitchen with them now; her dressing gown wrapped tightly around her and her hair still wrapped in curlers. Her voice dropped a tone or two as she said, "Are you still on with this football? Can't you talk some sense into our Vi? It's bad enough a girl like you playing, but no married woman should be out there — at least, not a respectable woman."

Violet didn't like the implication of what Billy's mam was saying, but at least Tessie didn't look offended.

"I was just preparing your breakfast, Mam, and then Tessie and I will have to be going. You don't mind her having a bit of toast with us, do you?"

Elsie harrumphed and didn't reply to the question. "Is there tea in the pot?"

Thankfully Vi had already brewed the tea and poured out two cups for Elsie, which were now ready for her to take back upstairs. Vi handed her the tray.

Once she'd gone, Tessie pulled a face. "I take it Mrs High-and-Mighty isn't coming to watch us then?"

"No," Vi replied thoughtfully, "but I rather think Billy's dad is hoping to."

Tessie began buttering the toast. "I don't much fancy your chances later if she's been sitting here all day brooding on her own."

Violet sighed. "No, you're probably right."

"Blimey, Vi."

Tessie and Violet were standing on the turf at Whittingham Road, the Billingbrook United ground.

"I didn't know it was this big." Violet turned a circle, looking at the stands and the terraces. "It's a bit different to where we usually play."

It took a lot to put Tessie off her stride, but the girl had gone quite pale. "Do you think anyone will be able to see us?"

Violet laughed. "I think they'll be able to see the game, but was there anyone in particular you were hoping would see you?"

Tessie blushed. "It doesn't matter. He'll probably have to go away to fight soon, anyway." She looked down at her feet.

"Come on." Vi put her arm around the girl's shoulders and led her toward the changing room where the other girls would be.

The level of chatter was much higher than normal. Everyone was talking at once. Violet looked around at most of the others and felt old. Perhaps Elsie was right and she shouldn't be playing. She went to the far corner of the changing room where she could be on her own. She took her wedding ring off her finger, running it around in her hand and looking at it. Tucking it carefully into her favourite handkerchief, she pushed it deep into the pocket of her dress. If only Billy could be here. She knew her own dad, brothers and Tommy would be watching, and wondered if Billy's dad would make it. There was a light rain falling. How many of the crowd would be put off by that? It wasn't like when they went to watch Billingbrook play and nothing would stop them attending. There was very little team allegiance to a Caulder and Harrison women's team game.

Just before kick-off, Joe Wood brought them together. "If you do the things you've learned in practice, then you'll be fine. Most important of all, enjoy yourselves."

He looked across to Mr Giffard, who nodded and cleared his throat. "Just remember that everyone at Caulder and Harrison is very proud of you, and the money you are raising is going to a very good cause. There's a big crowd, despite the weather. Do your best, girls."

They then headed out onto the pitch, side by side with the girls from the Blackburn factory. Vi could have sworn the other team all looked taller and fitter than their team, but maybe they were thinking the same thing.

The Caulder and Harrison girls had improved since they'd played the men's team; now they could pass the ball between their own team much more effectively, and were less afraid to tackle the opposing players. From what they could see, the Blackburn team were of a similar standard and hadn't been pulled together just before the match.

Even though there were thousands of people watching, Vi's brother John and her Dad had managed to be at the front of the terrace with Tommy and Bobby in front of them. They probably couldn't see the whole of what was going on, but Violet was glad to know where they were and waved to them. She wished that Billy's dad was with them, but still hoped he might be in the stands.

The play from both teams was ragged in the first half. Vi knew she was in awe of the size of the crowd, and she suspected the others were too. She could cope with some of the shouts from the supporters, such as, 'Show us your legs', and wasn't put out by, 'Billingbrook United's players never looked as pretty', but what she really didn't understand was why someone would pay for a ticket, only to shout, 'They should be ashamed of themselves. It's not right.' None of the banter helped the girls to find their stride.

Violet was frustrated; she knew they could play better than this. The Blackburn girls weren't as badly affected by the taunts, but then it was a local Billingbrook crowd so most weren't directed at them. After twenty minutes, their team made the most of Billingbrook's disarray and scored from a corner. Vi's spirits sank even lower. She heard a taunt of, 'There's no point being here, they're rubbish'. At first she thought the man was probably right. Then Vi heard a voice as real as though it was next to her. It sounded awfully like Billy as it whispered to her, 'Show 'em what you can do.'

Vi paused where she was on the pitch and looked around. Of course there was no one there, but that didn't matter. She'd bloody well show them. Violet stopped taking any notice of the crowd. She looked around at the positions the girls were in and started calling out instructions; she moved Clara further forward so there were three of them up front. As the team started to sort themselves out, the crowd responded. The jeers were replaced by encouragement, and there was everything to play for.

Just before half-time, Clara passed the ball to Florrie on the other side. Florrie controlled the pass, but one of the Blackburn players was bearing down on her and she passed the ball back to Clara. Violet found space, and Clara saw where she was. Violet watched as the ball came in her direction. In one swift movement, she received the ball and brought it under control. Then she made a break down the field; every yard gave her a better chance of scoring a goal. This was as close as she would get before she was tackled by the Blackburn player who was behind her. It was now or never. Violet struck the ball, and it felt good. She watched as it cleared the goalkeeper's head into the top corner of the net, and heard the crowd cheering as the ball crossed the line. She punched the air and turned to see Tommy jumping up and down for all he was worth. It was definitely one of the happiest moments of her life; apart from giving birth to Tommy, it was quite possibly her greatest achievement. She had levelled the score. She went back to her position feeling lighter and happier and ready for more.

As the second half started, so did the heavier rain. It made the game much harder work, but Violet still enjoyed every minute. The Blackburn girls scored a further two goals, but Florrie also defeated the Blackburn keeper with a well-aimed shot into the bottom corner, so they were only one goal down when the referee blew full-time.

Before she thought about it, Violet said to their captain, "We should play a return match against you at Easter, to see if we can level things up."

Mr Giffard had been standing nearby and heard. "An excellent suggestion. I shall arrange that with their manager."

The girls were all chattering with the excitement of the game. Now her nerves had worn off, Violet would have liked to have been part of it, but she wanted to go off and find Tommy. She couldn't wait to hear what her dad said and to read the report in the *Billingbrook Mercury*.

"I'll come with you," Tessie said, picking up her bag.

"You were great," John said as they approached, but Vi realised he was looking at Tessie rather than her.

Tessie blushed, and Violet understood who it was that Tessie had her eye on; she hadn't seen that one coming. She shook her head and lifted Tommy up.

"Best game I've seen in ages, love." Vi's dad looked as excited as she felt.

Vi thought he might be exaggerating a little, but it made her happy to hear his praise.

"I'm cold, can we go home now?" Bobby tugged on Dad's sleeve.

Violet laughed and came down to earth. What else was she expecting from a young child, even if he was her brother? He'd been standing outside in the rain for the last couple of hours.

Dad shrugged. "Bye, love. See you soon."

Vi put Tommy down and took his hand.

He leaned his head against her arm. "I wish Daddy was here."

"Yes, my darling boy, so do I." Then as they walked, Vi turned to Tessie. "Why didn't you tell me it was my brother?"

Tessie looked uncomfortable, so Vi said no more about it.

The following day, Violet wanted to read the *Mercury* report before her mother-in-law saw it. When she did, she groaned. "The ladies wore pretty caps to top off their outfits..." What about the football? "Young Miss Skelthwaite was a particular favourite with the crowd..." Lucky Edith. This wasn't what the reporting of Billingbrook United's games was like. She'd never once seen a comment about the appearance of their goalkeeper. "Miss Tunnicliffe (23) is rather older than many of her teammates and remarkably light-footed." Well, that might be seen as being closer to the game. She sighed; no doubt Billy's mam would find something to say. She still didn't know if his dad had managed to watch. He could be remarkably silent when the need arose.

Vi waited anxiously to hear Elsie's response when they

sat down to tea that evening. She was certain something would be said. It was Alf rather than Elsie who brought it up.

"How much did the football raise, love?" he asked as they started on the toad in the hole.

"I don't know. Mr Giffard hasn't told us yet."

"It should be a sizeable amount. It was a large crowd," Alf said, taking another mouthful.

Vi frowned. She tried to remember the newspaper report. Had it said anything about how many attended? Perhaps it had. She was longing to ask Alf if he'd been at the match, but she didn't dare.

"I hear the second goal was the best." He kept looking at his plate as he said it.

Violet smiled. He'd seen her play; somehow, Alf had gone out for the afternoon and had been at the match. She didn't reply; she didn't need to. He'd told her what she so desperately wanted to know, and she was thrilled.

CHAPTER 20

Lots and lots and lots of shirts she sends out to the soldiers
And sailors won't be jealous when they see them, not at all
And when we say her stitching will set all the soldiers itching
She says our soldiers fight best when their back's against the wall
Sister Susie's Sewing Shirts for Soldiers - R. P. Weston & Herman E. Darewski - 1913

29th December 1915 - Momentous Cabinet Meeting on the Unmarried Shirkers - The Daily Mirror

Billy's first thought as Stan fell forward was that his mate was dead.

"Oh, God, Stan!" He took Stan's arm to feel for a pulse.

"Get off, you silly sod and help me out of here. It's my leg they hit."

Billy didn't know whether to laugh or punch his friend. He did neither. He dragged Stan into the slight ditch in front of them to give some cover while he worked. He couldn't give the sniper a second chance.

"Sorry." Stan's face was contorted with pain.

"Where?"

Stan rolled on to his side and Billy could see the red stain spreading out on the back of Stan's trousers. It was somewhere in his upper thigh, but it was hard to see how

208

bad the wound was. Here was not the place to try removing Stan's clothing to find out. He rummaged in Stan's tunic for his mate's emergency bandage and secured it tightly in a tourniquet around the wounded leg. He hoped, at the very least, that it would help to stem the bleeding; but he needed to take Stan back, and there was no way he was going to be able to walk, not without support.

It was already growing light. Billy didn't know how much blood Stan was still losing. He couldn't risk waiting until it was dark again to return to their own trench. The only option was to carry him and pray that they could make the last eighty yards before the enemy sniper took them both out.

Lieutenant Croft had said he'd have them covered. Now was the time to put that to the test.

"Sling this over your shoulder as well as your own." Billy removed the bayonets from both rifles and then handed the rifles to Stan. The last thing he wanted to do was fall and for either of them to be impaled on the bayonets.

He hauled Stan up so he rested higher on the bank, then rolled his shoulders and limbered up. He could do this. Billy squatted down so that Stan could pull himself onto Billy's back without standing and then held him tight.

Stan winced as Billy put his arm around the injured leg.

"Sorry, mate." There was nothing much he could do. Billy couldn't afford Stan to slide off when he broke cover. He took a deep breath. "Ready?"

Stan winced again in reply.

Billy went up the bank on the other side, getting used to the feel of carrying Stan. As he did so, he heard gunfire. "Shit." He couldn't stop now. He staggered forward, keeping as bent over as he could without Stan's weight overbalancing him. Then he realised that Lieutenant Croft had been as good as his word. The fire was from their own troops; they were creating a diversion so Billy and Stan could get back. If they managed to draw the enemy fire, then Billy stood a chance. He ran as best as he could toward safety.

He could have been running ten thousand yards, rather than under a hundred. Route marches with full pack and assault courses didn't seem so stupid now. Billy told himself he could do it. Each step felt like waiting for the final whistle to blow, knowing he was exposed in near-daylight to enemy fire. Even so, he couldn't afford to miss his footing. It would have been so much easier if he could just have looked ahead and run, but a wrong step might have them both sucked down into endless mud. Never had Billy prayed so hard.

Billy counted down the distance as they covered the ground. Fifty yards still to go. Twenty. Ten. He could see the trench just ahead. Five. They'd made it. Hands reached up to help lower Stan down before he was able to follow. Once he did, he fell back against the trench wall. "Jesus, Stan," Billy gasped, "that was close." He leaned over and retched.

Stan was already being loaded onto a stretcher to be taken for treatment. Billy would need to report to the lieutenant before he could do anything else; then he wasn't sure which he wanted most, a strong drink, breakfast or sleep. He started with a cigarette.

"Well done, Dobson." The lieutenant came up while Billy was watching Stan being carried away. "They're not as inactive as we thought they were. Sorry about that. We'll need to find a way to take that sniper out."

Billy wasn't entirely sure what he was supposed to say. "Yes, sir. Thank you, sir." He just hoped he wasn't being asked to go back to find the sniper.

"You did a good job of bringing Bradley back. Get some rest and then go and see how he's doing."

"Thank you, sir." Billy was definitely happy to do that. It would be a while before Stan had been assessed and treated, so Billy decided to make his way to the triage area and then settle down nearby for some kip. Chip had found him pretty quickly when he returned and tagged along, which Billy found comforting.

"Well, it's not a Blighty one," Stan said cheerfully later in the day when Billy was allowed to visit him in the hospital tent. "Flesh wound, so probably looks worse than it is."

"Do that again and I'll make you walk." Billy shook his head and grinned at his mate.

"At least it hasn't spoiled my good looks, which is a great help with the lovely nurses of the Voluntary Aid Detachment." He winked at one who was passing his bed. "To be honest, I'd get more kip in here if the poor buggers who came off worse than me didn't keep groaning."

"Make the most of it. You may not be as lucky the next time."

"And you may not be there to save me." Stan sounded serious for a moment as he said it. "Thanks, mate. I didn't think I wanted to bother going home until today, what with Mam and everything. But there's more to it than that. I want to see your Tommy growing up, and maybe I'll be lucky enough to find a girl like Vi one day. You're a lucky chap, Billy Dobson."

"I know," Billy said, smiling. He wanted to tell Stan that he needed him around, but his mate would think he'd gone soft if he said something like that. He was saved from finding the words by one of the nurses.

"Private Bradley needs to rest. Let's have you out of here." She ushered Billy away.

Stan winked at him before turning his most boyish smile in the nurse's direction. Billy had to laugh. His mate would never miss an opportunity to chat up a girl, however ferocious she looked; if it was anything like normal, she'd be lapping it up within seconds.

Billy went back to where he'd left Chip; the nurses hadn't let him take the terrier to see Stan. He patted the little dog. "Looks like it's just me and you for a day or two." He sat under a tree with the dog curled up next to him, and realised how comforting it was to have someone to tell everything to and who wouldn't repeat a word. He could even tell him how unbearable the thought of life without Stan would have been.

The rest of that deployment to the front line went without major incident for Billy, and he was glad when his four days were up and relief arrived. By the time he arrived back at base camp, Stan was already up and about.

"It's light duties for me for a few days. I don't want to give these up too soon," he said, waving his crutches. "I was rather hoping they might attract a bit of sympathy from the mademoiselles."

"Stan, if you're fit enough to walk into town, you don't need the crutches. And before you ask I've carried you far enough recently, so I'm not offering you a piggyback."

Stan gave him a look that was quite like the one Chip had given Billy when he was eating earlier. Billy sighed.

Looking away from Stan, Billy saw Davy coming over to them. He stood up and slapped the lad on the back.

"When did you get back? How's the arm?"

"Couple of hours ago." Davy raised his arm and lowered it again. "Almost feels normal, but not quite. I had to go for a debriefing before they'd even let me sleep. All I want now is my bed." He looked at Stan and ran a hand through his hair. "I thought I'd had a rough few days, but at least I'm in one piece. What happened to you?"

As Stan told a rather embellished story, in which his own heroics were prominent, Davy could hardly keep his eyes open.

"Come on," Billy said to Stan. "Now you've practised your story, let's give the lad a chance of a kip and see how it works on someone else."

"Now there you're wrong. I've already done my practising on the nurses. I'll be word perfect by the time I see that pretty brunette in the cafe."

Billy looked across at Davy and was about to shake his head, but the lad was already asleep.

The following day, Davy and Billy left Stan with his feet up and were sent to dig a new latrine. It was hard work, but safer than front line work; unless you were filling in the old latrine, when one slip could be both dangerous and extremely unpleasant.

"A bit of a picnic after the last few days," Davy said.

Billy laughed. "Not exactly a picnic, but who'd have thought that digging a bog could be seen as the best option for the day?" Despite the cold, Billy wiped away the sweat from his face.

"It gives me something to write to Mother and Father about. I never know what to include about our active service. I expect it would be crossed out by the censors if I did say anything about the last few days. That's not the reason I leave it out, though. It would scare Mother awfully if she knew what I was doing." Davy went back to digging.

"Mind you," Billy said, "I never thought I'd be as grateful for the privy back home."

"Don't you have a bathroom at home?" Davy asked in genuine amazement.

Billy laughed. "Only if that's what you want to call the tin bath in front of the fire each week." Billy couldn't believe that in the nine months they'd been together, Davy had never realised how different their lives at home were. At least being young, the lad had seen the privations of the army as an adventure, or maybe it reminded him of the school he'd been boarding at. Either way, Davy clearly had no idea how most people in Billingbrook lived.

"I told Mother and Father about Mrs Dobson playing football. I'd like to come and watch her when we're home, if that's all right?"

Billy laughed. "Of course it's all right, I'm looking forward to seeing her myself. I can't imagine it. I've tried to — the photo she sent helped a little. I still can't picture them playing. Mam seems to think it's awful what Vi's doing, but I'm proud of her."

"How long d'you think all this is going to go on for?" Davy asked.

"You're usually the one who knows stuff around here." Billy threw his shovel of mud onto the pile. "I wouldn't raise your hopes. It looks like they're bringing in conscription, I was reading about it in the newspaper."

Stan hobbled over to where they were. "Unless you're a bleedin' conchie. To be honest, that's starting to look attractive."

"I thought you were resting." Billy shook his head. He

hadn't been expecting to see Stan out and about.

"I was bored." Stan lit a cigarette and passed it to Billy.

"You'll have us all in trouble." Billy took a deep drag on the cigarette, then passed it to Davy.

"Give over. Anyway, the nurse told me I should take gentle exercise."

Billy shook his head. "By gentle, I don't suppose she meant you hiking halfway across France."

Stan shrugged and gave a boyish grin before taking the cigarette. "It's knocking off time, anyway. Come on."

Stan balanced on his crutches and watched as Billy and Davy finished off. "That was what was missing from my day. I've always liked watching other men work."

Billy threw some mud in Stan's direction; he wasn't able to move out of the way in time.

"I suppose I asked for that." Stan shook his head.

Returning to camp, Billy let out a low whistle. "It looks like things may have become a little more active along this stretch of the line." They stood back to let a line of men go by. Some were the walking wounded, others were being carried on stretchers. Behind that, a number of soldiers were escorting a group of enemy prisoners, who were not only wounded, but had the drooped shoulders and downcast look of defeat.

"I hope Major Shaw doesn't have any more bright ideas when we go back to the front line. Cats might have nine lives, but I'm not sure we do." The sight of the number of injured men had shaken Billy.

"You won't catch me complaining if we spend hours fetching and carrying supplies, that's for sure. It feels like a cushy number when you know more about the alternatives. Mind you, look on the bright side," Stan said, with an irrepressible grin, "if they patch up the enemy soldiers, maybe they can dig the bogs instead of you."

"I don't think that's allowed," Davy said. "But don't you think it's strange, the way the enemy look just the same as we do?"

"Except, Davy boy," Stan waved one of his crutches, "they're wearing the away team strip. Which means on principle, we have to win."

CHAPTER 21

It's a long way to Tipperary,
It's a long way to go.
It's a long way to Tipperary,
To the sweetest girl I know!
Goodbye, Piccadilly,
Farewell, Leicester Square!
It's a long long way to Tipperary,
But my heart's right there.
*It's a long way to Tipperary - Jack Judge and Harry Williams
1912*

*2nd March 1916 - 'Civilians Must Go Short or our Armies Must
Go Short': Great National Economy Campaign Opened - The
Daily Mirror*

After Christmas, life for Vi fell back into a routine. Their
return match against Blackburn was arranged for Easter
Monday, but although there were no other games until
then, the girls still practised once a week.

"It's best to be ready," Joe Wood said. "We might find
other factories who want to play against you."

"D'you think so?" Florrie asked. "We could end up
playing every week, like real footballers."

Violet quite liked the thought of playing more often.
She loved the game. She now understood why it meant so
much to Billy. In her letters she'd tell him about their

training sessions and the different tactics they were trying. He even made suggestions sometimes, which Vi would take back to Joe.

"You should encourage your brother to come down and watch us," Tessie said as she was lacing up her boots one day.

"Bobby?" Vi frowned. "He's always in the way. It's much better when he and Tommy are at Mam's."

Tessie stood to face her, hands on hips, and let out a heavy sigh. "Not, Bobby, silly. Your other brother."

Violet looked at her friend. Her reaction after the match at Christmas hadn't just been a one off. "Are you really sweet on our John?" She gave Tessie an encouraging smile. "I don't think he has a sweetheart. I'll have to ask."

Tessie gasped. "You can't tell him."

Violet laughed. "I'm not going to ask him. I'll ask Mam, I'm sure she'll know. He's a good lad, our John."

"He won't sign up, will he?" Tessie had a deep frown on her face.

"I don't know. He worships Billy — I've been worried he'd try following him. He's not quite sixteen yet, so I hope not. At least he still has a steady job, I think that helps. I can't promise though." Vi sighed and sat on the bench. "I don't think I could bear it if he went as well. It's a shame Ena's Percy hasn't gone yet, I suppose he'll be called up in a few weeks. I'm hoping that will make Ena's life easier. And that brother of his."

Other than complaining about Violet's football kit being hung out to dry, Elsie said very little about her playing, as long as she didn't leave Tommy at Ivy Terrace. With Alf, however, things were different. He said nothing at all at home. Then, one Saturday afternoon in February, Violet saw him standing on the sideline at the recreation ground, watching them practice. When they came to a break in the game, Violet went over to him.

"Dad, what are you doing here?"

He raised an eyebrow. "I'm on my way to do some errands for Mam — I took a bit of a detour. I heard you say that Tommy would be at your Mam's, so I guessed the coast was clear." He grinned and looked much younger than his fifty-six years.

Vi gave him a peck on the cheek. "Thank you."

"I know I don't have to ask you not to tell Mam."

"Mr Dobson!" Tessie had come running over to join them. "What are you doing here?"

"Enjoying watching some football. Takes me back to when I used to play."

Vi hoped he was going to say more about it, but Joe called them back over to carry on. The next time she turned to look he'd gone, presumably to complete Elsie's errands.

Every few days there was a brief letter from Billy, enough for her to know he was still alive. Each one brought enormous relief; if there was a gap of more than three days between their arrival, Violet found it hard to eat for the worry. She knew of people at work who had lost loved ones and however little she knew them she felt their loss keenly.

"Will Daddy be here for my birthday?" Tommy asked her earnestly one morning at the start of March.

Oh, how she wished she could say, 'Yes' to him. Billy hadn't had more than a day or so off at a time, and certainly nothing long enough to travel to Billingbrook and back. It had been nearly a year now since he'd left. Surely the war couldn't go on much longer.

"I'm sure Daddy will be here if he possibly can. If he isn't, then I know he'll be thinking about you and wishing he was here."

"What if he forgets me?"

"Oh, Tommy, Daddy will never forget you." She took him in her arms and held him tight. Then a thought occurred to her. "Tommy, are you worried you're going to forget Daddy?"

The little boy burst into tears and Violet rocked him gently.

"You look very like him. The same sandy hair." She ran her fingers through Tommy's hair. "The same green eyes." She kissed each one. "The same smile." Her own tears dripped down to join Tommy's.

Billy didn't make it home for Tommy's birthday in March, but to Violet's amazement he did manage to send a letter especially for his son, which arrived on the morning of his birthday. Violet was grateful that the post arrived before she had to leave for the factory; she would have hated to have missed the opportunity to read it to him.

'*My very dearest Tommy,*

I wish more than anything that I could be there to sing happy birthday to you on your fifth birthday. You must be very grown up now. I think of you and your mam every single day. You are the first thing I think about when I wake up and the last thing I think about before I go to sleep. Stan has a little dog called Chip. I think you'd like him very much. I hope we can bring him home when we come.

Take care of Mam for me and remember how much we both love you.

Daddy.'

Violet's voice was quivering as she read it, but she tried

hard not to spoil Tommy's birthday with tears. She bit her lip hard and then took a deep breath. "We should keep this safe somewhere so I can read it to you again later."

"Can I put it under my pillow?" Tommy looked up, pleading with those big green eyes.

Violet smiled. She had no idea if the boy would leave it there, but if that was where he wanted to keep it then she wasn't going to say no. "Only take it out when I'm with you, so you don't lose it."

They went back to the bedroom together and placed it under the pillow.

"Now I have to go to work, but I think as a treat Granddad is taking you to the workshop." She kissed Tommy's forehead and with a heavy sigh picked up her coat and headed out to meet Tessie.

"I've never been anywhere outside Billingbrook." Clara was getting ready for training. "How are we going to get there?"

"Mr Wood says the company's hiring a charabanc to take us all," Florrie said. "Can you imagine? My sister says if she'd known we'd have such exciting trips she'd have joined the team."

"I thought she said you were stupid playing football?" Tessie put her kit bag under the bench seat.

"Yes, she did. She said I'd never find a bloke and they'd just think I was a girl of 'easy virtue'." Florrie grinned.

"So what changed her mind?" Tessie asked.

"Michael Tanner got her pregnant and she had to marry him."

They all roared with laughter. Even Violet found herself chuckling. She hoped that wasn't what the men watching thought of her.

"Do you think there will be any spare spaces in the charabanc?" Tessie asked as they walked home later.

Vi thought it would be fun to go in a real motor vehicle. She couldn't wait to tell Billy about that. "I don't know. Who did you want to ask?"

Tessie didn't reply. Vi looked across at her and realised she'd gone red. "Is this still about our John?"

Tessie nodded but couldn't meet Vi's eye.

Vi smiled. "I'll have to ask Mr Giffard. It would be nice if there were some supporters on our side when we play." Of course, there were trains, but there was no way that her dad and John could afford the cost of that as well as an entrance ticket to the match. However, even if there were spaces on the charabanc, she presumed the other girls would have family they wanted to take too.

The following morning Vi planned to go to the management corridor to leave a message asking if she could talk to Mr Giffard, before heading to her bench.

She was just passing the gatehouse when she heard her name being called.

"Mrs Dobson."

She turned to see the man on the gate was beckoning to her. Vi turned to Tessie. "You best go on. I'll tell you what it's about at break."

Tessie looked disappointed, but waved to Vi as she went.

"There's a message for you. You're to go straight up to see Mr Giffard." The gatekeeper handed her the piece of paper.

"Thank you. I don't suppose Mrs Simpson said what it was about, did she?" Vi was frowning as she took the message slip.

"Sorry, miss." The gatekeeper touched his cap and

went back to his post.

Violet never ceased to be amazed at how the gatekeepers knew every single employee. She supposed if they were tasked with the safety of the factory and ensuring details were taken from visitors it was part of the job, but it couldn't have been easy. She turned in the direction of the management block entrance.

Even though Mr Giffard was very approachable and often came out to see them practice, Vi's hands felt clammy and she was folding and unfolding the piece of paper as she walked. She was glad to see Joe Wood was waiting too. She smiled. "It's not because I've done something wrong, then?"

"Not unless we both have. But I can't think of anything." Joe stood up and was about to move to the corner seat to give room for Vi, but Mrs Simpson came out and showed them straight into Mr Giffard's office.

"Do sit down." Mr Giffard indicated the chairs in front of his desk. "I won't keep you long. I've had a call from Major Tomlinson at Billingbrook Hall; he wondered if the girls would have a photograph taken with him and one or two of the soldiers there. He thought if we were in the *Billingbrook Mercury* it might help to encourage others to support their work. What do you think?"

"I… well…" Vi looked at Joe. "Well, I'm sure we could. I'm just surprised that he thinks it will help so much."

Mr Giffard gave a warm laugh. "You really don't realise how delighted they are with your support. The amount of money you girls have raised has been a huge help to them. I think he's rather hoping we might arrange some more matches."

Violet could feel herself smiling. She didn't want to stop playing, but she had never imagined they might have the opportunity to carry on. She felt a little bolder and cleared her throat. "There was one thing I was going to ask." She glanced at Joe. She wished she'd had the opportunity to discuss her idea with him, so she knew she would have some support.

"Fire away." Mr Giffard had a twinkle in his eyes.

"Is there any way that some of the girls' families could go with us to see the match?" She wanted to explain the entire idea before he responded, and her words began to tumble out. "Most of us can't afford the normal cost of travel and, well, I was wondering, is there any way that maybe the company could arrange for a special train just for our supporters, at a cheap rate for the day." There, she'd said it. She'd seen in the newspaper there were sometimes special cheap trains to places like Blackpool and hoped there could be something similar.

Joe was nodding, his eyebrows raised. "I know some of the other workers would like to go. They've been asking me about it."

Mr Giffard steepled his fingers and rested his chin on top. He nodded. "I'll need to make some calls. I can't promise anything, but it's an idea. Leave it with me, I'll let you know about that and the photograph."

The photograph was arranged for the Saturday afternoon. Vi wanted to be part of everything that was going on, so took Tommy over to her parents' house before she needed to go to the recreation ground.

After greeting her, Vi's mam looked serious. "I spoke to our Ena yesterday. Percy's been sent his call-up papers."

"Oh?" Vi wasn't sure from her mam's tone if she thought it was a good or bad thing.

"That's not all there is to it. Don't ask me how, but he's

got a medical dispensation, so won't be going." Vi's mother shook her head.

"Percy? But he's fit as a fiddle." Vi was confused. Perhaps there was a mistake.

"That shows how much we know, doesn't it? He's found some doctor to say he has a dicky heart and not fit to fight. I don't know if our Ena believes it, but I certainly don't." Vi's mam was shaking her head in disgust. "There's your Billy, volunteered when he didn't need to, and Percy won't go when he should. I wish she hadn't married him. No good can come of it."

It was the first time her mother had expressed the strength of her feeling against Percy to Vi. It made it easier to realise her mam thought as much of him as she did, but she decided it was still not sensible to raise her concerns about Percy hitting Ena. The last thing she wanted was for her lovely dad to feel he had to confront Percy. That sort of meeting wouldn't end well.

The photographer was already at the training ground when Vi arrived. Mr Giffard was with him, as were a number of men in military uniform. Vi headed for the changing rooms to put on her football kit and to find the other girls. She was still changing when Joe knocked on the door.

"Mr Giffard wants to know if you're ready for the picture," he called to them.

"How do I look?" Clara asked.

Vi was still putting her shorts on and was now fumbling in her haste. The others were laughing and giggling.

Eva came over to her. "Vi, your shirt's inside out."

Vi looked down at the football strip she was about to

pull over her head and laughed.

Eva put a hand on her arm. "It's not our first photograph — stop worrying. Besides, you're married and don't need to look your best."

Vi didn't know whether to be grateful or offended. She took a deep breath and sorted herself out. "Right, I'm ready." She tucked the last stray strand of hair under her mob cap and led the girls out onto the pitch.

"Good show, gals."

Violet smiled. Major Tomlinson was behaving as though he was in charge of what was happening and somehow in his presence Mr Giffard was looking smaller than he did normally.

The major soon corralled them into position for the photographer, while Mr Giffard looked on bemused. Vi was beginning to feel a little sorry for him.

Once the photograph had been taken, Major Tomlinson moved in front of the group. "I want you gals to know that we're all very grateful for what you're doing — the chaps need all the help we can give them. I'm rather hoping you might all see your way to coming up to the Hall to see them and cheer them up, it would lift their spirits no end. Carry on." He made an abrupt turn, paced over to Mr Giffard to say his farewells, and then marched back to the motor vehicle the men had arrived in.

"Well, I never." Edith was standing open-mouthed, watching them leave.

Mr Giffard coughed to gain their attention. He was still looking shrunken. "Thank you. There was one other thing — Mrs Dobson asked me whether there was a way to lay on transport to the match at a modest cost. I'm pleased to say…" as he spoke he seemed to be re-inflating, "the train company will lay on a 'football special' for us. Places will be limited, but they will be included in the ticket price for those travelling from Billingbrook."

Tessie clapped her hands together. "Oh, Vi, you will ask John, won't you?"

Vi laughed and nodded to her friend. "I promise I will."

The train wasn't due to arrive in Blackburn until close to kick off, so the girls were still travelling by charabanc. They all wrapped up warmly, as the weather wasn't great for the time of year, but even the heavy showers couldn't dampen their excitement. There was enough room for all of them to sit comfortably. In addition to the driver, there were all the girls in the team, Joe Wood and Mr Giffard. As they drove off Vi could see her dad with John, Tommy and Bobby, waving; they were all going on the train and were as excited about that as she was about the charabanc. None of her family had done something like this before. She wished they could all be going together. She waved for as long as she could see them, and realised Tessie was doing the same. Then they joined in with the general chatter; the girls were pointing out things they saw in the changing landscape as they left Billingbrook.

By the time they reached the outskirts of Blackburn, everyone was talking at once with the excitement; Violet wondered how they'd ever settle down to play the match. They drove through the town and out toward the ground. The mood changed as they approached Ewood Park, the ground where Blackburn Rovers played, and the girls fell silent. Violet clutched her bag, ready to climb down. It looked so impressive, even compared to the Billingbrook United ground. When the charabanc stopped, Violet didn't want to get out at all. Tessie led the way and the others followed her.

"Are you coming?" Mr Giffard said to her, not unkindly.

"Pardon? Oh, yes." Violet felt far away. "My Billy would have loved to see this." She sighed and on shaky legs went to join the others.

Once they were all ready, Joe addressed them. "Now, I want you to think that you're only out on the company pitch and we're practising. Ignore the crowds. Just play as well as you do when you're playing against each other."

"Never mind that," Clara called. "We have a score to settle, haven't we girls?"

Determination replaced anxiety and Violet wanted to win. From the moment that the whistle blew, she threw herself into the game. Time and again she found space so she could receive passes and take the ball forward. She scored her first goal after only ten minutes of the match, and her second, which turned out to be the winner, just before full time. Walking off the pitch to the cheers of her teammates after their win, Violet knew that however much anyone might disapprove, she did not want this to be her last match.

CHAPTER 22

When this lousy war is over, no more soldiering for me,
When I get my civvy clothes on, oh how happy I shall be.
No more church parades on Sunday, no more putting in
for leave,
I will miss the Sergeant-Major,
How he'll miss me how he'll grieve.
(sung to the tune of What a Friend we have in Jesus)

*20th May 1916 - Thrilling Deeds of Heroism at Loos: Official
Account of the Great Battle Published To-Day - The Daily
Mirror*

"Take this to the sergeant over there and ask for a long
stand, lad." Stan gave a piece of wood to one of the new
recruits who'd just arrived from England.

Billy was starting to feel like an old hand, even without
Stan's pranks. These men were at least still volunteers,
although most of them had realised their call-up papers
would be on the doormat within weeks. They arrived with
a look of zeal: with some of them, it was as though they
believed that now they'd arrived the battle could be won
in days. Billy couldn't blame Stan for wanting to take some
of them down a peg or two.

"'Ere, Granddad, Sarge says you need to see him." The
youth was back, looking as cocky as ever.

Billy had realised how much the war had aged him

without the new lads calling Stan Granddad; even Davy now seemed more of a seasoned veteran. It was seeing the lads of fifteen who'd lied about their age which upset Billy. How bad must their lives at home have been to make this a better option? He was miles away, thinking, when Stan gave him a kick.

"Daydreaming's over. Work to do — we're on prisoner duties." Stan shrugged and looked as though he didn't know what that meant.

Billy got up off the log he'd been sitting on and brushed himself down. He, Stan and Davy went over to Corporal Brown. "Dobson, Bradley and Moore, reporting for duty."

"Over there please, lads. We need you to take over as escort for the group of prisoners of war that we're holding. They need taking to the secure camp." Corporal Brown indicated for them to join other British soldiers who would be leading the prisoners on the march cross-country to the camp.

When they'd first arrived Billy got the impression that no one had thought about what to do with prisoners, but now their arrival and escort was becoming more commonplace. They joined the other men and waited for their consignment of prisoners to be handed over to their care.

It was a few miles to where the men would be housed. It was the job of the escorts to take the German soldiers there in one piece and without any of them going AWOL. The last thing they needed was more Germans free to go back and fight, quite apart from the trouble they'd be in if it happened.

It was a relatively slow march and they plodded on along a broken track. The prisoners were dishevelled and dispirited.

"Woher kommen Sie aus?" Davy said to the man nearest to him as they marched.

"D'you hear that?" Stan said to Billy. "The lad only speaks German as well as French. Bet you've not told our superiors that one. You'd have been on special assignments long before…" Stan's voice trailed off.

Billy realised at the same time as Stan had that it might account for the times Davy had indeed been taken away on other duties, which he had not been able to tell them about.

"Ich komme aus Bayern," the prisoner replied.

"He comes from Bavaria," Davy said, for the benefit of Billy and Stan. He turned back to the prisoner. "Und, eure Familie, sind sie noch in Bayern?"

"Yes, they are still there, my wife and infant son." The prisoner switched to English, with almost flawless pronunciation.

"Bloody hell," Stan said, "they even speak better English than I do."

"Not all of us. But yes, we learn in school." The man seemed to have relaxed slightly as they spoke to him. "My son was born after I left. I have not seen him yet."

Billy felt a shiver run through him. Seeing a man as his enemy was hard enough without seeing how many similarities they had. Once he saw the person underneath, the thought of what he had to do just became harder.

He put such thinking out of his mind. At least for these prisoners, the fighting was over. Billy couldn't let his guard down; if he did, he'd be the one to cop a bullet. He fell back a little in the group so he wouldn't hear any more of the conversation.

Before Billy joined up, his whole world was Billingbrook. Now, he'd met men from as far away as New

Zealand. His experiences had changed the way he saw the world. It wasn't that he particularly wanted to travel, and certainly not without Vi; however, it did make him think he wanted to better himself. Getting to know Davy had started him thinking that. He knew now he should have taken school more seriously. When he returned home, would it be too late to do anything about it?

"And what delights are we facing today?" Stan said when they heard the morning call the following day. "I wouldn't mind more escorting prisoners. As things go, that wasn't so bad."

"Come on you lazy sluggards." The sergeant was already rounding them up. "Look lively."

Lively was one thing Stan rarely looked at this hour of the day. Even the thought of it made Billy smile as he pulled his boots on.

The sergeant directed them to the end of the rail line, where their task was to help unload all the arriving ordnance, stack it into carts and help move it from the station to the storage points, without incident.

"Anyone would think there was a war on," Stan lifted yet another shell box onto the stack.

The three of them worked well as a team, and as they moved crate after crate they developed a good rhythm.

"That's that then." Davy passed the last one down and straightened up.

Sergeant Penney was grinning. "I don't think so, laddie. There's another train due in when this one pulls out."

"You have to be kidding. I thought we were going with the carts?" Stan did not look happy.

"I'm keeping you three on unloading. You're doing too

good a job to move you to something else." The sergeant leered, and Billy worried for a moment that Stan would feel an urge to wipe the grin off his face. Fortunately, before any of them had time to react, Sergeant Penney had turned and marched off along the line of trucks.

Even as fit as he was, Billy ached by the end of the day; the unloading had been relentless. Next day after breakfast, when he saw Sergeant Penney waiting outside the mess tent, he groaned.

"Same again, lads. Off you go, at the double."

Billy nodded and dragged Stan away before he could say or do anything.

Either other mugs had been doing this task until now, or there was a lot more ordnance arriving than had been the case previously. As their work continued day after day, Billy realised a major offensive was in the offing. A sense of urgency came over the camp, that wasn't triggered by just the ammunition arriving; the number of men had increased too. A new attitude prevailed. There was an overriding belief amongst the lads that this was the big push that had been spoken about, and within weeks they'd be victorious.

After more than a year away, Billy felt ready to face whatever lay ahead. He was not exactly excited, but prepared to get on with it. Stan was fully recovered, with only a slight limp to show for their earlier incident, and even that Billy suspected was more for show than any real discomfort. When they played football, Stan showed little sign of the injury at all.

The artillery bombardment of the enemy line began late in June. No one could have been in any doubt that this was different from the war on the Western Front so far. The air rang with the sound of shells exploding, and the news that came back from the front line was encouraging.

Night and day Billy could hear the shells and feel the vibrations through the ground from the onslaught. Under such a sustained attack, he couldn't imagine the enemy staying around long to find out what would follow.

When the three of them were told to prepare for their next stint on the front line, everything was different. This time many more men were being sent forward. The line was long, but Billy couldn't help thinking it was going to be overcrowded.

He sat down to write to Vi.

'*... The noise is like nothing I can describe. It's almost constant. Like the worst thunderstorm that never stops. Hopefully, it means I will be with you and Tommy soon. I can't wait to see you. I love you, Vi. I don't think I realised just how much until I came here.*

I'll be home soon.

Yours always

Billy.'

He had enough time to make sure he sent it before they set off for the reserve trenches. Maybe this would be the last time they had to do this; surely the Germans would surrender in the face of this barrage? He was whistling as he found Stan ready to set off.

"Sure you're fit? You could probably swing another week or two of light duties back here with that limp."

"What and let you see all the action without me? Not bloody likely." Stan grinned. "Besides, the girls have moved on to the next round of casualties. My charms have waned." Stan became serious. "I've been thinking, if I die, there's no one to receive a pension. That'll be it, army's duties over."

Billy didn't want to listen to this. "That's enough. You aren't going to die. Don't start thinking like that."

"No, hear me out. I've had an idea."

How many times over the years had Billy heard that line? He knew he should just leave Stan to it and not listen, but they were mates. He'd been drawn into more hairbrained schemes than he could count. He supposed that would always be the case. "Go on." Billy sighed. "I'm listening."

It was a warm day, close to the end of June. Having to carry full pack was a nightmare when it was like this. At least they didn't have too far to go, but with the zigzagging and the difficulties of moving about, it still took a fair time. They'd spend a few days in the reserve trench and then be on the front line again in early July.

"You have to be kidding me." Stan did not look pleased when they were assigned their first tasks. "I thought I'd seen the last of these."

The size of the imminent operation was evident. The crates of shells and other ammunition they had unloaded from the trains and waved off to the stores now needed bringing to the trenches ready for action. There was no letup.

For a moment, as he carried one of the wooden boxes encasing the shells, Billy wondered if it might have come from the factory where Vi worked. He smiled, feeling they might be working as a team.

On the 30th of June, still with the sound of the artillery as a constant orchestra, they moved forward to the front line. Every able-bodied man was on standby.

"Get what rest you can, lads." Lieutenant Croft went along the line of troops. "Tomorrow's the big one. We'll have them on the run before you know it."

Despite the sense of anticipation, nothing was going to stop Billy sleeping after the last few days of constant work. First light would be with them all too soon and then, by all accounts, it would be the big push. This would be no skirmish; this would be full-scale battle.

"King and country," Stan said, punching Billy's arm.

Billy nodded. It was impossible not to be caught up by the atmosphere of it. Now there was no fear, just an urge to get on with the job.

"We will be in the first wave." The lieutenant was once again going along the line.

Billy looked at the sandbags making up the wall of the trench. They were the only thing that now stood between him and the enemy. When they heard the command, they would go up the ladder and run like hell in the direction of the enemy lines, rifles and bayonets ready for action. There were thousands of men ready to fight. Not just their company, but others along the line. This is what everything until now had been building up to.

The lieutenant was chivvying along soldiers who were still packing up their kit. "The artillery should have made sure the way's safe. They will have cleared away the barbed wire and any of the enemy gun placements. Straight over no man's land and give them hell."

"Nice idea," Stan muttered.

"Right men, the first wave is off on the dot of 07.30. Ready yourselves." The final seconds ahead of action ticked by. The lieutenant's eyes were fixed on his watch. Finally the whistle was blown, and as fast as they could the men began to climb the ladders over the side of the trench and charge.

Another of the officers was standing by to keep them all moving in a continuous line. "Look lively. Ours the glory, boys."

"Glory, my arse," said Stan. "Just don't think of turning round. If Fritz doesn't shoot you from behind, this herbert will shoot you from the front." He glared at an officer positioned ready to shoot any of his own men who lost their nerve and failed to advance. "Makes you wonder who we're bloody fighting."

Billy heard no more of Stan's words. Heart pounding, he climbed the ladder. His senses sharpened. He was one man among many. They all had the same goal. A team.

He must have been about two hundred yards behind the leading men. As he ran, his mind couldn't process what was happening around him. There was machine gun fire. This wasn't coming from behind them; it wasn't British machine guns aimed at the Germans. This was coming from in front, aimed at their advancing line. The German guns hadn't all been taken out by the Allied artillery, as they'd been told. The German machine guns were firing, and they were firing directly at Billy and Stan and Davy and every other soldier they knew. Men were falling. Other soldiers were having to run over the bodies of their comrades, onward toward the enemy line. Onward toward the firing guns. Billy ran blindly after them, aware of gunfire, screams, groans and broken men. But he ran on. He had a job to do. This was what he came here for.

CHAPTER 23

So don't talk to me about invasion,
Nor say that we are in a sorry plight,
There's not another nation in creation,
That dares with us to fight.
Our soldiers they are just as brave as ever,
Our soldiers too, who fight upon the wave,
And with volunteers ashore, what on Earth do we want more
To protect the little island of the brave?
Don't Talk to Me About Invasion - 'Jolly' John Nash (1830 - 1901)

30 June 1916 - British Attacks Increasing - Russians Take 10,000 Prisoners - The Daily Mirror

When Vi came in from playing in the yard with Tommy, Alf had been to buy a Sunday newspaper. She could see the headline, 'British Troops Sweeping On'. Her heart leaped. Would it all be over soon, as people were saying? Oh, she did hope so. She wanted to read the rest of the piece but could see no more than, 'Enemy Surrounded'. She'd have to wait until Alf had finished with it later; or buy her own, which seemed a waste.

In her head Vi began to believe that soon they could be a family again, and life could return to normal. She'd put every spare penny away in her savings jar, ready for them to find their own place to live when Billy came home. How good that sounded. 'When Billy comes home,' no longer 'if'. With things going this well, surely it would be a matter of weeks, or maybe even days. She sang to herself as she prepared the Sunday dinner. She'd take Tommy out in the afternoon, maybe call in on her parents.

"Will Daddy still look the same when he comes home?" Tommy asked as they walked.

"Of course he will." Vi realised she'd said it automatically. Would he have changed in fifteen months? She didn't think she'd changed, but then she supposed in small ways she must have done. "He'll still have eyes just like yours, and the same lovely smile."

Ena and Percy were at the Tunnicliffes' house when Vi arrived. Vi stiffened. She was in no mood to have a conversation with Percy about the war; his pride in having evaded being called up was a sore point with all the rest of the family. She didn't need his goading.

Tommy went out to find Bobby. John was with them, so they wouldn't find too much trouble. She'd looked at John differently since she'd realised that Tessie was fond of him. He wasn't her little brother anymore; he was a man and not a bad one, even if she did say so herself. He'd look better when he'd finished growing and filled out a bit, but there was no rush.

"Play us a tune, Dad," Vi said, as much as anything to avoid conversation with Percy around.

"It's Sunday, love," he said by way of apology. "It won't do to disturb the neighbours."

Vi sighed. "I think I might go for a walk in the sunshine for half an hour. Anyone want to come?"

Mam looked as though she'd like to take up the offer, but shook her head.

Vi went down to the river. The stepping stones were easy to reach just then and she went across to sit on the rock. Before the summer was out, she wanted to be back here with Billy and Tommy. They'd had a picnic the day before Billy went; maybe they could have another to celebrate his return. She watched the water for a while and thought about how good it would be to have him back.

All the talk in the factory on Monday was of the great success that the boys were having on the Western Front. The girls were so proud of the role they were playing, providing the munitions. The atmosphere was lighter than it had been for ages.

"Do you think we'll still have a job when it's all over?" Eva asked Vi.

"I don't know, I hadn't thought of that. It will just be so good to have everything back to normal. Maybe the hat factory will be taking people on again, and I can go back to making hats. I did love doing that."

Tuesday's and Wednesday's headlines seemed to confirm all that Vi was hoping. Advances were being made, German prisoners were being taken; success was within the country's grasp. She couldn't wait to hear all Billy's news. The letter which arrived Monday had been written before all this took place.

At lunch break they were having a kickabout in the yard when Florrie came running over.

"Have you heard? There's a whole trainload of wounded men been brought to the hospital. There's hundreds of them. They've no idea how they're going to cope with them all."

Vi's heart missed a beat. Surely Billy couldn't be among them? No, she'd have heard if he was wounded.

"Mr Giffard says he wants to arrange another football match to help raise money," Florrie continued.

Vi began to worry. There'd been nothing in the newspapers about high levels of casualties. She wanted to ask someone what was happening, but didn't know where to start. There were others in the factory in the same position; for some it was husbands, for others brothers or sons.

"We could go up to the hospital to ask?" Florrie said. "I wonder if they'd let us have an hour off work to go."

"Why don't we ask Mr Giffard?" Edith looked with disgust at the fingernail she'd been biting and pulled a face. "I should have washed my hands before doing that. Will I never learn?"

It broke the tension and they laughed.

"It's a good idea. Come on, Vi, why don't the two of us go to see if the old dragon will let us past to see Mr Giffard? If we go now, there's still time before the shift restarts." Florrie took Vi's arm and propelled her in the direction of the management corridor.

"Do you think we should be going without Mrs Johnson's say so?" Violet looked back across the yard.

"What she doesn't know can't hurt her." Florrie sounded determined. "Mind you, that woman seems to have eyes everywhere."

Violet didn't want to lose her job, but Florrie was right. She had to find out if there was any news.

Florrie, whilst still only sixteen, had more confidence than Vi. She marched straight into Mrs Simpson's office and, before the woman had time to react, launched into an explanation. "We'd like to go to Billingbrook Hall to see if they can give us any news on Vi's husband and my brother. We thought Mr Giffard could authorise us to take an hour out of our shift to go."

Violet was fully expecting Mrs Simpson to ask them to leave and make an appointment to see Mr Giffard. Instead, she smiled sadly and said, "Sit down, ladies."

Florrie deflated and sat in the chair in front of Mrs Simpson's desk, whilst Vi sat in the one by the door.

"I'm expecting Mr Giffard back at any moment. That is exactly where he's gone, to see if he can find out what's happening." She looked down at some papers on her desk and moved them out of the way. Then she moved them back to their original position and looked up. "My own brother went out there too."

Violet was taken aback. She'd never thought of Mrs Simpson as being human, never mind having a brother who was fighting. She nodded but said nothing.

Mrs Simpson carried on with her work as Florrie and Violet waited. It must have been around ten minutes before Mr Giffard swept in.

"Ladies," he said to them, nodding his head in acknowledgment as he went through to the inner office.

Mrs Simpson followed after him, pen and notebook in hand. She closed the door and Florrie looked at Violet and shrugged. Five minutes later, Mrs Simpson opened the door and invited Florrie and Violet to go in. They remained standing and Mrs Simpson stood in the open doorway.

"I'm afraid it's a bad business. I don't have any information on particular soldiers, no one seemed to know. Casualties are high. All they could say to me was that the War Office would contact families as and when it was appropriate. They don't even have a complete list of their patients, never mind any others of the local regiments. I'm sorry."

"Thank you for trying to find out." Violet tried to smile. "I guess we just have to wait."

Florrie and Violet went back to their benches, and although Vi was a few minutes late, Mrs Johnson said nothing.

A week passed and Violet was feeling a growing sense of unease. Whilst there'd been nothing from the War Office, there had been no letter from Billy either. She hoped it meant he was too busy to write, or maybe that the post wasn't being taken back and forth to the Front because of the fighting. She tried to tell herself all the acceptable reasons that she might not have heard, and paint on a smile for Tommy.

Florrie didn't come into work on the following Tuesday. Whispers around the factory were of some families having heard that loved ones had died. Violet bit her lip every time she heard any of the stories. *Please God, not Billy.*

That night when she got home there was still no news, and she sent up a silent prayer of thanks.

When Violet arrived home on Wednesday, Billy's mother was weeping.

"Mam?" Violet dropped down onto the floor in front of her.

Billy's mam didn't respond.

"Mam?" Violet said a little louder.

The older woman waved her hand in the direction of a piece of paper on the table beside her.

Hands trembling, Violet picked up the open telegram and read.

'It is my painful duty to inform you…'

Violet froze. She realised her mother-in-law was speaking to her.

"I'm sorry I opened it. I had to. Oh, Violet, it was awful. I was talking outside to Mrs Brown. We saw the telegram boy at the end of the road, and she said, 'I wonder which house he's calling at.' It wasn't one house. He went first to one, and then to another. He must have delivered fifteen or more telegrams the length of our road. When he handed it to me, I collapsed. Mrs Brown had to help me in. I didn't know what to do. I said to Alf we should come to you at the factory, but he said you wouldn't want that. He's taken Tommy out, even though it's late. He didn't think he should be here when you found out." Elsie Dobson broke into convulsing sobs as soon as she'd finished speaking.

Violet felt numb. She stayed where she was, kneeling on the floor, feeling sick and empty. He couldn't be dead. The papers were talking about victory; how could they do that if so many men had died or were injured?

She heard Alf bringing Tommy back through the kitchen and straightened up. "Best be putting Tommy to bed." She tucked the telegram into her pocket and shakily walked to the door. She continued to go through the motions of hugging the boy and taking him upstairs to bed. She would have to tell him about Billy at some point, but not tonight. She sat stroking Tommy's hair as he drifted off to sleep, and wondered if there had been anyone to sit with Billy as he went to sleep for the last time. She tried not to let the tears fall. She was scared that if she started crying, she might never stop.

Once Tommy was sound asleep, she went back down to see Alf and Elsie.

"He died a hero," Alf said quietly.

"He was already my hero. I didn't need him to be a hero for anybody else." Vi had to go out; late as it was, she needed some fresh air. At least it wasn't quite dark. She had no idea where she was going, but simply walked along Victoria Street away from town.

She hadn't gone far when she heard footsteps behind her.

"Wait up."

Violet turned to see Tessie running after her.

"Mam told me. I'll walk with you."

Tessie was still very young at fifteen, but she'd become a good friend and Violet was grateful for her company. They didn't say much. Once they were away from the houses, Vi stopped and looked up at the sky. With clenched fists raised she shouted, "Why, Tessie? Why?" And then the tears came, great racking sobs which overwhelmed her whole body as Tessie held her.

As dusk began to close in, Violet felt thoroughly spent and wiped the last of the tears away. She squeezed Tessie's hand. "Thank you." She still didn't really want to talk, but Tessie seemed to be fine with that and slipped her arm through Violet's as they walked back.

When they neared the edge of the housing, Vi stopped. "I need to go to tell my parents. I'll walk you back and then go over."

"Don't be daft. I'll be fine walking back." Tessie frowned. "No, I'll come with you, then we can walk back together."

"It'll be late by the time we're back."

Tessie smiled. "I'm a big girl now, Vi. I'll be fine. It's you I'm worried about."

Vi wondered if it was because Tessie wanted to see John, but when they were at the corner of the road Tessie said, "I'll wait here. Take as long as you need, I'll be fine. I don't want to intrude." She sat on a low wall at the end of the terraces and shooed Violet on so she wouldn't argue.

Vi opened the front door gently, not wanting to disturb any of the house who were already asleep.

"Oh, you gave me a start," Mam said, standing up from her chair. She took one look at Vi and fell back. "No!"

Vi nodded and with a shaking hand passed the telegram for her father to read.

"Oh, Vi love." Her mam pushed herself back up out of the chair and enveloped her daughter in her arms. "Frank, get a brew on."

Dad tucked the folded telegram back into Vi's hand and patted her arm as he went over to put the kettle on the stove.

"I won't stop long, but I thought you'd want to know." Vi took out her handkerchief and dabbed her face.

"Why did it have to be Billy? Why couldn't it have been Percy?"

"Mam, you can't go saying things like that." She'd thought it herself, but hearing it said was shocking.

"That's as maybe, but it's not right." Mam paused. "I don't suppose you've heard anything about Stan, have you?"

Vi shook her head. She didn't know how she could find out if Stan was safe.

When Vi went back to find Tessie, another figure stood up from the wall and moved away as she approached. "John?"

"I... I was just..."

Tessie came up and stood by him. "It's all right, John. Vi knows."

"I'd best go in. I'm sorry about Billy." John scurried back to the house before Vi had the opportunity to say anything further.

Vi was pleased that Tessie and John were getting closer.

She didn't feel like talking about it now, though. She slipped her arm into Tessie's, as much to reassure Tessie as for her own comfort, and began the walk back to Ivy Terrace.

Vi was careful to go into the house without making a noise. By this time of night on a normal day, everyone would have been asleep for hours. She closed the back door and tiptoed out into the hall. She heard a noise from the back room and stopped. She realised there was a little light beneath the door. She'd best say goodnight and reassure whichever of Billy's parents had waited up for her that she was all right.

When Vi opened the door, Billy's mam was on her knees with the box from under the sideboard open in front of her. She was clutching a tiny cardigan and sobbing. Around her on the floor were an assortment of bootees, letters and even a photograph.

"Mam."

Elsie looked up and gasped. She tried to gather the treasures up quickly. Vi sank to her knees next to her mother-in-law and wrapped her arms around her. The two of them stayed like that, crying together for long enough for the lamp to start to flicker.

"I'd best pack these away." Elsie pulled away from the embrace and lifted an infant's pink jumper. Without another word to Vi, she began to pick up each item and lay them in the box with tender care.

Vi sorted the lamp so that it wouldn't go out while Elsie needed it, and then left the room and went upstairs.

Violet didn't know when she'd eventually fallen asleep; long enough ago to still feel thick-headed, recent enough for her pillow to still be wet from the tears. Her face felt puffy and her eyes raw.

Her first thought was that the sheet was cold as she rolled over. Worse than that, it was smooth and crumple free. Even though she should have been used to that by now, it felt new — different. That wasn't what mornings were supposed to be like. She wanted to reach for Billy and have him pull her to him, to feel the strength of his arms as he drew her into his warm embrace. Not today. Not any day. She lay there, tired, wrung out. Most of all, she wanted to curl into a ball and pull the covers over her head. The sun was squeezing its way through a gap in the curtains. How dare it? How bloody dare it? How could it be so heartless? There was no room in her day for sunshine.

"Mam. Mam."

If Billy wasn't here beside her, she didn't want to be 'Mam'. How could she face looking into the green eyes that he'd given, but which were no longer his? That sandy tousled hair, so like his but framing a younger face.

Violet wanted to scream. She wanted to scream that it couldn't be true.

"Mam."

The lad was only five. He needed her to carry on; he'd lost his hero as much as she had. She rolled to a sitting position on the edge of the bed and there it was, on the night-stand. The telegram. *'It is my painful duty...'* She could almost smell the cordite and hear the shells falling.

Today there was no place for regrets. She had to be mother and father. She had to be everything their son needed. But who would be there for her, and how would she break the news to Tommy?

CHAPTER 24

She's only a bird in a gilded cage,
A beautiful sight to see,
You may think she's happy and free from care,
She's not, though she seems to be,
Bird in a Gilded Cage - Arthur J. Lamb and Harry von Tilzer
1900 approx

12th July 1916 - Saving the Wounded: A Nameless British Hero
Who Carried in Twenty Men While Under Fire - The Daily
Mirror

Violet decided that however much trouble she would be in as a result, she wouldn't go to work that day. She wondered how many others wouldn't be there and shuddered. Tessie would explain. What Violet had to do was to tell Tommy. She sat down and had breakfast with him first; thankfully, Alf had already eaten, and Elsie had stayed in their room.

Once she'd cleared the plates, she sat back down at the table with him. "Tommy, love, we had some bad news yesterday. Daddy isn't going to be coming back from the war." Violet was determined that she would not make it worse for the child by him having to deal with her own emotion and she fought back the tears.

"Not ever?"

Violet bit her lip and shook her head. "No, Tommy, not

ever. He did a very brave thing fighting for his country, but he died in the battle." It was almost impossible to keep her voice steady.

Tommy nodded earnestly, a tear forming in the corner of his eye. "Won't I ever see him?"

Violet shook her head.

Tommy frowned. "I don't remember him very well. He's been gone a long time."

Violet nodded but could say nothing.

"Will you always be here?" Tommy looked up at her, his green eyes wide with fear.

"Oh yes, my darling boy. I'll always be here for you." She wrapped him in her arms and held him close.

"Will Uncle Stan be coming back?"

"I don't know, darling. We'll have to find out. I hope so." She'd been thinking about that last night. If Stan was still alive he'd write to her, she was sure of that. It meant if she didn't hear anything, then Stan hadn't pulled through either. All she could do was wait.

"You put on your shoes, I'm going to take some tea up to Grandma and then we'll go over to Nanna's so you can play with Bobby." Vi didn't know what to do with herself. There was no funeral to arrange, no grave to lay flowers on. She had questions she wanted answering, but there was no one to ask.

Tommy was subdued, but she didn't know how much he'd understood. She made some fresh tea and took it upstairs. She knocked on Elsie's door but received no reply. Elsie didn't reply when she knocked again and then opened the door. Billy's mother was sitting in bed, staring straight ahead. She didn't even turn when Vi went in. Vi put the tea on Elsie's night stand. "Mam."

Elsie looked toward Vi as though surprised to see her

there.

"I've brought you some tea. Can I get you anything else?"

Elsie shook her head but said nothing.

"I'm going to take Tommy out for a while. He won't disturb you then. "

Elsie put her hand out to Vi, and Vi took it in hers.

"I'm sorry, love," Elsie said.

Vi sat on the edge of the bed and put her arms around Billy's mam. "I'm sorry, too." They stayed like that for a few minutes until Vi heard Tommy calling.

"Mam."

She stood up from the bed. "I'd best go. I'll be back later."

Elsie nodded and resumed staring into space.

Vi returned to work the following day. She couldn't afford to lose her job. She had no idea if there would be a pension from the army, and for now she needed to make sure there was enough money to keep her and Tommy. She was quiet as she and Tessie walked to work, only half listening to what the girl said.

"You'll play then?"

"Pardon?" Violet realised an answer was required.

"In the matches that Mr Giffard wants to arrange. You'll play?"

"I don't think so, it wouldn't be right. And I really don't want to upset Billy's parents now. I can't afford for them to throw me out." It was a horrifying thought. She had no idea if the older couple would want her to stay now. She knew her mother-in-law didn't like the bother of Tommy, but she still loved him. Then there was the money; she didn't think they'd want to give up her income. Maybe it would be all right, but she didn't know.

Tessie gave a theatrical sigh. "Mam says they'll want you to stay as your Tommy is all they have left of Billy."

"Maybe," Violet said quietly. She just didn't know. Either way, she wouldn't be part of the football team. Not now.

It was hard for Violet to focus on her work. Several times she realised she was at risk of making serious errors; that was something she couldn't afford to do. She wondered if she should ask for some time off, but they were short-handed and their work was still needed.

At lunch break Eva said, "Are you coming down for a kickabout in the yard?"

Vi shook her head. "I'm going for a walk."

She headed out of the gate and walked toward the town centre. There was a church, St Michael's, right near the main shopping area. She tried the door and found it was unlocked, so went inside. To Vi's surprise there were other women already there, sitting apart from each other, heads bowed in prayer. As she sat in one of the pews and kneeled on a hassock to pray, she wondered if the other women had received the same news she had. Was there a God? She had no idea, but she couldn't bear to think that Billy had just gone from the world and wasn't somewhere better. A few words couldn't hurt, whether there was someone listening or not. Right now, she needed to believe. She needed something to trust in.

Vi had been kneeling with her head bowed for a few minutes before she looked up. She was surprised to see Tessie sitting a couple of places along in the pew. Vi frowned.

"I followed you," Tessie whispered. "When Eva said you were going for a walk, I was worried about you. I just thought I'd be here, in case you needed someone."

Vi didn't know whether to laugh or cry at Tessie's overwhelming kindness. She got up from her knees. "Shall we go?"

They came out of St Michael's into the sunshine. Vi turned her face up to it as tears rolled down her cheeks.

"I just don't know where to start. I suppose I need to talk to Billy's parents, but I don't know where to begin."

"They probably don't know what to say to you either," Tessie said, as they walked back toward the Caulder and Harrison factory.

Vi thought about that. Tessie was probably right.

The following day was Saturday, and as she was not going to football, it gave a good opportunity to take Tommy to her parents and then spend some time with Billy's parents.

"Won't you stay, love?" Queenie said as Vi made to leave.

She would have loved to spend the day with her own family, feeling the warm embrace of their love; but she had hardly seen Elsie or Alf and she needed to speak with them. She hesitated. "I'll be back this afternoon. I'll stay longer then." She kissed her mam's cheek and walked back to Ivy Terrace.

Alf was in the kitchen when she went in. "I thought you'd be going on to football today. I was just making a brew for Mam." He indicated the tray.

Vi took a deep breath. "Can I come up and talk to you both?"

"Of course you can, love. It might do Mam good. I've been trying to persuade her to get up, but she's not having any of it." Alf added another cup and saucer to the tray. "There's enough in the pot, come up with me now."

Alf went into the room ahead of Vi. "Our Vi's come up too," he said, as though speaking to a child.

It was only a couple of days since Vi had seen Billy's mam, but she was shocked by the change she saw. Elsie's cheeks looked hollow and sunken, and she seemed to have aged years in that time; there was none of the fight and spirit that Vi was used to seeing. She suspected that Alf's pampering might not be what was best for her mother-in-law, even though it was fuelled by his love and kindness. She also wondered if that was Dad's way of coping with the loss.

Vi sat on the edge of the bed. This wasn't going to be easy. "I know you didn't think I was good enough for Billy." Dad's face looked pained, but she ploughed on before she lost her nerve. "And I know you only had me living here because of him. I quite understand that now Billy's gone, you may not want me living here anymore. The thing is, Tommy and I have nowhere else to go right now. I can try to find something, but it might take a while. Could you give us a bit of time to sort ourselves out?" Vi realised her eyes had filled with tears and she felt cross with herself. She didn't want to show how hard this was for her.

Dad opened his mouth to speak, but it was Elsie who spoke first. Her face had become animated and alive compared to how it had been moments before.

"You'll do no such thing."

Vi was confused. She thought Elsie was saying she had to go immediately and was about to respond, to beg for longer if she had to.

Elsie continued. "You will not move out from living here. I think I can speak for Alf as well as myself when I say we want you and Tommy to stay and see this as your home."

Alf nodded, his eyebrows raised as though he was as surprised by this outburst as Vi was.

Elsie's jaw was set when she added, "You're our family now, you and Tommy. I may not have been as welcoming as I should have been, but we can't lose you too. You're all we have."

Vi looked at her mother-in-law. Did she mean the words she was saying? Concluding that she did, Vi said, "Thank you, that's a big relief. We want to be here." Vi moved along the bed and hugged Elsie.

After a brief time, Elsie pulled back. The fire seemed to be back in her eyes. "Just don't go getting any ideas about taking over. This is still our house, mine and Dad's." She turned to Alf. "Now, will you open those curtains for me, love. It's about time I was out of this bed."

Alf's eyes were wide with surprise, and as he went to the window he mouthed the words, "Thank you," to Vi, who smiled in reply.

Setting aside her biggest worry of where she and Tommy would live gave Vi room to grieve. In some ways, with Billy having been away over a year, nothing had changed. However, with the removal of hope everything had changed, and the future stretched away as a daunting void. Every day was a case of forcing herself to do even the most basic of tasks. If it hadn't been for Tommy, then she had no idea what she'd have done. He was starting school in a couple of weeks, and was disappointed that he wouldn't be with Bobby, but that couldn't be helped.

Tessie was full of all that was happening with the football. "Mr Giffard's trying to arrange a cup. There are some of the other factories who have women's teams who might want to play."

Vi smiled sadly. "That's good."

"Beattie Norris is taking your place up front, but she's not as good as you. And Nellie Pearce has joined the team. Please, won't you change your mind?"

Violet had lost count of the number of times Tessie had asked her. She missed the games and the closeness of the team, but it wouldn't be right. She still had a kickabout with Tommy when he asked, but he was more often busy playing with his own friends these days. She guessed that would be even more the case once he was out at school. "Have you seen our John?" Vi asked, changing the subject.

Tessie blushed. "He's taking me to the picture house on Saturday night."

Vi squeezed Tessie's arm. "That's wonderful. It is nice to hear something happy for a change."

When Tommy started school, Vi wished more than anything that Billy could have been there to see him. He looked so grown up all of a sudden. "Look at you. Your Dad would be so proud of you."

Having to find the money for some clothes for Tommy, given he'd grown out of the cast-offs he'd been wearing, had been one of the things that had kept Vi focussed on her work over the last few weeks. She needed to keep her job. It was so difficult to get answers out of the War Office on what she and Tommy would be entitled to.

"We have a match arranged in October," Tessie said as they walked home from work one day. "You will at least come and watch, won't you?"

Violet smiled. She could go with her Dad and John; they could take Tommy and Bobby. Maybe Billy's dad would like to go with them all, they'd all enjoy that. "Who are you playing?"

"A team's coming all the way from Blackpool." Tessie looked very proud.

Violet stopped. "Billy said when he came back, he'd take us all to Blackpool for the day."

"You could still go one day, take Tommy."

"It wouldn't be the same. I'm not sure I could." How Violet missed the companionship. She didn't have much confidence doing things like that on her own.

Every day Vi and the girls at work would go through the newspaper looking for the lists of those killed or wounded and any news they could glean. Occasionally it was through the paper that one of the girls would first find the fate of one of her relatives, but there had still been nothing about Stan.

When the day of the football match arrived Violet was excited; it would be the first time she'd watched from the stands. She hadn't talked about the game at home, and hadn't even told Tommy she'd be watching rather than playing.

"Why aren't you down there?" Tommy asked as they took their places on the terraces.

"Because your Mam would rather be up here with us today," his granddad said.

Her dad looked at Vi kindly and she smiled.

In the end, Billy's dad hadn't gone. She did ask him, but he said he'd rather stay at home with Elsie. Vi suspected he just couldn't face the fight it might lead to if he went.

Violet enjoyed watching the game and commenting on it to her dad. "Oh, Beattie shouldn't have missed that. She hasn't found any space. She'd have been better to pass it back to Tessie."

"Is that what you'd have done, love?" her father asked.

"Well, I'd want to swap Clara around with Florrie for a start — I think she's better on the left. Then I'd make Beattie do some practice on losing the person marking her. I'd…"

Her father chuckled.

"What?"

"And you wonder why the girls say they're missing you?" He shook his head.

The team from Blackpool beat the Caulder and Harrison team by three goals to nil, and as they walked home Tommy said, "It isn't so much fun watching when you aren't playing."

"It might be if they won," his granddad said.

Violet couldn't wait to read the newspaper report of the match. She wanted to see if their correspondent's thoughts on the game, with his greater experience, were the same as hers. When she did read it she was back at the Dobsons' house, and despite her intention to avoid any mention of the game, she couldn't contain herself.

"Have you seen this? All the practice they've done, and the paper still only talks about what they were wearing and what nice girls they are. What about the football? What about all the money they've raised for the hospital?" She stopped, realising where she was.

"Yes," Elsie Dobson spoke sternly. "I wanted a word with you about that."

"Mam, I didn't play. I've given up. You don't need to say anything."

"Don't I, young lady?"

Violet could tell from her tone that this wasn't going to be good, and wished more than anything that she'd kept to not saying a word.

"Why isn't your name listed amongst the players? That's what I want to know." Elsie was standing hands on hips in front of her.

"Excuse me?" Violet was blinking fast. Elsie must think she'd used an assumed name.

"I asked, young lady, why you were not playing in the football match. I'm told you're rather good and that they might have won if you'd been on the team. Our Billy was proud of you playing football and raising money for the hospital. Is that really any way to honour him now he's dead? Are you just going to stand back and see your team lose?"

Elsie was serious. Violet couldn't help but burst out laughing. Her mother-in-law was actually cross with her for not playing, after all she'd said before.

"But I thought…"

"That was before. You should be playing as Violet Dobson and be proud of it." Elsie was still looking stern.

Violet was so happy that she couldn't stop herself. She hugged her mother-in-law and then kissed her cheek. "I don't know what to say."

"There's nothing you need to say, just get yourself back into the team."

Elsie marched out of the room and Violet stood shaking her head in wonder. Doing the ironing would give her time to think. She went into the kitchen to put the iron onto the stove to heat.

Of course she wanted to play, that wasn't in question. She didn't want to push one of the other girls out though, that wouldn't be fair; she was the one who'd left the team. There was the smell of scorching and she realised she'd left the iron on Alf's collar too long. She took it off quickly to see how bad the damage was. Folded over no one would see, or so she hoped.

She could at least start to practise with the girls again. She kept it as a secret for the next few days; there were no matches planned, so whether she would be on the team wasn't really an issue. The following Saturday, she wanted her return to be a surprise. She waited until Tessie had already left for practice and then followed a little way behind. As she walked, she felt nervous. Perhaps the rest of the team wouldn't be glad to see her back; it had been three months since she'd played. She suddenly wished she'd talked to them in advance.

"Vi?" Tessie said, when she saw her friend coming over to join them. "What are you doing here?" Then Tessie looked at the bag Vi was carrying. She gasped and jumped up and down. "Oh, do say you're playing again?"

Vi nodded and most of the girls cheered. The new ones looked confused, but they didn't know Vi, so that wasn't surprising. Even Joe Wood was delighted to see her arrive, and before long she was running along the pitch as though she'd never been away. She'd forgotten how good it felt to be out here.

"If there's a match arranged, I'm happy to start as a substitute. I don't want to take anyone's place," she told Joe.

"That's good of you, thank you. The younger girls can be difficult at the best of times."

From the pained expression on his face, Violet wondered just what had gone on in her absence and was surprised that Tessie hadn't said anything, unless of course she was the cause. She nodded but said nothing.

Discussions to start a women's football cup between a number of the factories were still in progress, but the following Monday Mr Giffard announced to the team that a return match at Blackpool had been arranged for the following month.

"I know I said I'd start as a substitute," Vi said to Joe Wood, "but I can't — I'm sorry. I'm not ready. I can't face going to Blackpool, not without Billy." She had to walk away; even after more than three months she just couldn't talk about it. Maybe one day she'd go to Blackpool and take Tommy, but that would be a while off yet.

As she returned to her bench to work that afternoon, she felt overwhelmed by a fresh wave of grief. Packing the shells with explosives, she couldn't help but wonder what other families might be left without a husband, father, son or friend as a result of each one of them. Would this war never be over? She tried to keep hold of the thought that the shells would help the Allies to finish the war. If the troops weren't well equipped, there'd be far more families in the position she was in now, and that thought was unbearable.

CHAPTER 25

I lie awake from six o'clock
Waiting for his welcome knock
Just to read what my pal writes
'Cos I think about him all the days and all the nights
And sometimes he will pass you see
And look and say there's none for me
Then I say, 'Now, can't you find me one?'
And look with great surprise
'If it's only just a little one
Well, I don't mind the size.'
Good Morning Mr. Postman - Paul Pelham & Herbert Rule - 1908

2nd November 1916 - Allies Make Another Successful Move on Somme - The Daily Mirror

"Oh, Vi, you should have seen her." Tessie had come rushing straight to the Dobsons' house the minute she came back from the match at Blackpool. "She was lying there with her leg at the oddest angle. It looked awful — Clara felt quite faint just seeing it. How Florrie coped with the pain, I don't know. They had to put her onto a stretcher and carry her off."

"Will she be all right?" Violet was finding the news of Florrie's broken leg hard to take in.

"She's going to be off work for a few weeks, but Mr

Giffard says they'll still pay her, otherwise he wouldn't find any of us to play. I suppose it'll be a long time before she's fit again."

Violet nodded, relieved that she would still be paid. She couldn't afford to be off work, and she presumed the same would be true for Florrie.

"Anyway, Florrie said to tell you that you'll have to take her place — at least until she's back on her feet. Well, I think that's what she was saying. There was the odd groan in the middle of it." Tessie laughed at the recollection. "I bet it'll be in the papers. She was ever so brave."

"I'll go round and see her, try to cheer her up. You could come too." It felt strange to Vi hearing about the events after they'd happened.

"You will play now, won't you?" Tessie looked anxious as she spoke.

Vi smiled and nodded. "I just couldn't face going to Blackpool yet." Maybe one day she'd go, when she was ready.

They went to see Florrie the following afternoon.

"You know," Florrie said, "if this is how much it hurts just to break my leg, I can't imagine how awful it must have been for some of the soldiers. Did Tessie tell you, a few of the men from the Blackpool hospital were brought to see the match?"

"They did look smart in their uniforms," Tessie said. "It's a shame you didn't meet them afterwards, Florrie. There was one who was ever so handsome."

"Tessie, what about our John?" Vi was horrified by what her friend was saying.

"None of them were as good looking as John, silly. I was just thinking that it was time we found someone for

Florrie."

Violet relaxed. Tessie seemed to mean what she was saying, which was good. Vi had quite grown to like the idea that one day Tessie might be part of the family, but maybe her thoughts were running away with her.

It was strange at work without Florrie there; Vi hadn't realised how fond of the girl she'd become. She'd grown close to most of the other team members while she was playing football and had missed that over the last few months. It was good to be part of the team, not just for the fresh air and exercise, or even the fact she loved playing, but because of the bond between them all. Florrie would miss that over the next few weeks. Vi resolved to go over to see her as often as she could during her recovery.

Now that it looked as though there would be more games, the girls started training regularly. There were still few men's football matches being played, and the women's games proved popular, even though they were friendlies. One of the things which spurred them on was that the more often they played, the more they could raise for the hospital.

Mr Giffard arranged their next match for three weeks later, and this time Violet would be in the starting lineup. For the first time she would be playing using her married name, and she felt quite excited about that.

She pressed her football shirt. She wanted to look her best; not in a way to attract attention, but to be smart and look professional. She was proud of their team and knew that the other girls felt the same.

"Would you like to come to the match, Mam?" she asked Elsie as they were having tea one evening. Vi had been waiting to find the right moment to ask, but realised she simply had to do it.

Elsie looked up, wide-eyed. "Oh, I don't think I could do that." She looked across at Alf.

He looked as though he had no idea what was the right thing to say, and Vi stifled a giggle.

Elsie put her knife and fork down. "No, I don't think so. I'm sure Alf can tell me everything that happens."

That at least was progress. Vi could see a curl of a smile on Alf's face. She was delighted that this time he could watch her play without any subterfuge.

When match day arrived, Violet felt a surge of excitement knowing so many of her family would be on the Whittingham Road terraces to watch the match. It was funny now, regarding Billingbrook United as their 'home' ground.

This time it was a team from Calderley who were the opposition. As the crowds cheered them onto the pitch, it felt good to be back. Whilst Violet had lost none of her fitness in the last few months, and she could still keep up with any of the younger girls, she was impressed by how much some of the others had improved. They were playing more as a team and by half time were leading by two goals to one, with the opening goal scored by Violet.

The second half was slower and both teams were keen not to concede any more goals. The crowds cheered every play and often men whistled when the girls went close to their areas of the stand. Some of the younger girls called back to the banter that was shouted down to them, or gave a little wiggle, acknowledging that they'd heard a compliment. Violet sighed. It was no wonder the newspapers forgot to report on the games themselves, but she couldn't blame the girls; maybe she'd have done the same when she was younger, if she'd had the confidence.

The score was standing at three goals to two in Billingbrook's favour, when in the final minutes of the game Clara passed the ball to Violet. There was an open field ahead of Vi and she had a clear path to the goal. This could give them a convincing win. Violet could see that Clara had moved up the field, but decided to take it all the way if she could. She had a good view of the goal and was about to shoot, when one of the Calderley players brought her down in a ferocious tackle. Violet was expecting the referee to blow the whistle — it was a penalty. Violet stood up slowly and turned to where she presumed the ball would be. She was confused; the referee had let them play on. It had been a foul, there was no question.

The Calderley girls had already moved the ball down to the other end of the pitch, as the rest of Vi's team had assumed the same as she had.

Violet watched as though it was happening step by step, as the Calderley player sent the ball rocketing toward the corner of the goal. Edith came forward, but the ball sailed straight past her and into the net as the referee blew for full time.

The match had finished as a draw and to Violet's horror an argument broke out amongst the girls. This was not what she wanted to see the newspapers reporting; if Elsie Dobson read this, she would have Violet's guts for garters. Violet marched over to the others and stood between the two teams. She positioned herself in front of the Calderley player who had committed the foul.

Vi held out her hand to the girl and the others fell silent. The Calderley player was hesitant to hold out her own hand to shake Violet's, clearly wondering what Vi was going to do.

As they shook, in a very clear voice Violet said, "If this is the way we behave, the newspapers will never take our football seriously. Next time, I hope the best team wins." She'd made her point, and as she turned away no one spoke. Vi's team followed her to the changing room where she sat down on a bench, shaking from head to toe.

"Did you really just do that?" Tessie asked. "I thought you were going to sock her one."

"Perhaps she should have done," Eva shouted. "I nearly did it for you." Then she started laughing, and before they knew it the girls were all in uncontrollable laughter, although none of them knew quite why.

"You should have come, love," Alf said to Elsie that evening when they were all back at home.

Tommy looked at his grandma with concern. "Why can't grandmas watch football?"

Vi stopped at his words. It might be the women playing, but it was still only the men of the family who were watching. She hadn't even thought about asking her own mother and sisters to watch.

"Of course they can watch." Elsie said it as soon as Tommy had spoken.

Vi didn't fancy the chances of anyone telling Elsie she couldn't do something, and wondered if this might be enough reason for her mother-in-law to come to the next match.

"I could take you," Tommy said earnestly.

Even Elsie smiled at that. "Then perhaps I should let you do that the next time your mam plays."

Thankfully the newspaper was brief in its mention of the confrontation. Violet was pleased with the report that they'd been robbed of the game and that *'a penalty should have been given to Mrs V. Dobson when she was brought down in the penalty area'*. Finally, the *Mercury* was beginning to talk about the game, even if it had taken an extreme circumstance for that to happen.

Tessie had taken to walking over to Vi's parents with her on a Sunday afternoon. She and John were still enjoying each other's company, and Vi's parents were as happy about it as Vi was.

"At least he's not so likely to sign up early," Mam said while Vi was having a cuppa and Tessie and John had gone for a walk. "I'm hoping this war's over by the time he turns eighteen."

"I'm hoping it's over before he's seventeen," Vi said. "That still gives us another few months. Surely it has to end soon."

When Tessie came back in, her cheeks flushed and her eyes bright, Vi thought back to the days when she and Billy had been courting. It was lovely to see the same in two people she cared so much about.

There was no letup in the orders for shells from the factory, and Vi's days passed quickly trying to keep up with what was asked of them. She could have worked extra hours, but she decided the time with Tommy was more important. Besides, now she wasn't saving to move out, there was less need for the extra money.

The highlight of the day was having a kickabout in the yard, and the best times were their football training sessions at the recreation ground.

"The newspaper would like to do a report on how the money is helping the hospital," Mr Giffard said when he'd called the girls together at the following week's practice. "They want to send a photographer to take a picture of us handing over the latest cheque."

"Are we all going?" Eva asked.

"We should take Florrie too. She'd fit right in on her crutches," Edith said.

Mr Giffard cleared his throat to bring the girls back to order. "I'd like Violet to be the one to do the presentation, if that's all right with everyone." He looked around for agreement.

Violet's eyes widened. "Me? I couldn't do something like that. I…"

"Whyever not?" Mr Giffard was frowning. "I thought…" He hesitated. "Well, what with your husband…"

Violet nodded. He was right, Billy would want her to do this, but she was much happier to be part of the crowd. "But everyone will be looking at me. I won't know what to do."

"Go on, Vi." Tessie nudged her. "If you can stand up to that Calderley girl, you can do anything."

Vi frowned. "That was different. I'm not quite sure how, but it was." She looked around at the eager faces. "All right. I'll do it." She felt nervous even thinking about it.

Vi was very glad the other girls were all there for support when they went to Billingbrook Hall. When she'd mentioned it at home, she almost thought Elsie was going to ask to come too; it was funny seeing her mother-in-law impressed.

Vi had only ever peeped over the wall into the grounds before. Even though she knew it was now a hospital, and not the grand house it once had been, she still felt she should be going to the servants' entrance.

It was a fine but cool November day, and the first thing which struck her as she neared the hall was the number of servicemen in wheelchairs or sitting on benches with blankets wrapped around their knees. It wasn't the men themselves, it was the bandages covering every conceivable part of their bodies, and in many cases the absent parts. Perhaps Billy would have been happier to die than to end like one of these; he'd never have been satisfied if he couldn't run after a ball with Tommy, or go to the pub under his own steam. She shuddered and tried to put Billy out of her mind, impossible as that was. She didn't want to break down this afternoon; she wanted to do a good job for Caulder and Harrison. She wanted Mr Giffard to be proud, not just of her but of the entire team. She took a deep breath and focussed on the house itself.

They were all quiet. Each of them she supposed was wondering if there were servicemen here that they knew. There were probably lads who'd been to the local school at the same time as some of the girls, although the classes had all been separate after the first couple of years.

"Have you seen this?" Edith was standing open-mouthed in front of a large oil painting in the entrance hall of the house. "Can you imagine having something that big in your home?"

"Can you imagine having a home big enough to put it in?" Eva did a little twirl as though she were dressed in fancy clothes. "The whole of our house would fit in this hallway."

"More than once," Beattie said. "I bet they don't share a privy with half the road."

They all laughed.

"Or do their own cleaning," Vi said, imagining how many people that might take.

From the entrance, they were led through a large room where all the furniture had been moved aside to make way for hospital beds, with small screens separating them from each other.

Violet felt sick at the thought of so many wounded, even though she realised this was comparatively few of the total number. She was glad when they went out of the other end of the ward into a bright and well-lit library, where the newspaper photographer was already waiting for them.

Violet recognised the very upright and smartly dressed army officer who walked briskly in their direction. He had been the one who had been photographed with them at the training ground. Major Tomlinson held out his hand to Mr Giffard. "I'm delighted you and the gals could join us. I'm sure it will brighten the day of our patients to see some pretty faces around here. Don't tell Sister I said that." He winked at Vi and his eyes sparkled.

After the Major had made some introductions, they stood in front of a floor-to-ceiling bookcase while Violet presented the cheque. Her hand was shaking as she waited for the photographer to take the picture and she hoped it wouldn't show.

"Now that's out of the way, I thought your gals might like to have tea with some of our walking wounded."

The major was clearly not someone who took 'no' for an answer, and without waiting for a reply he led the way into the neighbouring dining room, expecting them to follow.

There were small tables around the room, rather than the big dining table that Violet had imagined a house like this would have. Whilst there were some soldiers standing, others were sitting at the tables looking eager for the girls to join them.

"Spread yourselves out," the major commanded. "We'll serve tea to you at the tables."

The girls looked at each other and giggled. Vi had little time to think about the fact that she was expected to talk to a complete stranger, as she was guided toward a table near the bay window. Two men were seated there, and one pushed himself up to standing as she approached.

"Forgive me if I don't get up." The other indicated his missing legs as he wheeled himself slightly away from the table. "I'm told I'll be given prosthetics once I've healed sufficiently." He held his hand out to shake hers. "Private Gibbins."

Violet introduced herself to Private Gibbins and to the other gentleman, a Sergeant Holdsworth.

She let the men lead the conversation and, whilst she introduced herself as Mrs Dobson, she said nothing of what had happened to Billy. She couldn't bring herself to talk about it to men who had seen the sorts of things which might have led to Billy's death. She drank her tea as she listened, but didn't feel much like taking a sandwich or a slice of the sponge cake that was on the table.

"It's a damn fine thing your team is doing," said a lieutenant who had come over to check everything was all right. "Have you told her, Gibbins?"

"It's thanks to you I'll be getting my new legs." Private Gibbins spoke quietly, as though far away.

Violet was moved by seeing the gratitude of the men. These men had given so much, and what she and the girls were doing seemed so little in comparison.

She enjoyed the opportunity to talk about the football and how the idea had begun, as well as the funnier moments they'd had; such as the dog walker who, when they were training, had said their husbands should have them under better control.

"Perhaps the more able-bodied might attend some of the matches, like the soldiers in Blackpool did," she suggested to Mr Giffard as they left that afternoon.

"Excellent suggestion." The major was just ahead of them when she'd said it. He turned around to her. "Do you think some of you gals would visit again? I rather think it's done the men good."

Violet could feel herself blushing as the major looked at her. "I'm not sure."

"Husband wouldn't like it, hey? Not to worry."

Vi felt the tears coming to her eyes. "No, Major, my husband died in battle. Seeing the men has been very difficult."

Vi walked briskly away from where the group was standing. She didn't want them to see her cry.

She stood facing the trees and took a few deep breaths. She shouldn't have said that, it wasn't the major's fault.

"Are you all right?"

Vi turned to see the lieutenant standing there.

"I'm sorry, I overheard what you said. We didn't realise — the major can be a bit of a brute at times. Your visit has done the men good, it would be marvellous if you could see your way to coming back — but of course, we'll quite understand if you won't."

Vi looked at the kindness in his eyes. "I'm sorry — I'll think about it. I'd better apologise to Major Tomlinson, he must think me very rude."

"I wouldn't worry about the major. He upsets people all the time and rarely notices." He laughed.

They walked back toward the group and the major was still talking as though he hadn't even realised she'd gone.

"Thank you," Vi said to the lieutenant. "I'll think about coming back. Maybe it would do me good too."

CHAPTER 26

Once upon a time I loved a chap called Jim
He wasn't werry 'andsome, but I took a like to 'im
And vough that is some time ago, a tear comes to my eye
To fink as how when fust we met, to court me he did try.
*He Didn't Seem to Know Just What to Say - Harry Pleon 1861
- 1911 (words as original song)*

*11 December 1916 - Business Men in Mr. Lloyd George's New
Cabinet - Lord Devonport to be the New Food Controller - The
Daily Mirror*

"I'm sorry, Mam, but I said I'd go." Vi didn't want to have
to justify herself to Elsie. She just wanted to do a good
deed, there was no more to it than that.

"And what about our Billy?"

Elsie was looking at her with such fierceness that Vi
wanted to step further away. She counted to ten silently.
How could she say to Elsie that Billy had been dead for
nearly six months? Besides which, she was only visiting
the soldiers out of kindness. What did Elsie think she was
doing?

Vi had a thought. "Mam, you could come with me. We
could both go."

Elsie gasped. "I'm not doing that. I don't think you
should either."

Vi took a deep breath. "Look, Mam, I still love Billy as

much as I always did. Besides anything else, he'll always be Tommy's father. I don't want another man in my life, that's not why I'm going to visit. I just want to help if I can. Tessie's coming too and she's walking out with our John. There are six of us girls going, just to have a cup of tea and to brighten their day."

Elsie deflated into a chair and Vi sighed. She was already going to be late and felt exhausted before she'd started. She felt bad that Elsie was likely to spend the afternoon being miserable, but she had to go.

Vi went out of the back gate to the road.

"I thought you were never coming. I nearly knocked," Tessie said, linking her arm through Vi's.

"It's good you didn't, I was having a bit of a ding dong with Elsie again. The rate things are going, I may end up having to find somewhere else to live. I just can't live my life the way she wants me to — she'd have me wearing widow's weeds for the next fifty years."

Until the argument with Elsie, Vi had been looking forward to going back to the hospital. The girls had decided it would be easier if they could sit at the tables in twos; then if conversation was difficult, they'd at least have each other for moral support.

One of the Voluntary Aid Detachment nurses led Vi and Tessie to a table near a large picture window, looking out onto the grounds. Vi couldn't stop looking out. She would love to live somewhere which had views of greenery instead of more terraced housing.

"It's beautiful, isn't it," the soldier seated at the table said. "If I have to convalesce somewhere, then it's not such a bad place to be."

"Do you live locally?" Tessie asked.

Vi was grateful that Tessie could strike up a

conversation with anyone, as she never knew where to start.

"Over near Garstang. It's a bit far for my family to come to visit. I'll be glad when I can go home."

They talked about families and places and what the men had done before the war. They'd just moved on to talking about the football when Matron came over.

"There was one of the soldiers asking after you following your last visit. Poor man, he's one of our long-term patients — terrible injuries. I thought talking to you might cheer him up. I told him you'd be here this afternoon, but I can't find him anywhere. Perhaps he's lost track of time. He can't have gone far, I'm sure I'll find him. Can I ask someone to bring more tea over to you while I have another look for Private Bradley?"

"Bradley?" Violet froze. "Not Stanley Bradley? About my age, local?"

"I couldn't tell you about his background without looking at the records, but his name's Stanley all right."

Violet felt the colour drain from her face. "He's alive?"

"Well, he wouldn't be here otherwise." Matron shook her head as though she were talking to a child who wasn't understanding her.

Stan was alive. Why hadn't he been in touch? Violet didn't know how she felt. In part she was angry. How come her Billy had died but Stan was alive? It wasn't fair, Billy should be alive too. But there was part of her that was delighted and wanted to talk to him, wanted to know about all the time Billy had been away. She realised the matron was still talking.

"He can't have gone far. He has difficulty wheeling the chair without someone to help."

Chair. Long term. Vi started to piece together the things

Matron had said. "How seriously injured is he?"

Matron pulled a face. "It's a miracle he's with us at all. I've no idea what will happen when he has to leave our care."

Violet nodded and wondered about Stan's brothers and sisters.

She no longer felt like talking to the men at the table while she waited for Matron to come back. She wanted to be on her own so she could take in what Matron had said.

"Have you known Private Bradley long?" one of the soldiers at the table asked.

Vi tried to focus. "Pardon? Oh, sorry, yes. Most of my life. He was…" She didn't want to say 'my husband's best friend'. She didn't want them asking her about Billy. "He was at school at the same time."

Tessie must have seen her discomfort and took over the conversation. After a while Vi looked at the clock; they had already been there longer than they'd planned, and she knew that Tessie was supposed to be meeting John that evening. There was no sign of Matron.

Edith and Eva were getting up from the table they'd been sitting at, so Vi took her cue from them. "I'm afraid we need to be leaving, but it's been lovely meeting you."

"Thank you for coming." One of the men got up from the table. "Can I help you with your coats?"

They were just saying their goodbyes when Matron marched over to them.

"Most peculiar, there's no sign of him at all. I just can't think where he can be. Would you be free to come again next Saturday, so that I can have him ready to see you? I wouldn't bother you, but it would do him so much good to have something to look forward to."

Of course Violet wanted to see Stan. "I could come

sooner, if that helps? Tomorrow, maybe?"

"We're a little short of staff at the moment. Next Saturday would be best if you could make it?"

Violet nodded.

"If you're here for two o'clock sharp, then I'll make sure Private Bradley is comfortably seated ready for you." Matron nodded to Vi and then turned to go back to her work.

There were many things Vi wanted to ask Stan about Billy, but it would be good to see him even without that; he'd been an important part of their lives for so long. Tommy would be desperate to see his uncle Stan, but it might be best for Vi to see Stan on her own first. She had no way of knowing if Stan was ready to cope with a visit from a bouncing five-year-old. It made fundraising all the more important to her. She wasn't sure if she should tell Alf and Elsie, but they'd been fond of Stan, they'd want to know.

It was already the start of December and Violet was glad it was going to be a busy month. Tommy seemed to deal with his dad not being around better than she had expected, but she knew Christmas without him would be hard for all of them. It had been difficult enough the previous year when they at least knew he was still alive. She would be glad not to have too much time to think. The football match on Boxing Day was something to look forward to, especially because it would be the first time that the whole family would be going to watch. She hoped that Elsie would at least be polite to Violet's own mother, even if they didn't have much in common, other than her and Tommy.

In the time before Christmas, Vi had presents to make as well as being busy at the factory. There was no letup in demand for shells; munitions were needed for the Front as much as they had been all year. There was no sign of the war being over. Even the previous Prime Minister's son had been lost in battle. Everyone was suffering.

Vi didn't want to take on extra hours unless she had to; her time with Tommy was too precious. She was grateful that they were still given some time on a Wednesday for the football team to practise. That really helped.

It was lunchtime when she finished work the following Saturday. Tommy would spend the afternoon playing with friends and she didn't feel like going back to Ivy Terrace to sit with her in-laws, or worse still, in her bedroom on her own. She wasn't due at the hospital until two o'clock, so she had over an hour to spare. She headed for the warmth of the library. She could always read the newspaper if nothing else.

Mr Lloyd George had taken over as Prime Minister that week and the political parties seemed to be agreeing to work together. Vi didn't really understand much about politics, but presumed working together would be a good thing.

She turned to the sports pages to see if there were any women's sports being reported, but could find nothing. She left the comfort of the library and went out into the grey December day.

There was a brisk wind and Vi was cold by the time she arrived at Billingbrook Hall. She felt nervous about the prospect of seeing Stan; she wondered how disfigured he might be and didn't want to offend him in any way. What if she couldn't bring herself to look at him?

By the time she reached the hospital, Violet was apprehensive. She was punctual and Matron was waiting for her.

"He should be right here." Matron marched across the hall to the dining room once again. She stopped abruptly. "He was just there only ten minutes ago." She pointed to the table. "I wheeled him in myself." Matron turned to the men at a neighbouring table. "Has anyone seen Private Bradley?"

If they did know where he'd gone, none of them broke ranks. Whilst Violet sat on the edge of a chair and talked to the men, Matron went off in search of her errant charge.

"Now why would Bradley want to hide from a lovely lady like you?"

The soldier winked at her.

Vi moved her chair a little further away from the man. Why indeed? It was what Violet was wondering. Much as Stan was a joker, he would want to see her, wouldn't he? She talked politely to the men at the table for half an hour before Matron came back, looking red-faced and confused.

"Very strange. No one seems to have seen him. He can't have gone far. I don't know what to suggest."

"He's in a pretty bad way," one of the soldiers said. "I don't blame him for not wanting to be seen by someone such as yourself."

Violet blushed at the implied compliment. She'd seen some of the other patients in the hospital and she thought she could deal with seeing Stan; besides, she cared about him. What a pity that he couldn't face seeing her. He must be terribly sad and lonely.

Walking home that afternoon, Violet wondered what to do. She would like to see Stan, but perhaps she should write to him first. She thought about the fact that there were only two more Saturdays until Christmas and wanted to take a present to the hospital for him. She could always leave a note with the gift. The present should be something that showed she cared, and she'd given some thought to what he'd like; Billy would have wanted her to do that. She turned her thoughts to what to take. The boys had appreciated her fruitcakes most whilst they were in France; at least that was what Billy said when he wrote to her. It was something Stan could share with the other soldiers if he wanted to.

Violet still didn't want to tell Elsie what she was doing. She knew Billy's mam would be full of questions if she knew that Stan was alive; until she'd seen him, Violet didn't want to face a barrage of things it would be impossible for her to answer. She found the time and money to buy the ingredients for two cakes. One she would bake for the Dobsons and the other she would take to Stan; at least that way the smell of the cake cooking would be accounted for, as long as Elsie didn't open the oven door to see them both. It just meant staying up late to take the cakes out of the oven, but that was a small price to pay.

Vi was working again the next Saturday morning, but went straight to the hospital when the shift finished at twelve noon. Arriving at lunchtime might mean Stan would be easy to find. She hadn't made any arrangement with Matron, hoping that if she turned up unannounced, there would be no opportunity for Stan to disappear, but had written a note just in case.

She felt silly worrying about how she looked, given that Stan was unlikely to be concerned by that. She'd taken a sandwich with her to eat for lunch, but couldn't face it. She felt sick as it was. Walking up the driveway, Vi tried to think of the words that she would say if she saw him. How might she convince him to talk to her? Nothing seemed quite the right starting point.

By the time she reached the entrance, Violet was having doubts about arriving unannounced. Perhaps she should go home again and post the letter to him. She was just about to turn around when one of the Voluntary Aid Detachment nurses was coming out through the front door and held it open for her to go in. Feeling as though she didn't have any option, Vi thanked the girl and stepped inside.

She'd only gone a pace or two when a soldier on crutches spotted her. "It's Mrs Dobson, isn't it? We talked when you came to do the presentation." He held out his hand to shake hers.

Floundering to recollect the man's name, Vi struggled to keep hold of the tin whilst shaking his hand.

The soldier smiled. "Private Hanley."

"Ah yes, of course. I'm sorry, I was miles away." She looked all around the hall in case she spotted Stan; not that she was sure she'd recognise him from what Matron had said.

"Are you looking for someone in particular?"

"Pardon? Oh yes, sorry. I'm looking for Private Bradley — well, actually, I was looking for Matron. I thought she might take me to Private Bradley."

Private Hanley gave a sharp intake of breath and shook his head. "He doesn't seem to want to talk to anyone very much. Maybe it will be different with you. I'll see if I can find him. Follow me."

"Please, don't go to any trouble. If you can tell me where to go, I'm sure I can manage." Violet looked at the poor man's crutches as he made slow progress.

He turned to face her. "I need to do some practice. I'll be going home next week, and I can't expect Mam to run around after me."

Violet wondered how old he was. From how he'd spoken he'd seemed older, but now she came to look at him, he couldn't have been more than a teenager. She nodded and followed behind so as not to be in the way of the crutches as he moved.

He went over to a figure sitting hunched in his wheelchair, alone in the corner of the room. "Bradley, you have a visitor." He paused with his weight on his crutch and indicated with his hand that Violet should approach.

She clutched the tin close to her coat and took a tentative step. The man in the chair did not turn around.

Violet almost tiptoed forward. "Stan," she said quietly, as she might to a frightened animal. "It's me, Violet." She saw the man stiffen and wondered what to do next. There was an empty chair close by which she could move across next to him; she thought that might be best. She put the tin on the table in front of him. "I brought you a present. It's not much, but Billy used to say you liked it."

The man gave a start and Violet frowned. He put his remaining hand down to the wheel of the chair as though to move out of the way.

"Please, don't go." Violet didn't know what to say. If he didn't want to see her then there was little she could do, but he was her closest link to Billy and she wanted to talk to him. She wanted to help him; for Billy's sake, she wanted to help.

His head was down, but as he tried to manoeuvre the chair he looked up. Violet saw his face clearly and gasped. Her hands went to her mouth and she fell back into the chair she'd moved over. She had to be wrong about what she'd seen. It just wasn't possible.

As the man continued to move the chair away, he knocked the table over and the cake tin went clattering along the floor. Several of the soldiers around the room ducked or moved away at the noise.

The man in the chair gave up, defeated, as Matron came over to see what was happening.

"Is there a problem here?" she asked. "Ah, Mrs Dobson, you've found him at last, I see."

Violet nodded mutely.

"Take me away," the man muttered as he tried once again to move the chair.

Violet was desperate. "No, you can't go. You can't."

Then he looked at her properly. "I didn't want you to see this. Why do you think I didn't get in touch? I'm not fit for anyone to see — it would have been better if I had died along with all the others. What right do I have to live when they lost their lives? I should have died alongside them. And look at me, what's the point?"

"I'm sorry, Mrs Dobson. Rather than helping, your visit is causing my patient too much distress. I think you'd better leave Private Bradley in peace."

Violet was shaking and struggled to get any words out. "No, Matron, I can't go. You see, he's not Private Bradley."

CHAPTER 27

All at once he sent me round a note
Here's the very note, and this is what he wrote
"Can't get away to marry you today,
My wife won't let me".
Waiting at the Church - Fred W. Leigh 1906

16th December 1916 - Thrice Wounded V.C.: Utter Contempt for Danger - The Daily Mirror

Matron stared at Violet. "Whatever do you mean? Of course he's Private Bradley. Why would he tell us that if he were someone else? And why would he have been wearing Private Bradley's army dog tag?"

Even through the scarring Violet could see he was frowning at her. She scanned the face, wanting to be sure; he was so disfigured that it would be hard to be certain except for one thing. It was the eyes. Stan's eyes were paler; Stan's eyes were more grey than green in colour. There might only have been an inch difference in their heights, and of course Stan's hair had been darker — at least it was when they went away — but only one man she knew had those piercing green eyes.

"I don't know why, Matron, but I do know that this man here is Billy Dobson, my husband, and not Stanley Bradley. It is you, isn't it, Billy?" She dropped down on her knees in front of him and took his hand in hers. She looked intently into the eyes and saw the pain, saw the shame, saw her own darling Billy.

Matron didn't miss a beat. She'd clearly seen a great deal in her days of nursing and calmly took hold of the handles at the back of the chair. "I think you may need to do a lot of explaining and it would be rather better in my office." She began to wheel her charge. Violet gathered up her things and followed.

Matron asked for one of the volunteers to bring them some tea. Rather oddly, Violet found herself worrying about where the fruitcake had gone and in her nervous state she almost laughed at the absurdity. Once they were sitting in Matron's office, Violet looked at Billy once again. She wanted to take his hand, but there was only a bandaged stump on her side. She bit her lip. Where on earth could they start?

Thankfully, Matron seemed unfazed by the situation and took charge. "Private Bradley or Dobson, whichever it is, this has clearly come as rather a shock to all parties, and I think it might be time for an explanation if you are able. You have been under my care for your physical disabilities for some time, but at no point have I had cause to doubt your mental capability. This does not look like a case of amnesia to me, and believe me, I have seen a few of those in my time."

Violet wanted to speak kindly and softly to Billy. She wanted to tell him that whatever happened, she still loved him, but maybe Matron's no-nonsense approach was the right one to take. Violet couldn't know what Billy had been through, what he was still going through. Perhaps Matron was owed as much of an explanation as she was, but she doubted the older woman was feeling any of the pain she was experiencing at the thought that her husband didn't want her anymore. And what of Tommy? Didn't he deserve a father, whatever state that father was in?

Matron was standing with her hands firmly on her desk and looking at Billy for a reply. Violet suspected it was a look which had reduced many a grown man to tears.

Billy didn't look up. As he began to speak, Violet realised that the scarring around his mouth must be uncomfortable and wanted to gently apply cream to soften the scars and help him heal.

"It was Stan's idea."

Violet groaned. It was always Stan's idea if there was trouble. No matter what it was, Billy followed along, ever since boyhood.

"We swapped dog tags the day before the battle."

When Billy hesitated, both Violet and Matron spoke at the same time. "Why?"

Billy's voice was unsteady as he continued. "I don't think Stan ever had any intention of coming back. He said if I came out of it alive, but the War Office thought I was dead, you'd receive a pension. I didn't think it through. You know me…" He shrugged and turned toward Vi for the first time. "I never really did think things through, I always trusted that Stan had it all worked out. So I agreed. I realised afterwards that I'd have to go on pretending to be him and it would all be very weird." He looked up sharply. "That wasn't why I carried on pretending to be Stan, I'd forgotten all about that. For all I knew, Stan might still be alive. I did it because I couldn't bear you to see me like this. I'm no use as a husband anymore."

At that point tea arrived. Billy looked grateful for the break as it was poured out. Once the nurse left the room, he went on without further prompting.

"By the time I had any idea what was going on around

me, several weeks had passed and you would have already been told I'd died… I wished I had. What kind of freak am I now? An arm gone, part of a leg, a face that's almost unrecognisable. I'm not Billy Dobson anymore. You're better off without me. You have the chance to move on. I didn't think you'd want me like this. I'm only ever going to be a burden to you."

"We made vows, Billy. For bloody better or worse, and I meant every word. When I said I loved you, when I said 'I do', that's what I took you for — better or worse, sickness and health. 'As long as we both shall live'."

Billy was quiet for a moment. Then he looked up, and with tears in his eyes said, "You promised to obey." He swallowed. "I'm telling you to leave here now and not look back. Find someone new who can give you more children, someone who can take care of you and who doesn't need nursing."

Violet balled her fists and brought them down hard on the edge of Matron's desk, causing the ink stand to jump. "Then I'm going to do something I never thought I'd do. I'm going to break one of my wedding vows and that's the one I'm going to break. You'd better get used to it, Billy Dobson, because if you talk nonsense I won't obey you now, and I won't obey you in the future. I'm taking you home so I can nurse you and love you and spend the rest of my life with you, and nothing and no one is going to stop me. Least of all you."

Matron coughed. "Fine words indeed, Mrs Dobson, but actually for the moment it will be me stopping you. Private Dobson is not ready to be discharged. The surgeon still wants to operate on him to reconstruct his nose, and he has a prosthetic leg to be fitted and some work to do on rehabilitation. It shouldn't be too much longer that he has to stay with us, but for the time being he needs to remain resident here at Billingbrook Hall."

Violet sat down, anxious that she might have said too much. "Yes, of course, Matron. I'm sorry. I didn't mean…"

Matron waved her hand in a gesture that suggested no apology was needed, and Violet turned back to Billy. "I love you." She moved closer to him and put her arm around him.

Billy lay his head on her shoulder, all the fight gone out of him and wept. "You're a good woman, Violet, you know I love you. But I'll only ever be a burden."

"I'll be the judge of that." She stroked his hair with her free hand and then tentatively ran a finger down the scarring on his face. "I will love you to my dying day. I've always loved you." After a few moments had passed, she added, "I'm sorry about Stan."

Billy nodded.

Violet hadn't noticed Matron leaving the room; surprising really as she was not a small woman. However, when she returned she was carrying the cake tin, as well as a folder of papers. She put the tin down on the mahogany desk, which Violet could only assume was part of the Hall's original furnishings and not standard army issue.

"I thought this might help whilst we go through some paperwork." Matron took the lid off the tin, clearly thinking she had as much right to a slice as anyone in the circumstances. "I've seen a lot of things in my time, but this is a first. I will need to notify the War Office, and no doubt there will be one or two complications."

"I need to tell Billy's mam and dad too — and our son, Tommy. I'd like to bring Tommy to see his Dad if that's allowed."

Billy shrank away from her. "He can't see me like this."

Matron shook her head. "And how else do you think he's going to see you? The reconstruction will help, but trust me — children are resilient. How old is he?"

"He'll be six in March," Violet replied.

Billy turned to face her. He was staring. "Tommy was only just four when I went away. It's best he forgets me."

"Private Dobson, your wife has made quite clear that you are to stop talking like that, and frankly I think she's right. Children of that age cope with far more than we ever expect them to. I suspect seeing him will do you the world of good. He at least still has a father — thousands haven't. We'll find a side room for you to meet in, I don't want the boy running around where the other patients are. Perhaps you should bring him on Christmas Day."

"But that's only just over a week away. I'm not ready." Billy sounded horrified.

"Private Dobson, if this was left to your timing, I fear you'd never be ready. I will be guided by your good wife." Matron opened the file on the desk and began going through the papers which had related to Private Stanley Bradley. She took up the pen and began to write some notes.

"Now," Matron said, looking up from her papers. "I'm sure you two would like some time to talk in private." She turned to Violet. "You do need to be aware that your husband will tire easily. We also find that our patients often don't want to talk about the things they've been through. I'm sure you'll understand."

Violet did understand, but she had so very many questions. It was going to take some time to work through what had happened, and know how life would go on. She was feeling many mixed emotions and she didn't know where to begin. She was confused and angry that he hadn't trusted her, hadn't wanted to see her. She loved him so much. She didn't know if she wanted to shout at him and beat her fists against him, or hold him and cry with relief.

When they were at last in a quiet area on their own, Violet said, "Do you think it would help for you to write a letter for me to take to your parents?"

Billy looked at her and snorted. "Haven't you seen? I can't write anymore. I've lost my arm."

"Billy," she said quietly. "I'm not going to give up on you, and you aren't going to give up on yourself. You're going to have to learn to be left-handed."

He looked at her in confusion, as though the thought had not occurred to him.

Violet began to feel more determined. "Having your love helps me be the best person I can be. With you there, I can do anything. Without you, I don't have confidence in myself. I love you, Billy Dobson, and we're going to get through this together. I've even learned to play football. Who would ever have thought I could do that?"

Suddenly, Billy broke into a smile. "I might not be able to write, but I could watch you play."

"Oh, Billy, yes. I haven't told you all that's happened — there's so much to tell you. We're playing on Boxing Day — maybe Matron could find a way for you to come. That will be the first match that your mother comes to — if she can overcome how she felt about me playing football, anything is possible."

"Mam?" Billy looked incredulous.

"Yes." Vi smiled. "For the first time, the whole family is coming." She hesitated. "At least, it will be the whole family if you can come too."

"Do you really think we can do this?" Billy reached out

his left hand to her. It was the first time he'd done that.

Violet slipped her much smaller hand into his. "I know we can. There is nothing we can't do together. For today, if you can't write to your parents perhaps you can dictate it and I'll write it down, but I expect you to try to learn."

Through the scarring, Violet could see that he'd broken into a grin.

"I was never much good at writing with my right hand."

She laughed. "Then maybe you'll do better with the left. You and Tommy could learn together — it will help him to see how important it is. You see, Billy, you're not useless. You could teach your son."

"You may not want me when you realise how hard it is to have me around. I still have nightmares. I wake up in the night screaming because I'm back there on the battlefield." He looked away.

Violet was unsure how to reply, conscious of what the matron had said. "We'll get through it together. We'll just keep trying."

CHAPTER 28

Hullo, I've been looking for You
For you, for you, for you-oo-oo
Looking all over the place, I have
For your beautiful face, I have
Baby kiss your Daddy dear!
What do you say? 'Tain't true?
A case of mistaken identity?-
No fear! I've been looking for you.
Hullo, I've Been Looking For You - Performed by Marie Loftus
1857 - 1940, author unknown

23rd December 1916 - Christmas Spirit Despite The War.
Children Who Forget Everything But Santa Claus - The Daily
Mirror

Violet didn't want to leave the hospital that afternoon; part
of her was frightened that Billy would somehow disappear
again. She clutched the letter they'd written together and
which she would give to his parents as soon as she arrived
home. She wanted to tell them while Tommy wasn't
around; she planned to tell him separately and take him to
see his dad the following Saturday, just before Christmas.
Matron said she was happy for Billy's parents to go as soon
as they could. In the meantime, Vi needed to decide how
she would explain this to Tommy. She felt sick thinking
about it. Even halfway home she felt as though she should

be turning around and going back to Billingbrook Hall to make sure it was true.

"Is that you, Vi?" Elsie called as Violet let herself into the kitchen.

Violet took a deep breath. There was going to be no easy time to do this, and she couldn't put it off. The letter had become a little damp and creased from her clutching it, and she hoped the ink wouldn't have run.

Elsie was knitting when Vi went in, and Alf, as usual for a Saturday afternoon, was smoking his pipe and reading the paper.

Without taking her coat off, Violet sat on the edge of a chair. "I have a letter for you both."

"Put it on the side, love, I've just dropped a stitch." Elsie was squinting at the knitting and was trying to work a stitch up a couple of rows.

"I think you might want to read it right away." Violet suspected there was going to be more than one dropped stitch before Elsie had finished.

Elsie looked at her and frowned, but she put the knitting down and took the letter. "It's in your writing. Are you moving out?"

Violet sighed. "It's not from me, Mam."

"Then why's it in your writing?"

Violet counted to ten under her breath. "Please, just read it. It's important." She didn't even want to explain that the writer had needed to dictate it. She didn't want the story coming out through questions.

Violet was trembling as Elsie opened the letter. She watched her mother-in-law's face as she began to read. The frown dropped away and her mouth fell open. Elsie swallowed and began to move her mouth as though trying to form a sentence. There was no sound. As the colour drained from Elsie's face, Violet began to wonder what she should do. Alf was still behind his newspaper and hadn't so much as looked up.

Violet coughed. "Dad," she said in a voice which he would be unlikely to ignore. "You need to read this letter."

Alf moved his paper down and took the pipe from his mouth. After he had waved away some of the smoke, he looked across at Elsie and everything changed. He put the pipe in the stand and threw the newspaper onto the floor. He went over to her as she held out the letter. "Are you all right, love?" He looked from Elsie to Vi. "You'd best bring Mam some tea."

Elsie managed to break her silence. "Tea, tea, I need something a bit stronger than tea. I need a medicinal brandy and no mistake."

Violet went to fetch the brandy and put the kettle on the range. She guessed both would be needed before they'd finished.

By the time she joined them again, Alf was sitting in the chair next to Elsie, holding her hand. Violet had never seen them like that and felt almost embarrassed to intrude. She crept in and put the tray on the table, poured a brandy for each of them and offered them the glasses. Elsie took hers immediately and downed the drink. She held the glass back out to Violet.

Violet blinked. She hadn't seen Elsie have one drink of alcohol before, never mind want another, but she didn't question it and poured a little more. This time Elsie at least sipped it, whilst Alf still held his glass. He looked up at Violet.

"How bad is he, love?"

Violet sighed. "I don't really know all the details. He's still our Billy, but he's lost part of his right leg, from the knee down, and his right arm. His face is badly scarred, but Matron says that will improve, and they're going to do some work on his nose." Her lip quivered as she talked.

"You look like you could do with a brandy too," he said gently.

Vi smiled. "I'm all right, thanks, Dad. I still have to tell Tommy when he comes in."

Alf took a sip from his glass. "Can we see him?"

Vi nodded. "Matron says to ask for her when you get there and she'll find you a private room — you can go any time. I'm taking Tommy next Saturday all being well." As she said it, she heard Tommy come bounding through the kitchen door and gave a sharp intake of breath. "I'll give you some time while I talk to Tommy."

Tommy had been playing football with other boys in the road and was red-cheeked and full of life as he came in from the cold. "We couldn't see the ball anymore," he said and shrugged.

Violet led him upstairs and listened to his chatter about the football. Once they were in the bedroom, she sat on the edge of the bed and lifted him into her lap. "I have some very important news for you." She'd been thinking about how to explain. She didn't want to tell Tommy that Billy had chosen not to contact them. "When we heard from the War Office to say that Daddy had died, they made a mistake."

Tommy began to frown. "You mean, he's not a hero?"

Violet smiled and swept the hair away from his forehead. "He's still a hero, and a very special one. But he's still alive too."

"Is he here?" Tommy had jumped from her knee and clapped his hands together.

"No, my darling boy, he's not here. He's in a hospital,

not very far away."

Tommy looked serious. "Will he be all right?"

There was no easy way for Vi to explain this. Whatever she said, she doubted that Tommy would understand until he saw his father, and possibly not then either.

"I hope so, but he was very badly injured. He's lost an arm and part of his leg, and his face is badly scarred." Violet bit her lip, waiting to see how Tommy would respond.

The boy looked sad and with tears in his eyes looked up at her and said, "But he is still my dad and he does still love me, doesn't he?"

Violet let out the breath she'd been holding. "Yes, my love, he will always love you and he'll always be your dad."

Tommy nodded, as though processing the information. "When can I see him?"

Violet wished that Matron had said she could take Tommy sooner than the following Saturday. The wait was going to be impossible.

Billy's Mam looked decidedly pale when she and Alf set off for Billingbrook Hall after lunch on Sunday. Violet wished she could go with them, but she knew they needed time alone with their son. She also feared that Elsie might shout at Billy for what he'd put them through and Vi didn't want to be there for that. She understood why Elsie was upset, God knew she had some of the same feelings herself, wondering why he hadn't trusted her love for him. However, above all that, Vi felt intensely protective of Billy, and would probably end up getting cross with Elsie if she showed her anger to her son.

Instead, Vi set off to visit her own parents to break the

news to them. She was still thinking about how to explain to them when she and Tommy arrived at their house. Tommy went running in as soon as the door was opened.

"Daddy's alive and he still loves me, even though he's hurt."

Violet could have wept for the simplicity of a child's priorities. She followed behind and saw the startled look on her mam's face. Violet broke into a wide smile. "It's true, Billy's alive."

Her mam came over and hugged her. "Oh, that is good news, but…"

Violet held up a hand to stop all the questions. "Let's wait until Tommy has gone to play with Bobby and I'll explain it all."

"Well, I never did," Mam said when Vi reached the end of the story.

"How long will he be in the hospital?" Dad asked.

Vi shrugged. "I don't know. Quite a while yet, from what Matron said. He still has to have an operation on his face, but they want him to have recovered a little more first. Then there's his rehabilitation — I think he's been pretty resistant up until now. He's just been saying he will never be any use to anyone. How could he even think that?"

"It's a rum business." Dad reached for his pipe and began to fill it.

"How will you cope, love?" Mam asked.

"I haven't even started to think about that. I suppose it will depend how much he can do when he comes home. I'd not long managed to sort all the pension arrangements out — now we need to see what money there will be to support him as an invalid." She took a deep breath. "I'm trying not to think about that though." She smiled. "I just want to focus on the fact that he's alive and we're still a family."

Mam came and patted Vi's shoulder as she went over to put the kettle on the stove.

Violet left Tommy with his grandparents when she went home. She thought Billy's parents may want to talk about their visit to Billy and she'd rather not have Tommy there to hear it. However, when she returned to Ivy Terrace, Elsie had gone to bed.

"It's all been a bit overwhelming for her," Alf said. "We didn't stay with him long. You know what Mam's like, she wanted to ask him lots of questions — I know she didn't mean to, but in the end she was upsetting him so much that the nurse asked us to leave." He sighed. "I remember well enough what war was like — it's not something you want to talk about with people who haven't seen it. It's taken me a long time to come to terms with what happened. I never talked about it with Billy back then — he must have been about seven when I joined up. It seems a daft thing to have done now looking back, to leave my family behind." He shook his head sadly. "Mam's been through a lot of worry over the years. She'll be all right, just give her time."

Tessie had already heard the news by the time they walked to work on Monday.

"I can't believe it — all this time. Has he been at the hospital since July?"

Violet shook her head. "He's not been there all that long, I don't think. We didn't really go into the detail of that. I have so many questions to ask him. I guess I'll have to be patient." She thought for a while. "Raising money for the hospital is even more important to me now."

Later that day Vi knocked tentatively at Mrs Simpson's office door.

"I don't want to disturb Mr Giffard," Violet said when she'd been admitted. "I'd just like to leave a message for him if I may, please?"

Mrs Simpson wrote down what Vi had to say, with only a twitch of emotion when Vi explained about Billy. The main point of the message was to ask if they could find a way for the team to play fortnightly, or even weekly, to raise more money for the hospital.

"Thank you, Mrs Dobson. I'll give the message to him when he's free."

Violet walked back to her bench wondering what would need to be done to set up a league, including themselves and other factories, as she'd suggested. She knew they'd been talking about a cup, but a league would mean more regular games. The few men's matches which were being played involved weakened sides, due to the number of first team players who'd gone off to fight. There must be room for regular women's fixtures.

Violet had never counted down the days of a week in the way she did that one; Saturday couldn't come soon enough. At the same time, she was filled with apprehension. Billy's mam had still talked very little about hers and Dad's visit to Billy the previous Sunday, for which Violet was grateful. She was still coming to terms with her own thoughts as well as worrying about Tommy. They had had one exchange, when thankfully Tommy was sound asleep.

"You shouldn't be taking him to see his dad like that," Elsie said, quite out of the blue one evening.

"Mam, if I don't take him when he's 'like that' as you put it, he'll never go to see him. Billy isn't going to suddenly get better, this isn't an illness that he'll recover from. We all have to accept that."

Elsie harrumphed and went quiet again. Violet wondered if Mam simply couldn't deal with Billy's injuries and if that explained her having made no mention of when she next planned to go to see Billy. She hadn't even said if she'd go on Christmas Day.

Violet wished she didn't have to work on the Saturday morning; concentrating was impossible. When the claxon sounded, Violet left her bench and hurried from the factory. She'd have run if it hadn't been against the rules. Once she was out of the gate, she did run; she hitched up her skirt and ran all the way back to Ivy Terrace. She reckoned it was good exercise for her football practice.

To her surprise Elsie had given Tommy some dinner and made sure he was ready. He was wearing his best clothes and sitting in the kitchen looking awkward. Vi was touched.

"Thanks, Mam." She gave Elsie a quick kiss on the cheek before heading straight back out with her son. Although Elsie had saved her some food, she couldn't have eaten anything and would have it later. As they walked to the hospital Vi tried not to think. When her thoughts strayed to the afternoon ahead she felt a sense of rising panic, as much about how she felt as about Tommy's reaction. Tommy was clearly excited, and she was dreading having to deal with how upset he might be.

When they arrived at the hospital they were shown into a small room toward the back of the house; it seemed like the sort of room that staff might have used as an office, but it was nice enough and had a view out onto the garden.

Tommy was bouncing up and down and Violet was trying to keep him occupied whilst they waited for Billy. They were looking out of the window when Violet heard the door open and turned around to see Matron wheeling Billy into the room.

Before any of them had a chance to say a word, Tommy ran to his father and wrapped his arms around him. "I've missed you, Daddy." He climbed up onto Billy's knee, and although Violet saw Billy wince with pain, Billy used his good arm to pull the boy up and hold him tight. Tommy looked into his father's scarred face and simply carried on as though nothing had happened. "Mam says you won't be able to play football, but you can watch me and Mam play and tell me how to do it better."

Tommy turned to Vi. "Is Daddy coming to watch the football with me and Grandma?"

Vi could feel a lump in her throat. "As long as Matron says it's all right."

"You just try stopping me," Billy said, closing his eyes as he held his son to him.

Vi could feel the tears streaming down her face as she watched them. This was it, her family. She had no idea what would lie ahead, but none of that mattered. They were together, and she couldn't be happier.

THE END

PLEASE LEAVE A REVIEW

Reviews are one of the best ways for new readers to find my writing. It's the modern day 'word of mouth' recommendation. If you have enjoyed reading my work and think that others may do too, then please take a moment or two to leave a review. Just a sentence or two of what you think is all it takes.

Thank you.

BOOK GROUPS

Dear book group readers,

Rather than include questions within the book for you to consider, I have included special pages within my website. This has the advantage of being easier to update and for you to suggest additions and thoughts which arise out of your discussions.

I am always delighted to have the opportunity to discuss the book with a group and for those groups which are not local to me this can sometimes be arranged as a Skype call or through another internet service. Contact details can be found on the website.

Please visit http://rjkind.com/

SOURCES OF INFORMATION

This is not a study of history, so I may not have provided every last reference in the manner you would like, however the following have all been interesting and useful sources if you want to do any further research yourself.

BBC History Magazine
Roger Domeneghetti - From The Back Page To The Front Room: Football's Journey Through The English Media - ISBN-13: 978-1910906064
Tim Tate - Secret History Of Womens Football - ISBN-13: 978-1782197720
Gail J Newsham - In A League Of Their Own: The Dick, Kerr Ladies 1917-1965 - ISBN-13: 978-1782225638
Kate Adie - Fighting on the Home Front The Legacy of Women in World War One ISBN-13: 978-14444759709
Patrick Brennan - The Munitionettes ISBN-13: 978-0-9555063-0-7

Dick, Kerr Ladies' Team
https://en.wikipedia.org/wiki/Dick,_Kerr_Ladies_F.C.
www.dickkerrladies.com/

General History sources
www.bbc.co.uk/history/british/timeline/worldwars_timeline_noflash.shtml
https://en.wikipedia.org/wiki/1914_in_the_United_Kingdom
https://en.wikipedia.org/wiki/1915_in_the_United_Kingdom
https://en.wikipedia.org/wiki/1916_in_the_United_Kingdom

www.theguardian.com/artanddesign/gallery/2014/jan/04/
1914-life-before-war-in-pictures
www.paimages.co.uk/collections/1041

British Newspaper Archive
www.britishnewspaperarchive.co.uk

Hat factory conditions
www.worldwar1luton.com/blog-entry/unhealthy-
conditions-hat-factories

Munitionettes history
https://en.wikipedia.org/wiki/Munitionette

Working hours
https://www.bbc.com/worklife/article/20190912-what-
wartime-munitionettes-can-teach-us-about-burnout

Songs
https://en.wikipedia.org/wiki/Music_hall_songs

Life of soldiers
https://www.iwm.org.uk/
https://www.bl.uk/world-war-one/articles/slang-terms-at-
the-front
http://www.lancashireinfantrymuseum.org.uk/the-
regiments-in-the-great-war-1914-18-3/

Soldiers' Songs and Slang of the Great War - Martin Pegler
- Osprey Publishing 2014

Short, Magazine Lee Enfield
https://en.wikipedia.org/wiki/Lee%E2%80%93Enfield

Machine Guns
www.firstworldwar.com/weaponry/machineguns.htm

Battle of the Somme
www.history.com/news/why-was-the-battle-of-the-somme-so-deadly

Pals battalions
https://en.wikipedia.org/wiki/Pals_battalion#:~:text=The%20Pals%20battalions%20of%20World,being%20arbitrarily%20allocated%20to%20battalions.

Army structure
https://history.stackexchange.com/questions/37732/how-did-the-british-army-unit-size-and-structure-in-wwi-change-from-1915-to-1918
www.longlongtrail.co.uk/

Films
Oh What a Lovely Way
They Shall Not Grow Old
1917 - Universal Pictures

YouTube
Walking the Battle of Ypres - Living History
Walking the Battle of the Somme - Living History
World War 1 in Colour - GunstarGizmo
Tactics of 1914 - The Advance and Assault - Highland Subaltern
Infantry Recruit Training in 1914 - Highland Subaltern
Conditions in Trenches - Dan Snow's Battle of the Somme - Discovery UK
What it Was Like To Be a Trench Soldier in WW1 – Weird

History
The Secret To Shouting Military Commands - Forces TV
Life in The Trenches (WW1 Documentary) - Becky Towle
British Recruits Joining Up (1914-1918) - British Pathé

ALSO BY ROSEMARY J. KIND

The Blight and the Blarney (Prequel to Tales of Flynn and Reilly)

Ireland has suffered from potato blight since 1845. Friends and neighbours have died, been evicted or given up what little land they have in search of alms. Michael Flynn is one of the lucky ones. His landlord has offered support.

Michael and his family have done all they can to help their immediate household, but as the famine and its aftermath continue, have their efforts been enough?

With the weakening brought about by hunger, there are some things he is powerless to protect his family from. Is it time for the great Michael Flynn to take his family in search of a better life?

New York Orphan (Tales of Flynn and Reilly)

From fleeing the Irish Potato Famine, to losing his parents on the ship to New York, seven-year-old Daniel Flynn knows about adversity. As Daniel sings the songs of home to earn pennies for food, pick-pocket Thomas Reilly becomes his ally and friend, until he too is cast out onto the street.

A destitute refugee in a foreign land, Daniel, together with Thomas and his sister Molly, are swept up by the Orphan Train Movement to find better lives with families across America. For Daniel will the dream prove elusive?

How strong are bonds of loyalty when everything is at stake?

Unequal By Birth (Tales of Flynn and Reilly)

1866 - Daniel Flynn and Molly Reilly's lives have been dogged by hardship since their orphan days on the streets of New York. Finally, the future is looking bright and Indiana is the place they call home. Now they can focus on making Cochrane's Farm a success.

The Civil War might have ended but the battle for Cochrane's Farm has only just begun. The Reese brothers are incensed that land, once part of their family farm, has been transferred to the ownership of young Molly. No matter that their Daddy had sold it years previously, jealousy and revenge have no regard for right. Women should know their place and this one clearly doesn't.

How far will Daniel and Molly go to fight injustice and is it a price worth paying?

Justice Be Damned (Tales of Flynn and Reilly)

1870 - William Dixon will not ignore injustice. The Reese brothers have been released from prison and no one has been made to pay for the life they took, nor the damage they caused to Cochrane's Farm. As his sister, Molly and her husband Daniel set out to rebuild their farm, William takes the fight onto the political stage.

Whilst his wife, Cecilia, runs Dixon's Attorneys' office in Pierceton, William begins on the campaign trail. He may not have the backing of the establishment, but his oratory is outstanding. The Fifteenth Amendment has broadened the electorate, but politics is still a white male preserve. William sets out to speak for those who have no voice. He stands on a ticket of equality and fairness. Lauded by some and vilified by others, everyone has a view on William

Dixon. Some will go to great lengths to stop his progress.

How do you fight for justice against those whose interests it does not serve? William Dixon is about to find out.

The Appearance of Truth

Her birth certificate belonged to a baby who died. Her apparently happy upbringing was a myth. Does anyone out there know – who is Lisa Forster?

The Lifetracer

Connor Bancroft is more used to investigating infidelity than murder, and when he's asked to investigate a death threat he's drawn into a complex story of revenge. He uncovers a series of, apparently, unlinked murders. He is nowhere close to solving the crimes but now his eight year old son, Mikey's life is in danger and Connor has little time left to find out – Who is The Lifetracer?

Alfie's Woods

Alfie sets out to befriend a money-laundering hedgehog when he is recaptured following his escape from the Woodland Prison. Hedgehog is overwhelmed that any other creature should care about him, finds the strength to change his life. Alfie's Woods is a story of the power of friendship and the difference it can make to all of us.

Embers of the Day and Other Stories

From the movingly beautiful, to the laugh-out-loud funny. This collection of short stories covers the breadth of Rosemary J. Kind's fiction writing in her usual accessible style.

Lovers Take up Less Space

A humorous review of the addictive misery of commuting on London Underground.

Pet Dogs Democratic Party Manifesto

Key political issues from a dog's point of view by self-styled political leader Alfie Dog.

Alfie's Diary

An entertaining and thought provoking dog's eye view of the world.

From Story Idea to Reader

Whether brushing up your writing skills or starting out, this book will take you through the whole process from inspiration to conclusion.

The Complete Entlebucher Mountain Dog Book

This book provides a complete insight into the Entlebucher Mountain Dog. Whether you are looking to add an Entlebucher to your family, get the best out of your relationship with a dog you already own or are interested in the story of the breed itself and its development in the UK, this is the book for you.

Poems for Life

Poetry collection including the inspirational 'Carpe Diem'.

You can find out more about the author's other work by: visiting her website http://www.rjkind.com

ABOUT THE AUTHOR

Rosemary J Kind writes because she has to. You could take almost anything away from her except her pen and paper. Failing to stop after the book that everyone has in them, she has gone on to publish books in both non-fiction and fiction, the latter including novels, humour, short stories and poetry. She also regularly produces magazine articles in a number of areas and writes regularly for the dog press. As a child she was desolate when at the age of ten her then teacher would not believe that her poem based on 'Stig of the Dump' was her own work and she stopped writing poetry for several years as a result. She was persuaded to continue by the invitation to earn a little extra pocket money by 'assisting' others to produce the required poems for English homework!

Always one to spot an opportunity, she started school newspapers and went on to begin providing paid copy to her local newspaper at the age of sixteen.

For twenty years she followed a traditional business career, before seeing the error of her ways and leaving it all behind to pursue her writing full-time.

She spends her life discussing her plots with the characters in her head and her faithful dogs, who always put the opposing arguments when there are choices to be made.

Always willing to take on challenges that sensible people regard as impossible, she set up the short story download site Alfie Dog Fiction which she ran for six years. During that time it grew to become one of the largest short story download sites in the world, representing over 300 authors and carrying over 1600 short stories. Her hobby is developing the Entlebucher Mountain Dog breed in the UK and when she brought her beloved Alfie back from Belgium he was only the tenth in the country.

She started writing *Alfie's Diary* as an internet blog the day Alfie arrived to live with her, intending to continue for a year or two. Fifteen years later it goes from strength to strength and has been repeatedly named as one of the top ten pet blogs in the UK.

For more details about the author please visit her website at www.rjkind.com For more details about her dogs then you're better visiting www.alfiedog.me.uk

ACKNOWLEDGMENTS

I am deeply indebted to Martin and Kate Pegler for their help and advice on the Great War.

As always thanks to my writing buddies - Patsy, Sheila and Lynne - who make an enormous difference to my work. Also, my husband Chris for your support, encouragement and improvements - thank you.

No book would be complete without mention of my wonderful cover designer Katie Stewart. I am so lucky to benefit from her skills.

Alfie Dog Fiction

Taking your imagination for a walk

visit our website at www.alfiedog.com

Lightning Source UK Ltd.
Milton Keynes UK
UKHW020205070521
383232UK00008B/186

9 781909 894464